Lorraine Mace is the critically acclaimed author of the D.I. Sterling thrillers. *Rage and Retribution* is her fourth instalment in this dark and gritty series. In addition, she is the humour columnist for *Writing Magazine* and the head judge at *Writers' Forum* where she also writes two columns. Lorraine lives in the warmer and sunnier clime of southern Spain.

Praise for Lorraine Mace:

'A dark, cleverly plotted tale . . . I was gripped from the opening scene and raced through the book to its final, shocking end. Crime writing at its very best' Sheila Bugler

'Gritty, topical, sometimes lacerating, but always enthralling. A truly compulsive read' Abbie Frost

'Her assured and fluid writing style truly brings characters and scenes to life on the page' Rachel Abbott

'D.I. Paolo Sterling is instantly engaging – *Children in Chains* is a dark, gripping and unflinching read' Louise Phillips

'Delve into the dark side. Well-constructed with unflinching plots. Satisfying enough for the most discerning crime reader' Ruth Dugdall

'Fast-paced and compulsive reading with tension ratcheted to the max. D.I. Paolo Sterling's humanity is tested b̶ ̶ ̶ ̶ ̶ ̶ ̶hing crimes and dam̶

'A visceral, no-punches-̶ ̶ ̶ ̶ ̶
Crime Noir at its̶

D1333994

RAGE
AND
RETRIBUTION

A **D.I. STERLING** Thriller

Lorraine Mace

ACCENT

First published in 2020 by Headline Accent
An imprint of HEADLINE PUBLISHING GROUP

1

Cataloguing in Publication Data is available from the British Library

ISBN 978 1 7861 5 6853

Typeset in 10.5/13pt Bembo Std by Jouve (UK), Milton Keynes

Printed and bound in Great Britain by Clays Ltd, Elcograf S.p.A.

HEADLINE PUBLISHING GROUP
An Hachette UK Company
Carmelite House
50 Victoria Embankment
London EC4Y 0DZ

www.headline.co.uk
www.hachette.co.uk

This book is dedicated with much love to my wonderful children David and Michelle

Chapter One

I opened the door and smiled at the scene. The naked man was splayed face down on the table. He looked as if he was still unconscious. Surely not? Moving into the room, I slammed the door closed to see if that stirred him. He spun his head at the sound. Good. He was awake at last. Blindfolded and gagged, he wasn't about to have a chat with me about how he'd ended up here. That conversation would come soon enough. I checked to make sure he couldn't make any sudden moves. Not that it was likely he'd been able to free his limbs. His feet rested on the floor, each ankle tied to a leg of a small square table with butcher's string. There was no way the knots would ever work loose. When the time came, I'd have to cut him free. His arms hung down on either side of the table and were fastened to the other two legs. Bent over the table at the waist, his backside was vulnerable and ready for action.

I reached forward to untie the gag. Letting them talk during the process was good – a chance to hear them trying to make excuses, or better still, begging for forgiveness. A quick tug released the material from the man's mouth, leaving him gasping for air. When he finally caught his breath, his anger erupted.

'What the fuck do you think you're doing,' he spat. 'Let me go.'

'Not yet. We've got some games to play first.'

Even after so many times of using it, the sound coming through

1

the voice distorter came as a shock. It was weird to speak, but not hear my own voice. I sounded like a Dalek on speed. Some of my visitors wet themselves with fear on hearing the strange sound, but not this one. It seemed to inflame him even more.

'Stop pissing about now and let me go.'

Time to give him the ground rules. 'Not today,' I explained. 'On the third day you can go, but not before that.'

'What the fuck are you on about? When I get out of here—'

I hated it when they were difficult and I had to set straight in with the punishment, even though they all deserved it. I picked up the tazer and held it against the man's scrotum, then pressed the trigger to release a five second burst of pure agony. That was usually enough to get their attention. As the man's screams died away, the only noise left in the room was the sound of his sobbing.

Leaning forward and grabbing a handful of hair, I lifted his head and hissed, 'If you get hold of me, you'll what? By the time I let you go, you'll be begging to do anything I say.'

I dropped his head and moved away to pick up the man's jacket from one of the armchairs. He didn't have much in his pockets, just his house and car keys and some loose change, but I needed to find his wallet. I found it eventually in the button down back pocket of his trousers. Opening it up, I was pleased to see it contained all the information I needed.

'Right, let's see who you really are. Hmm, your driving licence says you're Jason Corbett. That's not the name you used in the club last night. Naughty, naughty. I might have to punish you for telling lies. Would you like another little burst from the tazer?'

'Fuck you, you bastard,' Jason screamed as he heaved against the ties, the thin string cutting into the flesh of his wrists and ankles. As he slumped back down, his stomach flattened against the solid wood of the table.

'You should conserve your strength,' I warned him. 'You're going to need it.'

'You mad fucker. You can't keep me here for three days. Someone will hear me yelling.'

2

I grinned. They all trotted out that line. 'Let me fill you in on how your stay here is going to go. You can make as much noise as much as you want. This room is soundproofed. Some visitors yell so much it gives me a headache, but then I use this beauty to give them a reason to scream.'

I stroked the tazer against Jason's scrotum. A strong stench of urine filled the room as he lost control of his bladder.

'Don't. Please don't.'

I sighed. 'It's just as well the floor's tiled. You all end up pissing on it.'

Jason squirmed. 'I'll give you anything you want. Anything! Don't use that thing. Please don't. Just let me go. Please let me go.'

'Ah, that's my cue,' I said, putting the tazer on the chair on top of Jason's clothes and picking up a clipboard from the other chair. 'What should I say next? Or rather, let me put it another way. What did *you* say to *your* victims? I've got your exact words here on my notes. "Shut the fuck up unless you want me to cut your fucking throat." Does that sound right to you? It seems a bit cliched to me, but I know it's been effective. You know that as well, don't you?'

Jason began to shake. I think he finally realised the trouble he was in. I patted his naked buttocks.

'You're a bit hairy. Have you ever thought of shaving? No? Oh well, beggars can't be choosers. I'll put up with it for now. Maybe I'll use some hair remover on you tomorrow, but that's going to be very painful because you'll probably have open wounds by then. Let's see how it goes today.'

I pushed against Jason's quivering flesh, but didn't enter him. Not yet. I wanted him to feel the same fear he'd inflicted on his victims.

'It's nice and hard, isn't it? All I need now is for you to say you want to be fucked. I won't do it unless you ask me. That's how you operate, isn't it? Make your targets beg you to fuck them so that you won't kill them? Well, it's time for a bit of role reversal.'

Jason mumbled something, but I couldn't make out the words.

'Come on now, Jason. You've got a choice to make. Say you want to be fucked, or get the tazer on your balls again. What's it to be?'

'Please don't . . . please.'

'Tazer or fuck, Jason. Your choice.'

'I . . .'

'Last chance to answer, Jason. If you don't choose, you get both. Wanna be fucked up the arse, Jason? Or have your balls electrocuted? Which is it? Huh?'

Jason sobbed. 'No, please, not the tazer.'

'So you want to be fucked, do you? Then say it. *Say it!*'

'Fuck me,' Jason whispered.

'Okay, if you insist.'

The sweet music of Jason's screams filled the room, keeping time as I thrust deeper and deeper.

Chapter Two

Detective Inspector Paolo Sterling looked around at the assembled company and felt an unaccustomed surge of civic pride. Most of Bradchester's business leaders had turned up for the opening ceremony of the renovated youth centre, even though many of them had initially rejected pleas for funding. Paolo had needed to work hard to convince them that giving the young people in the town a place to call their own would make any difference to the numbers arrested in drink and drug related crimes. Bringing them round to his point of view had meant being more persuasive than he'd ever thought he could be. Looking at the youngsters huddled at the back of the hall, he knew he'd go cap in hand to big business all over again if he had to. This wasn't just important to the present generation of unemployed teenagers; it would affect the lives of those as yet unborn if somehow this generation could find their way into work.

It was time for the bit he dreaded. Making speeches was not something he enjoyed, but everyone seemed to feel it was for him to declare the youth centre open. For once, the press would have something good to report. He noted that all the major newspapers were represented and the local television station had the event covered as well.

He glanced over at his daughter and her boyfriend and smiled. They were standing at the edge of the crowd, waiting for the unveiling of the official plaque. Katy and Danny had been pretty much inseparable for nearly a year. Where one went, the other was sure to follow. Not that he minded. Danny might not have been Paolo's choice when his daughter first started seeing him, but the more he got to know the young man, the more he liked him. In fact, it was entirely down to Danny that Paolo was now standing up on a stage about to cut the ribbon and proclaim the renovated youth centre open. Without Danny's urging, Paolo might not have become so involved in the fundraising activities that had brought in the cash to update the facilities.

The only important person missing was the woman who'd shared this dream with him. God, he missed Jessica now that she was away so often. The downside of Jessica becoming better known in the psychiatric field, from Paolo's point of view, was that she spent more time than ever in London. Not that they saw much of each other when she was in Bradchester. The demands of their two careers made sure of that. Paolo stifled a sigh. In truth, he was the biggest culprit. At least when Jessica was in Bradchester at weekends, she made time for him. All too often, though, that time was taken up by the demands of his job and she'd end up eating alone, or, worse still, sleeping alone.

He forced his mind back to the reason for his attendance tonight and cleared his throat. Better get it over with.

'This has been a long time coming,' he said, 'but now that we have finally reached this point, I have no intention of focusing on the negatives we had to overcome on the way. The centre has changed a great deal in the last couple of years. From a rundown building that offered little in the way of amenities, it now boasts a multisport hall, snooker tables and a cafeteria. The swimming pool has been completely refurbished and the council has employed a qualified coach, Derrick Walden, who will offer free lessons to beginners three days a week. For those already able to swim, Derrick will be available for coaching on a fee paying basis. That is the only time anyone will have to pay to use the facilities here. Everything else will be covered by the trust fund we will establish using the surplus donations, generously provided by our business leaders.'

Paolo waited for cheers from the back of the hall to die down before continuing.

'But this isn't just a leisure centre. This will be a place for our young people to come for help in finding work, whether it's in an office, an apprenticeship or into the performing arts. There will be skilled people on hand to help with education and training programmes, counsellors for those who need a safe place to talk, as well as members of our local drama group who will be running workshops. The intention is to put on a performance each year, in addition to a pantomime at Christmas. This renovated centre is a wonderful achievement and it wouldn't have been possible without the financial support of Bradchester's business community.'

As the applause died down, he picked up the scissors from the lectern and turned to face the velvet curtain covering the plaque.

'It gives me great pleasure to announce the reopening of Bradchester's Youth Centre,' he said, cutting the ribbon and allowing the purple cover to fall.

The gasp from the assembled audience was almost deafening. Defacing the plaque in vivid red letters were the words: MASONS A CRUK.

Paolo turned back into the glare of flashing lights as the press photographers fired off shot after shot. The reporters clamoured forward, shooting questions without giving him chance to answer.

'What do you know about this?'

'Are you going to investigate?'

'Did this come as a surprise to you?'

'What are you going to do about it?'

'Will you arrest Councillor Mason?'

'Is there money missing? If yes, why haven't you arrested the councillor?'

Paolo held up his hands in the classic position of surrender and shouted to be heard over the cacophony.

'At the moment I know as much about this as you do.'

A strident voice interrupted him. 'I repeat: are you going to investigate? Did you know money was missing? After all, you were the main fundraiser.'

Paolo couldn't see beyond the flashing bulbs, but recognised the voice and sighed. A query that loaded could only have come from Gordon Hennessy, muckraker supreme for the *Bradchester Sport*. He should have known that piece of slime would put the worst possible interpretation on anything to do with the centre.

'Yes, there will be an investigation, but as of this moment I have no reason to suspect the councillor of any wrongdoing. This could simply be an attempt to smear his name by someone bearing a grudge.'

'Is it true the councillor is a friend of yours? Is that why you're so quick to defend him?'

Paolo looked through the glare to the spot from where he thought the last question had been yelled.

'I am not defending anyone, Mr Hennessy. I have said there will be an investigation and there will be one. However, at this moment all we have is an accusation scrawled in what looks like lipstick. Until I find evidence of wrongdoing, it would be premature of me to accuse anyone of a crime. However, to answer your question, no, Councillor Mason and I are not friends. We do not socialise and have only come together on this project. Outside of this, we have no contact. I trust that puts your mind at rest.'

Paolo permitted himself an inward smile. Far from being friends, he and Montague Mason had locked horns on just about every aspect of the renovation project, but he had no intention of sharing that with the press – the gutter variety or the more responsible kind.

He held his hands up again and kept them in the air until the noise abated.

'Gentlemen and ladies of the press, clearly there is something here for me to look into, even it is nothing more than a case of defamation of character. I'm afraid I must ask you all to clear the hall as I need to close this area off to allow tests to be taken of the substance on the plaque. Perhaps you would like to make your way to the cafeteria, where I believe refreshments have been laid on for this evening.'

'What do you—'

Paolo shook his head. 'No more questions tonight. Let me get on with my job.'

He waited until the assembled guests, media and workers had filed into the adjoining room before turning to Katy and Danny who were standing quietly to one side of the plaque.

'I need both of you to go next door as well.'

Katy nodded. 'I know that, Dad. I just wanted to give you a hug. It's not fair. We've all worked so hard on this and the night got hijacked by some idiot who can't even spell.'

Paolo grinned. Trust Katy to pick up on that. If there ever was such a branch of the force as the Grammar Police, she'd be made up to Chief Superintendent in no time.

'Don't fall into the trap of believing everything you read. How do you know the words weren't deliberately misspelled to make us think it was someone semi-literate?' He hugged her. 'Don't dwell on what's happened tonight. From tomorrow, the centre will be up and running. It's amazing what's been achieved here.'

She nodded. 'You're right, but it still pisses me off.'

'Katy!'

She blushed. 'Sorry, Dad. Forgot who I was talking to. Come on, Danny, let's go and grab some food before it all disappears.' She looked back at Paolo. 'You coming?'

He shook his head. 'No, you go on. I'm going to call Dave. Unfortunately, this is such a public accusation, it has to be dealt with as a crime, even if one hasn't been committed.'

Paolo sat in the centre's administration office opposite Montague Mason and wished for the hundredth time he found the man even a tiny bit likeable. There was something almost repellent about him, but Paolo couldn't quite pin down what it was that made him feel uncomfortable in Mason's company.

'Montague, it's no good saying the same thing over and over.

That sign was uncovered in the full glare of a media spotlight. Whether I want to or not, I have no choice but to look into the centre's fundraising books. You know as well as I do, an investigation has to be carried out in the open.'

Montague scowled. 'No, Paolo, I don't see that at all. Some idiot woman scrawls a message and suddenly I'm seen as a thief? How would you like it if that happened to you?'

'I wouldn't like it, but I'd have to deal with it. That's what you've got to do. Deal with it so that everyone can see the accusation has no foundation. First of all, we don't know it was a woman. Anyone can buy lipstick and a man could easily have decided to use one to make us think it was a woman. Secondly, if we don't investigate it's going to look as if we're covering up for you.' Paolo held up his hand. 'Yes, I know you say you've nothing to hide and nothing to cover up, but the press will have a field day if we don't show we're taking the accusation seriously.'

'Fuck the press! I'm sick to death of all of them. They've done nothing constructive to help with this project. Instead of supporting and encouraging us to make a place for young people to go, the bloody headlines have been all about how much public money has been wasted on drug-taking louts and unmarried mothers. What they've been screaming for is for us to fix potholes and turn the canal into a tourist attraction! And we all know why the canal project became the press darling, don't we!'

Paolo sighed. 'This is not the time to go into your rivalry with Fletcher Simpson.'

Montague snorted. 'Isn't it? You heard that bastard Hennessy making his snide accusations. Why would he do that? Because he writes for the paper Simpson owns, that's why. And why was Simpson so keen to get the canal project financed instead of this centre? Because he happens to own the three businesses on the banks of the canal that would benefit most from getting it cleaned up and turned into a tourist attraction. If you want to investigate wrongdoing, try looking at that bastard and leave me alone. In fact, I wouldn't mind betting it was someone working for Simpson who defaced the plaque.'

Paolo looked across at Detective Sergeant Dave Johnson who'd been silently taking notes. Dave grinned. This was the fourth time Montague had made the accusation. Clearly, in his mind, it could only be Simpson or someone working for him who would do such a thing. Paolo thought he might well be right, but he still had to look into other possible motives.

'Montague, let's get down to business. I will arrange for someone from financial crimes to make sure all is as it should be with the account keeping. In the meantime, the sooner we think about who had access to the plaque, the sooner we can call it a night and get some sleep. Who has been in the hall since the plaque was put in place? Actually, more to the point, who has had access since the curtain was put up?'

'Lots of people,' Montague said with a massive sigh that made Paolo want to shake him. 'Council members, cleaning staff, the caretaker, the new tutors and instructors, people bringing in books for the youth library, you name an occupation, they've been in the hall at some point or another.'

'I'm going to need you to be a bit more specific. I want you to write down every name you can remember. Ask your secretary to do the same. If neither of you know the names of individuals, write down the company, so that I can follow up on it,' Paolo said.

He stood up and waited for Dave to finish scribbling and close his notebook. They said their goodbyes and headed for the door, but stopped when Montague called out.

'Of course, there are a couple of helpers who have been here most days. I suppose one of them could have it in for me.'

Paolo looked back. The way Montague had spoken it was clear he felt the two concerned needed investigating.

'OK, add their names to your list and I'll look into their backgrounds.'

'You're not going to need to look far,' Montague sneered. 'It's your daughter and that boy she hangs about with. He's bad news if you ask me.'

Chapter Three

I never enjoyed the second day. The bastards still retained just enough arrogance to believe they would get back at me when they were free. It was also the day I had to teach them some manners and that was never easy with people who'd never had any to start with.

I opened the door and recoiled at the stench. Jason had soiled himself overnight. They all did eventually. That was one of the reasons there was a drain under the table. The ability to hose down the men was a necessity.

As I closed the door, Jason moved his head in the direction of the sound.

'Water, please, so thirsty,' he whispered.

I smiled. It was almost as if he'd read my mind. He was going to get water. Lots of water. I intended to clean him up inside and out. Purify the body and purify the mind.

I walked across and turned on the tap, allowing some water to trickle from the hose. Jason's head spun in my direction. I knew how he felt. That longing for water must be overriding all other emotions right now, even fear. That would change.

I turned the tap to full force, pointed the power hose at Jason's rear end, and pulled the trigger. He'd asked for water, so I let him have it. A fierce ice cold jet rushed out, pummelling Jason's exposed flesh and removing the faeces.

Jason screamed as the water connected with his raw wounds from last night's activities. I needed to wash away the blood and skin so that he would be nice and clean for me to go at him again.

'Turn it off, please. I'm begging you,' he screamed. 'It hurts. Fuck, it hurts.'

'Yes, I know,' I yelled over the sound of the rushing water and stepping closer to point the jet directly into the man's cheek crack. 'I have to make sure I flush out all traces of your filth.'

As the soiled water ran into the drain under the table, Jason screams turned to whimpers. When I was certain he was as clean as I could get him, I turned off the tap and dropped the hose next to it. Walking back to the table, I smacked Jason's cheeks with my open hand. I'd need to put some alcohol on those wounds, but that was a job for tomorrow. A final gift before I released him.

'Let me go,' he whispered. 'You've had your fun. Please, let me go.'

'Is that what your victims said to you? Did they beg? Did they promise to do whatever you asked, if only you let them go?'

Jason went still.

'Ah, you didn't realise I know everything about your sordid secret life, did you?'

'I don't know what you're talking about,' Jason said. 'You've got the wrong man. That's what it is, you've made a mistake.'

I sighed again. So bloody predictable. They all said that on days one and two. By tomorrow, when it was time for him to go home, he'd have confessed to his crimes and would never be stupid enough to commit any more.

'You've had it easy so far. I'm going to leave you until this evening to think about why you're here. When I come back again, you can look forward to my visits every hour on the hour until I get too tired to service you. Bye for now.'

Jason must have realised I meant what I'd said, as he cried out.

'Wait! Please. I'm so thirsty.'

'Would you like some water to drink?'

13

Jason's body trembled. 'Yes,' he whispered. 'Please, if you take off the blindfold I promise not to look. If you'll just—'

'Just what? Give you a drink? Sorry, no can do. You have to take your punishment like a man. See you in a few hours.'

'No!' Jason begged. 'Please. I'll die unless you give me something to drink.'

'No you won't. I told you. You'll be here for three days. Nothing to eat, nothing to drink, but lots and lots of sex. Isn't that what you tell your victims? Don't you tell them they are there to provide you with lots of sex? Now it's your turn to find out what that feels like. Keep that thought in mind until I get back.'

Paolo glared at the files and heaps of paperwork covering most of his desk. No matter how much time he spent on it, the piles grew instead of disappearing. And now, when he was swamped with cases he needed to concentrate on, he was going to have to expend vital resources on the lipstick idiocy.

He thought back to his conversation with Montague the night before. What struck him as odd was the man's reluctance to have the books looked into. You'd think he'd be only too happy to show the people of Bradchester that he had nothing to hide, but it had felt as if he'd been on the verge of refusing access to the accounts. Interesting, Paolo thought, wondering if there was a bit of fire hiding inside the smoke.

He recalled the nasty look of glee on Montague's face when he'd mentioned Danny and Katy as possible suspects. Paolo sighed. Whether he wanted to or not, the fact that Montague had named them meant that Paolo would have to get one of his team to ask Katy and Danny if they were involved.

A knock on his door made him look up to see Cathy Connor peering round it. CC's hair over the last few months had been Ronald McDonald red. Paolo wondered how long it would be before she changed it again. He smiled, remembering the vivid blue that had lasted for just one day before word from above had come down ordering it to be dyed a more suitable colour.

'Nice to see you smiling, sir,' she said. 'I expected you to be scowling after the mess last night. Have you seen the papers?'

Paolo picked up the *Bradchester Sport* and showed CC the headline.

'Oh, that's not nice. *"Fundraising Copper in Bed with Councillor?"* Personally,' CC said, grinning at him, 'I couldn't imagine you and Mr Mason in bed together, but maybe they mean it figuratively.'

Paolo laughed. 'I certainly hope they don't mean it literally. My tastes definitely don't run in that direction. The clever use of the question mark keeps them on the right side of a defamation claim by me or by Montague. Talking of Montague Mason, I'm expecting someone from the centre to bring over a list of everyone who had access to the plaque.'

'That could be what the woman downstairs has come in for. That's why I'm here. A Miss Clementine Towers says she has information about the youth centre that you need to act on.'

'I don't need to see her. Ask her for the list of names and give it Andrea to check, will you?'

CC smiled. 'I would, sir, but she insists on seeing you. She has vital information and only the man at the top can deal with it. She needs someone with authority to act.'

Paolo laughed. 'That sounded like a quote.'

'It was, sir, almost word for word. She won't speak to anyone in a lesser position. To be honest, I think even you might be a bit too lowly for her, but I don't suppose the chief would be too pleased if I took her up there.'

'OK, bring her up, but once I get the list, I'll need as many of you as possible to eliminate possible suspects.'

CC turned to go, but stopped with her hand on the door handle and looked back. 'This is a bit OTT, isn't it, sir? I mean, it's only a bit of lippy on a plaque.'

'I couldn't agree more, but you've seen today's headlines. OK, they're not all as pointed as the *Bradchester Sport*, but most of them imply if I don't investigate it's because I have something to hide. I've been too active in the fundraising for the centre not to have mud clinging to me if there's any thrown. Anyway, go and get Miss Towers. The sooner we clear this up, the better.'

Five minutes later CC ushered in a woman Paolo guessed to be in her late sixties. She was dressed completely inappropriately for her age, wearing a flared denim skirt and bright striped tee-shirt in alternating lines of yellow and black. Paolo expected her to start buzzing at any moment.

'Are you in charge of what happens at the youth centre?' she demanded.

'I'm the investigating officer, yes. Won't you please take a seat,' Paolo said, gesturing to the chairs in front of his desk. 'I believe you have some information for me.'

'I do indeed and I hope you're going to do something about it. I couldn't believe my eyes. Really I couldn't. It's a disgrace. That's what it is, a disgrace.'

'Well, it's certainly unfortunate, but—'

'Unfortunate! How can you say that when you don't even know why I'm here? Unless you put them there. The way society is today, it wouldn't surprise me.'

Paolo thought he now knew how Alice felt when she'd dropped down the rabbit's hole. 'I'm sorry, I think we're talking at cross purposes. I thought you had come from the youth centre.'

'I have,' Clementine Towers said. 'I've just come straight from there and I want you to do something about it.'

'About what?'

'The books, of course. Why else do you think I'm here?'

Paolo thought he saw a glimmer of light. 'That is not for me to investigate. I've turned that over to financial crimes.'

'What? Why? What have the finances got to do with it? They are all donated.'

The light blinked out and Paolo felt like he was back with Alice.

'Shall we start again?' he suggested. 'Tell me, Miss Towers, are you here to bring me a list of names prepared by Mr Mason and his staff?'

She looked as bewildered as Paolo felt. 'No, why should I?'

Paolo smiled. 'No reason at all. It was just a misunderstanding. What can I do for you?'

'You can send in your men to remove the filth on the shelves in the youth centre.'

'I'm afraid you are going to have to be a bit more specific.'

'Books, officer! Books that will corrupt the minds of our young if we allow them to be read. I went there today. I go every day to see what I can do to help out. As a gesture of goodwill I took in all my old Richmal Crompton and Enid Blyton novels to donate to the open library. Do you know the young woman there was barely civil to me? She had the cheek to say those books were hardly likely to appeal to anyone. Old-fashioned she called them. Do you know what's on the shelves there? The complete range of the dreadful Potter books, that blasphemous Pullman trilogy, not to mention those subversive *Twilight* books and the Lord only knows how many others equally vile.'

Paolo realised too late that the woman had the light of an evangelist in her eyes. Silently promising to get his own back on CC for passing a madwoman on to him, he smiled at his visitor.

'I'm afraid the books at the centre are outside my remit.'

'Perhaps,' she said, 'but not outside your remit as a parent to explain to your daughter the error of her ways!'

'What on earth has my daughter to do with anything?'

'She was the one who was so rude to me! In fact, she told me to mind my own business.'

Paolo found himself silently applauding Katy and wishing he could follow her example, but he couldn't tell the woman to get lost, unfortunately.

'Look, I don't think reading a bit of fantasy hurt anyone.'

'That's where you're wrong,' she hissed. 'Fantasy leads young minds into the dark arts. It's because of books like that we have murders and rapes in the classroom!'

Paolo stood up. 'I promise you I'll look into it. Allow me to show you out.'

She smacked her palm down on his desk. 'Don't humour me, young man. I've been held against my will in the grip of evil forces. I know what it's like to be sucked into the depths of depravity. I'm going to keep an eye on things over at that centre and if there's any sign of—'

'You let me know if you spot any evil doings,' Paolo said, moving towards the door and opening it. 'I'll certainly look out for you and will take action if I see you again.'

She stood up and shook out her denim skirt, looking him up and down. 'You are responsible for this town's morals. I'm not sure you're up to the job, but I'll pray for you.'

'Thank you,' Paolo said, looking out into the main office and signalling to CC to come over. 'Please show Miss Towers out and then come back here afterwards.'

He went back into his office and shut the door. Leaning back against it, he allowed the laughter to seep out. He had no doubt he would receive another visit from Miss Towers. The only thing to decide was where to hide when she came looking for him.

When CC came back she held a list in her hand, which she silently passed over to Paolo.

'You look as if you're in shock, CC. Did the delightful Miss Towers favour you with her message about the dangers to our youth?'

CC nodded. 'Is she for real?'

'Sad to say, I think she is. She genuinely believes the children of today are corrupted by the books they read. Anyway, that's her problem, not ours. Let's have a look at this list. Who brought it in, by the way?'

'Mason's secretary, April Greychurch.'

He glanced down. 'No one stands out as a possible suspect for the vandalism.' He handed the paper back to CC. 'Give this to Andrea and ask her to work her way through the names. She might come up with someone who bears Montague Mason a grudge.'

CC laughed. 'I would have thought she could do that without even trying.'

Paolo grinned back. 'What I meant was, someone with a stronger than usual grudge against him. I know the man isn't exactly likeable, but someone went to the trouble of humiliating him publicly. Either that person loathes him, or feels the need to highlight a genuine concern. We have a duty to find out which it is.'

As CC went to close the door, Paolo called her back. 'Send Dave in to me, would you? I haven't seen a copy of his notes from last night.'

CC frowned. 'He's not in yet. He told me yesterday he might struggle to get in on time.'

Paolo looked at his watch. This was the third time this month Dave had been late. 'OK, when he shows up, tell him I'd like a word.'

She nodded and closed the door.

Half an hour later, it opened again and Dave came in.

'Sorry I was late, sir. It won't happen again.'

'Problems?'

Dave shrugged. 'Not really. Well, yes, in a way, but nothing to do with work.'

Paolo waited. If Dave wanted to unload, he would.

Dave moved across the room and pulled out a chair. As he sat down, a massive sigh escaped.

'It's the wedding, sir. It's taking over my life. Who'd have thought getting married would involve so much planning and preparation!'

Paolo grinned. 'I had a feeling that's what the problem was. I've been through it myself. Don't worry; it does come to an end eventually.'

Dave looked haggard rather than relieved at Paolo's words. 'Really, sir? But when? The wedding is still four months away, but it's all Rebecca and her mother talk about. Catering, flowers, clothes, cakes, venue for the reception and I don't know what more. It's driving me nuts.' He took a breath. 'Shall I tell you why I was late today? Apparently it was urgent that we made a decision on the type of buttonholes our guests would have. I got away as soon as I could, but if this is a taste of married life, I'm not sure I've made the right decision.'

'As I said, Dave, it will pass, but you need to explain to Rebecca that getting in on time takes precedence over wedding discussions.'

Dave looked up as if he'd been stung. 'I did apologise for coming in late, sir.'

'Yes, I know you did and, to be honest, I wouldn't normally have said anything, but after all that rubbish in the papers earlier this year about you getting preferential treatment because you're the Chief Constable's nephew, I want to make sure you don't get any further accusations thrown your way.'

'Has someone complained?'

'Not yet,' Paolo said, 'but you can bet your life it will happen. Now that word is out about your relationship to the man upstairs, anyone with even the smallest grudge will be looking to see if you get away with things that they don't. I'm sorry, but that's the way life is. You know that as well as I do.'

'I'm not stupid, sir. I've heard the whispers and seen the nudges. I just didn't expect you to join forces with the small-minded masses.'

'For Christ's sake, Dave, why the hell do you think I've spoken to you today? It's to stop the gossip, not join in with it!'

Dave looked as if he wanted to say something, thought better of it, and swallowed whatever words were trying to escape.

'You wanted to see my notes from last night,' he said, appearing to Paolo as if he was having to force each word out. 'Let's hope they are professional enough to stop accusations of my being on the team just because my uncle is top dog.'

Chapter Four

The light tap on his office door had never sounded more welcoming to Paolo. Dave looked as though he wanted to explode and Paolo didn't blame him, but facts were facts. Whatever Dave did was looked on by others to see if he was using his family connection as an unfair advantage.

'Come in,' he called out, not caring who was outside, just grateful for the interruption.

CC stuck her head round the door. 'Sorry to interrupt you, sir, but Andrea has whittled the list of those with access to the plaque down to more manageable proportions. Do you want to go through it now, or shall I come back?'

Paolo waved at the seat next to Dave. 'Come in. We'll go through it together and decide which names to follow up first.'

He waited while CC had got herself settled, pleased to notice there was no constraint between the two team members.

'Right, what have you got for us?'

CC laid the paper on the desk and angled it so that all three could read the names.

'First up is, of course, Montague Mason. I realise he's the one under fire, but we can't ignore the fact that he might have done it himself for some reason as yet unknown.'

Paolo nodded, even though he was pretty sure after the previous night's discussion that Montague was genuinely distraught at what had happened.

'I think we can rule him out,' he said. 'Who's next?'

'His secretary, April Greychurch. She has more access than most, as she's spent much of the time on her own during the last few days. As you know, sir, Montague has been out and about a lot, meeting and greeting the centre's sponsors.'

She tapped the page with her pen. 'The next one is interesting. George Baron was in a couple of times. He's the owner of that newish businessmen's club on the other side of town.'

'Triple B?' Dave asked. 'Was he one of the sponsors?'

'Not as far as I know,' Paolo said.

'Then why would he be at the youth centre?'

'Good question, Dave. I think you and I should go and find out the answer to that one. Who's next?'

CC grinned. 'You'll love this one, sir. It's our very own Miss Clementine Towers.'

'Not the woman who was here warning about books being subversive?'

'The very same,' she said. 'Apparently, she's there every day sticking her nose into what's going on. She's worried about the town's morals.'

Paolo laughed. 'I know she is. She told me I was supposed to be guardian of them but didn't think I was up to the job. To be honest, I agree with her.'

CC dropped her pen. 'You think books are subversive?'

'No, I meant I agree with her that I'm not up to the task of being guardian of the town's morals. I don't think anyone would be. Anyway, she is definitely one to watch. Let's move on. Who else do we have?'

'The new swimming coach, Derrick Walden. He's there at all hours, according to the information we received from the centre. The next one is my personal favourite, Fletcher Simpson. We all know how much he was opposed to money being diverted towards the centre's renovation project. It would suit him down to the ground to cast suspicion on the rival project.'

Paolo glanced up. 'Yes, it's common knowledge where he thought the money should have gone. I wonder what took him to the youth centre. Another one for us to visit, Dave.'

'The only other person of note is the caretaker, Arbnor Bajrami. I believe you know him, sir?' CC said.

Paolo nodded. 'I arranged the position for him last year after many of the Albanian businesses closed down. I can't see him putting his job in jeopardy when he was so grateful to find work, but I'll have a word the next time I'm at the centre.'

'That just leaves William Coburn,' CC said. 'He's the electrical contractor. I don't know why he was there after the plaque had been put in place. Maybe the spotlight shining down onto it needed moving or something.'

'Okay, CC, you go with Andrea to interview Coburn the electrician and the delightful Miss Towers. Dave and I will go to the centre. We'll speak to Arbnor and Derrick Walden, then we'll drop in on Montague's secretary to see what she knows about the visit from George Baron, then we'll call on the man himself and finish off with Fletcher Simpson. Busy day ahead for us, Dave.' Then he noticed the look on CC's face. 'What?' he said.

'You palmed Miss Towers off onto me when you know she only likes to speak to those at the top.'

Paolo laughed. 'Tell her you're planning a coup to replace me. That should put her firmly on your side.'

CC grinned. 'How do you know I'm not doing exactly that?'

Before Paolo could answer, Dave shoved his chair back and rose.

'If we're down to banter, I'd better go and catch up on the work I should have been doing this morning instead of choosing bloody flowers. I'll be at my desk when you need me.'

CC's grin faded as Dave left the room. 'What's eating him?'

Paolo sighed. 'Wedding planning blues, back biting gossip and some malicious whispers about nepotism. You've got your ear closer to the ground than I have. What've you heard?'

'Not very much, sir. I think everyone knows better than to slag Dave off in front of me. It's not fair. He probably works harder than any of us. I know I didn't like him when he first arrived, but he's kinda grown on me.'

Paolo nodded. 'Me too. The problem is this wedding of his coming up. He's been in late a few times and people get antsy about it.'

CC picked up the list and rose. 'Well, maybe they should consider the number of times he's first in and last out. I think he more than makes up for the odd hour he's late, don't you?'

Paolo stared at the door for a while after CC had left. She'd made a valid point. Who'd have believed a year or so ago that CC would be Dave's champion. He smiled. Funny how life turned out. Looking at his watch, he decided he just had time to call Jessica before going out on the interviews.

As he touched the screen to make the call, he found himself willing her to answer it, but his wish wasn't granted. It went immediately to voicemail.

'Jessica Carter's phone. Leave a message. I'll get back to you.'

'Um, hi, Jess. Just wondered how you were doing. Miss you. Call me.'

He clicked off the call and tried, unsuccessfully, not to dwell on the fact that his last four calls had gone straight to voicemail.

CC's words played on a loop through Paolo's mind while Dave was negotiating traffic across Bradchester. Dave was, without a doubt, the hardest working member of his team, but sadly that wouldn't stop the backbiters from making their snide comments.

As they pulled up outside the youth centre, Paolo turned to his DS.

'Look, about this morning. I wasn't having a go at you, I hope you realise that.'

Dave shrugged. 'I know. I'm sorry I snapped in your office, but all this crap since the press found out about my uncle is doing my head in.'

Paolo climbed out of the car and leant on the roof. 'Don't take this the wrong way,' he said when Dave's head appeared on the other side of the car, 'but would you like me to put you in for a transfer?'

'You want to get rid of me?' Dave said, slamming his door with more force than Paolo felt was necessary. 'I thought you said—'

Paolo sighed. 'I knew you'd take it the wrong way. I'm offering you a chance to move away from here. To transfer to a branch where no one knows your background. If you don't want to take it, that suits me just fine. I don't want to lose you.'

'I'm not going anywhere,' Dave said. 'If some back at the station don't like it, they can stick it.'

Paolo smiled. 'OK, that's that sorted. Shall we get started? Walden, Bajrami and then Greychurch. April has only been Montague's secretary for a few months, so I don't know her as well as his previous secretary.'

'What happened to the one he had before?' Dave asked as they walked across to the youth centre's main door.

'She retired. April is also on the team of sports instructors here. She'll be giving lessons in the evenings after she finishes work. I believe she has a black belt in one of the martial arts CC is so terrifyingly good at.'

Dave held the door open for Paolo to pass into the centre. 'Which one, sir? CC has belts in three, I believe.'

Paolo shook his head. 'No idea. All I know is that there is no way I would ever mess with either woman. I've seen them both bodily pick up men and throw them to the ground. I'd look like a right idiot being tossed about as if I weighed no more than a bag of sugar.'

Dave laughed. 'I can just imagine it. CC terrifies most of our bad boys. I'm quite sure they would far rather see you or me bearing down on them than CC determined to make an arrest.'

They made their way to the pool area, but there was no sign of Derrick Walden. Paolo walked over to the lifeguard to see if she knew where to find the swimming coach.

She shrugged. 'He was here just now. Have you looked in his office? His next lesson's not for another hour, so maybe he's gone to grab something to eat. Police, hey? Is he in trouble?'

'No, not at all. We're talking to everyone who was here in the

25

couple of days leading up to the opening ceremony to see if any-one spotted anything suspicious. Were you around then?'

She laughed. 'Nope, I only started here today. I read all about it, though. Stuffing up the plaque really put Mason's nose out of joint.'

Paolo raised his eyebrows. 'Nasty thing to do though, don't you think?'

Her eyes widened. 'Yes, I mean, no, I . . . Sorry, it seemed funny to me when I saw the headlines, but I suppose it wasn't really.'

'No, it wasn't, especially as people seem to have decided the allegation is true without any proof. You wouldn't like it if it happened you, would you?' He watched her face change as that thought settled in. 'We'll check out his office, but if he isn't there we've got a couple of other people to speak to, so we'll drop in again on our way out. If Derrick comes back, ask him to wait for us, would you?'

As they left the pool area, Dave held the door open for Paolo to pass through.

'Bit hard on her, weren't you, sir?'

Paolo shrugged. 'I don't particularly like Mason, as you know, but it gets on my bloody nerves when people read crap in the papers and decide whatever's been printed must be true. Whatever happens now, innocent or guilty, Mason will always have people thinking he must have done something dodgy. Anyway, if Derrick isn't around, we can chat to Arbnor Bajrami and see if he saw anything. His room is next door to Derrick's.'

They made their way to the swimming coach's office just off from the changing rooms and lockers, but it was empty. As was the caretaker's room next door.

'Not our day today. Another one to come back to after we've spoken to April,' Paolo said, leading the way to the staircase.

On the first floor, he and Dave were heading for the offices at the end of the corridor when Arbnor came out of one of the side doors and careered straight into Paolo. He looked ill-at-ease, as if Paolo was the last person he'd expected, or wanted, to see.

'Sorry,' he said. 'I wasn't looking where I was going.'

Paolo straightened his jacket and shrugged. 'Don't worry, no damage done. We were coming to talk to you, anyway. Shall we go in there and chat?' he said, pointing to the door Arbnor had closed behind him.

'No!' Arbnor said. 'Sorry, I have such a lot to do and need to get on. We'll talk later, yes?'

'Well, no. I'd like a quick word with you now, if that's OK.'

Arbnor made no move to open the door. He reminded Paolo of a guard dog.

'We can talk here,' he said. 'What do you want to know?'

'You're at the centre most days. Did you notice anyone acting suspicious after the plaque was covered? Any idea who might have decided to cause an upset?'

Visibly relaxing, Arbnor smiled. 'No, I didn't see anyone, but I wasn't surprised. There are many people who dislike Mr Mason.'

'Would you care to name some names?'

Arbnor shook his head. 'I'm like two of the three monkeys. I see nothing. I hear nothing. But if I had, I would tell you.'

He turned towards the stairs, but Paolo put his hand out to stop him.

'If you think of anything, no matter how small, that might point us in the right direction, you call me, OK?'

'Yes, I'll call if I remember anything, but there is nothing. Sorry, I must go. Very busy.'

As Arbnor fled down the stairs, Paolo turned to Dave. 'What did you make of that?'

'I get the distinct impression he has something to hide, but whether it's to do with the plaque, I haven't a clue.'

Paolo shook his head. 'Me neither, but that was very odd. I think I'll keep a watchful eye on Arbnor Bajrami. When the crime syndicate blew up last year I thought he was a victim, but maybe I was wrong.'

'He speaks very good English,' Dave said.

'Many Albanians do. Those that came here as children went to school in Bradchester. If they're going to have an accent, it would be a local one.'

They walked along the corridor and knocked on April Grey-church's door. She looked over the top of her computer screen and smiled when she saw Paolo. Sitting opposite her and sipping from a bottle emblazoned with a distinctive sports logo was the swimming coach. As usual, Derrick Walden's long hair was pulled taut off his face and tied back with a black band, giving the coach a permanent look of surprise.

'The long arm of the law. Come in,' April said. 'Mr Walden was just leaving.'

Derrick stood up, still clutching his designer bottle. Paolo was surprised at how tall the man was. He'd seen him around the place before, but this was the first time he'd stood next to him. Derrick towered over him by a good few inches.

'I was downstairs looking for you just now,' Paolo said. 'I'll be down after I've had a quick word with April. OK with you?'

Derrick nodded. 'Sure thing.' He turned to April. 'Chat again later?'

She nodded, but Paolo got the impression she'd rather have said no. He waited until Derrick had closed the door behind him before turning to April.

'Is he bothering you?'

She laughed. 'No one bothers me, Paolo. Anyone gives me grief, I know how to deal with them.'

Recalling his earlier words to Dave, Paolo imagined the slightly built woman felling the swimming coach with one blow. Derrick Walden wouldn't enjoy that experience.

'Are you here to lock up bloody Clementine Towers?' she said, grinning at him. 'You're too late; she left an hour ago. It would make my day if that lunatic was shut away somewhere.'

'Why, what's she done?'

April laughed. 'Nothing really, apart from try to tell everyone here what they are doing wrong and how she could do it better. That's why Derrick was up here. Clementine doesn't feel he should be teaching the girls. Says it's inappropriate for a man to see them in their costumes and that there should be segregation in the pool. Did you know she's put her name down on the volunteers list for everything you can think of, from working in the canteen to washing floors? No matter where I go, I bump into her. Some people think she's the best thing that ever happened to the centre, but I think she's a nosy interfering busybody with nothing better to do with her time!'

Paolo grinned back. 'I've met her. You're not a fan?'

'Fan? I'd drown her in the swimming pool if I thought I could get away with it. OK, so you and this gorgeous hunk haven't come to arrest our crazy lady. How can I help you?'

'We're just following up on everyone who had access to the plaque after it was put in place, April.'

She grinned. 'Oooh, can I be a suspect? Can this nice young man take me down to the station and force the truth out of me?'

Paolo laughed as a crimson tide flooded Dave's cheeks. Who'd have believed the misogynist who'd first come to work with him would be hiding a shy and easily discomfited man?

'Nice young man? Have you two never met?'

She shook her head. 'I would never forget that face and body,' she said, making a great show of looking Dave up and down.

'Behave yourself, April. That's sexual harassment and if someone spoke to you like that you'd be understandably angry. Besides, you're embarrassing the poor man. This is Detective Sergeant Dave Johnson. Dave, this woman winding you up is April Greychurch. Right, now that's out of the way, what can you tell us about the two days leading up to the unveiling?'

The laughter stopped and she frowned. Paolo was pleased to see she took the question seriously.

'Other than the list I prepared and dropped off at the station, not very much, I'm afraid. I put down all the names I could think of where people had been left on their own for short periods of time.'

'A couple of them seemed a bit out of place here: Fletcher

Simpson and George Baron. Any idea what either of them were doing here?'

She shook her head. 'Not a clue. I didn't see Baron myself. His name was given to me by someone and I just added it to my list.'

'Can you remember who told you about him?'

She shrugged. 'Not really. I went round asking everyone and wrote the names down as I went. I can find out for you if it's important.'

'No, don't worry at the moment. If it turns out we need to know, I'll come back again. What about Fletcher Simpson?'

'I put his name down. I spotted his back as he was going out through the doors.'

'But you don't know who he'd been to see or why he was here?'

'As I said earlier, I haven't a clue. By the way, have you been able to match the lipstick?' April asked.

Paolo shook his head. 'It's being tested at the moment, but I don't hold out much hope on that score. I doubt the lab results will show anything other than a standard easy to purchase brand.'

'Hmm,' she said. 'I have a horrible feeling it might be mine.'

'Did you do it?' Paolo asked.

She laughed. 'No, don't be daft. The thing is, I dropped my handbag near the plaque a couple of days ago and one of my lipsticks is missing. I have a feeling it must have rolled and I didn't spot it when I picked everything up.'

'Didn't you need it?' Dave asked.

April grinned. 'You think we ladies only carry one lipstick. One colour fits all occasions? I didn't want to use that shade until this morning and noticed it was gone. I'm not saying it was my lipstick that was used, but it could have been.'

Paolo tried to decide if she was telling the truth, or covering her tracks, but her face gave nothing away.

'Tell me, April, have you noticed anything odd about Arbnor? Does he seem to be acting strange to you?'

She shrugged. 'Not so that I'd noticed. What do you mean by

strange? You think he might have picked up the lipstick and got artistic with it?'

'No, nothing like that. We bumped into him coming out of one of the rooms along the hallway and he—'

'Which room?' she asked. 'There's no reason for him to be up here at all. He takes care of the centre downstairs, but up here it's just offices and storerooms.'

'Maybe he needed some supplies,' Dave suggested.

April shook her head and stood up. 'There's only office equipment, not cleaning supplies. Would you mind showing me which room it was?'

They walked back and Paolo pointed to the door Arbnor had come through. April opened it, but the room was empty apart from a desk adjacent to a day couch against one wall and a locked medical cabinet against the opposite wall.

'This is our sickroom,' April said. 'He shouldn't have been in here, but maybe he'd been having a sneaky nap and you surprised him.'

Paolo smiled. 'Could be,' he said, but didn't believe it. If anything, Arbnor had been wide awake and sweating a little.

'Who has the keys to the cabinet?' he asked.

April pulled a string from round her neck, showing a bunch of keys. 'I keep control of the medical supplies. Even the sports instructors have to come to me if they want anything from that cabinet.'

Paolo nodded. 'As you say, he was probably taking a nap.'

'Was there anything else, Paolo?'

'Yes, is Montague around? I'd like a word with him.'

April shook her head. 'He's out for the afternoon. No idea where. He didn't tell me.' She put her head on one side, as if considering whether to speak. Then nodded. 'Paolo, I honestly don't know who defaced the plaque, but . . .'

'But?' Paolo prompted when it became clear she wasn't going to finish her sentence.

'But I think there might be some truth in the accusation.'

'Really? What makes you say that?'

31

She shrugged. 'A couple of times I didn't think the numbers added up and mentioned it to Montague. He said to leave things for him to look into and on both occasions he found the error and put it right. The first time it happened I didn't think anything of it, but the second time he acted weird.'

'Weird in what way?'

'I don't know how to explain it. He was jumpy and raised his voice when he said he'd deal with it. I definitely got the impression he'd rather I hadn't picked up on the error.'

'Why didn't you raise this before?' Paolo asked. 'I've been here often enough.'

'Because it was only after the business with the plaque that it hit me how Montague had acted. Look, there's probably nothing in it and I imagined things that weren't there.'

Paolo smiled. 'Possibly, but financial crimes are going to look into the funding records. If there's anything even remotely dodgy, they will find it.'

They said goodbye to April and made their way back down to the pool area. Derrick Walden showed them into his office. It was a tiny space, but in the short time he'd been there Derrick had made it his own. A couple of Chelsea scarves were pinned to the wall above his desk and photos of teams through the ages filled every available wall space.

'We don't get many Chelsea fans round here,' Paolo said, pointing to the memorabilia. 'Like most places, we've got plenty of Man U fans that have never set foot anywhere near Manchester, but not many who support London clubs.'

Derrick smiled. 'I was born in London. Lived in lots of places over the years, but Chelsea's my team. Always has been, always will be. I believe in loyalty. Will this take long? I've got a lesson in half an hour.'

Paolo sat on one of the hard wooden seats opposite Derrick's desk and Dave took the other.

'We won't take up much of your time. We're just following up on everyone who was here during the time between the plaque being covered and the unveiling ceremony. Did you see or hear anything that might now seem odd, even if it didn't at the time?'

Derrick shook his head. 'Nothing I can recall, but most of the time I was down here, getting ready for the centre to open, planning my sessions and so on.'

'Forgive me,' Paolo said, 'but I have to ask. Did you deface the plaque, perhaps as a joke?'

'You must be joking! I'd never do anything to damage that man's reputation. If it wasn't for him, this place would still be a rundown dump and I wouldn't have this job. No way would I ever . . . bloody hell, I can't believe . . . I thought you wanted to know if I'd seen anything, now you're accusing me of doing it. Was it her? Did that bitch upstairs say it was me?'

'Calm down,' Paolo said. 'No one is accusing you of anything. What makes you think April would say such a thing?'

Derrick shrugged. 'I put two and two together. You've just come from there. She doesn't like me. I don't like her and so I thought . . . but obviously I was wrong.'

Paolo nodded to encourage him to keep talking. 'What's the issue between you two?'

'First of all, she's what we used to call a prick tease before the PC mob stepped in. She's all come on, big boy, show us what you've got, but shuts down completely if you take her up on it.'

'And secondly?' Paolo prompted.

'What?'

'You said, first of all, which implies there's another reason you don't get on with April.'

Derrick shrugged, picked up his bottle and took a sip before answering. 'I think she hates Montague, but pretends she's his best buddy and I don't like hypocrites. If you don't like someone, fine, but don't be all over them one minute, then badmouthing them the next. That's what she does.'

'If you don't get on, why were you in her office?' Paolo asked.

'As we have to work in the same building, I thought we should try to get over our differences, but she wasn't having any of it.'

Chapter Five

'What do we know about this club we're going to, sir? I can't say I've heard much about what goes on there.'

During the drive to the far side of Bradchester, while Dave listened to non-stop noise on the radio he swore was music, Paolo had allowed his thoughts to drift to Jessica and their lack of contact; was he seeing something sinister when the only problem was that she was too busy to call? At Dave's question, he dragged his attention back to job at hand.

'I must be honest, I know very little about Triple B, except that it's a private club. I tend to only take interest in those clubs where it's likely drugs are being peddled. Triple B has been open for just over a year and has never come up on our radar for any reason. Membership is by invitation only. I would imagine people get invited after existing members put names forward. I think the place operates as an old-fashioned men's club. You know the type of place I mean? Somewhere to go for good food and fine wine served in almost complete silence, apart from the snores of those who'd succumbed to an after-lunch doze in comfortable leather armchairs.'

Dave laughed. 'I can't imagine a more boring scenario.'

'That's if I'm right. And if I am, why would the owner of a place for retired businessmen be at the youth centre?'

'We're about to find out, sir,' Dave said over the voice of the SatNav telling them they'd reached their destination.

The car park was only half full, but there was a strong indication of the wealth of those enjoying membership. None of the vehicles looked older than a couple of years at most and they were all at the top end of the price range. Some serious money was using the club as a meeting place. Paolo decided he might need to revise his thoughts on the clientele.

They approached the porticoed entrance to a three-storey grand building that looked as if it might have been a hotel in the not too distant past. Wide steps led to an imposing lobby. A man who looked like he might have been a heavyweight boxer in a previous life stepped out from an alcove, preventing them from going beyond the doorway. Even though he was immaculately dressed, his demeanour was that of a bruiser ready for a fight.

'I'm sorry, gentlemen, but this is a private club. Members only.'

Paolo showed his warrant card. 'I'm Detective Inspector Paolo Sterling and this is Detective Sergeant Dave Johnson. We would like to see the owner, George Baron. I called earlier. Could you let him know we're here?'

'No need. I'm right here, aren't I! It's okay Chaz, I've been expecting this visit.'

Paolo looked across the lobby in the direction of the voice. The man who'd called out was nothing like he'd expected. Instead of a suave and polished upper-class man with a plum in his mouth, George Baron's speech showed he was from a working class background, but was trying to disguise the fact with a veneer of polish over his original accent. Paolo guessed London – probably south of the Thames. But it wasn't his voice which drew Paolo's attention. The right side of his face was covered in a dull purple birthmark almost in the shape of a question mark.

'Hello, Mr Baron. Thank you for seeing us at such short notice. Is there somewhere we can go that's a little more private?'

'Yeah, mate, come through to my office,' he said, leading the way back across the lobby to a door at the rear.

The room they entered was occupied by a woman in her mid-thirties, possibly a bit older, Paolo surmised. She looked up as they came in and Paolo had the impression she was sizing them up for some reason.

'This is my secretary, Trudy Chappell. Trudy, be a love and fetch some coffees for me and these nice officers, there's a good girl.'

Paolo hid a smile at the resentful look Trudy cast at George's back as he led the way into his own office through a door to the right of the secretary's desk. He noticed another door behind the desk and wondered where that one led.

'Come in, don't hang about out there,' George called. He settled himself behind a large mahogany desk and pointed to the two chairs facing him. 'Sit yourselves down and tell me how I can help you.'

Paolo sat down and waited for Dave to take out his notebook before continuing.

'Were you at the opening of the youth centre?' Paolo asked. 'I don't recall seeing you there, but it was pretty packed.'

George grinned. 'No, not my scene. I was invited, but didn't feel it was the type of evening I'd enjoy. Why do you ask? I've read the papers, so know what happened, but as I wasn't there I'm not sure what you think it's got to do with me.'

Paolo smiled. 'I don't suppose it has anything to do with you, but we're following up on anyone who was at the centre prior to the opening ceremony and your name came up. Forgive me for saying this, but I cannot imagine what reason you would have for calling in at the centre. As you've just pointed out, it isn't really your scene.'

George nodded as if he'd seen the light. 'I was there the day before opening, but it wasn't anything to do with the centre as such. I'd read in the paper that there was going to be a place where local businesses could advertise job vacancies. You know, get the unemployment figures down. I put up an advert for young men to come and work here – board and lodgings included.'

'Doing what, exactly?'

'Bar work, waiters, someone to help the gardener. We have quite a few vacancies here, but we're looking for the right type of young men. Those who won't repeat any business secrets they might overhear.'

There was a light tap on the door and Trudy came in bearing a tray. She placed it on George's desk and left without a word.

'That's going to be a bit hot. Would you like a look round the place while it cools down?'

'Thank you, yes,' Paolo said. 'I'd got it fixed in my mind that this was an upmarket old folk's refuge for retired businessmen. I take it I'm wrong?'

'Yes and no,' George said, picking up the phone. 'Hold on a moment. I just need to notify everyone we'll be coming round so that they can leave the public rooms if they wish to keep their anonymity. Chaz,' he said into the receiver, 'we're going to do a tour. Can you let the members know? Great. Thanks.'

He put down the receiver and smiled at Paolo.

'Our membership is a mix of retired and active businessmen. As well as private meeting areas, which I won't be taking you into, we've got bedrooms here so that our members can stay overnight if they so desire, but in the main most of them come for a few hours to unwind or meet their friends. Shall we go?'

He led them back into the lobby and then through one of the doors leading off from it.

'Through here we have the billiard room, which leads to the conservatory.'

After an exhaustive trip around the public dining rooms, various lounges, the library and television room, Paolo knew no matter how much money he might have, this would never be somewhere he could belong, or would ever want to. It was a place of privilege for those few at the top who wanted to keep the plebs at bay.

'What's on the upper two floors?'

'Bedrooms, private dining rooms, places for members to be alone if that's what they need. You've seen all the public areas now. What do you think of the place?'

'Very plush.'

'You sound disapproving,' George said as the crossed the marble floor of the lobby.

'Not disapproving, just not somewhere I'd feel comfortable putting my feet up on the coffee table and relaxing,' Paolo said, turning to frown at the laugh Dave managed to turn into a coughing fit.

37

As they re-entered the office, George shrugged. 'Our members are not really the type to put their feet on the coffee tables. Me, now, that's different. I often do exactly that at home, but then my background is more, let's say, earthy than theirs. Sit down again, do. Is there anything else I can help you with?'

'Not at the moment. Did you have any success with your advert at the centre?' Paolo asked, trying not to grimace as he swallowed a mouthful of lukewarm coffee.

'A couple of young men applied, but neither of them wanted to live in.'

'Does that matter?' Paolo asked.

'You've seen how far off the bus route we are here. The only way to guarantee workers without their own transport get in on time is to have them living in. Chaz, the man you met at the door, lives in and Trudy drives to work each day. Is that everything? I am quite busy and must get on.'

'Just one last question before we go,' Paolo said. 'Do you know of anyone who might bear Montague Mason a grudge? Someone who would deface the plaque in order to cast aspersions on him?'

'I can't think of anyone. Montague's always seemed pretty inoffensive to me.'

'Oh, you know him socially?'

'Not exactly,' George said. 'I see him from time to time, but we're not buddies or anything like that.'

'Is he one of your members?' Paolo asked with a smile.

George laughed. 'Now you know better than to ask me that. This is a private club and unless you have a warrant to see the members' list, I don't have to tell you who's on it, do I?'

'Nope, there's no reason you have to tell us anything. I'm curious about the name, though. Why Triple B?'

George hesitated and then laughed. 'Hubris. This is the third club I've opened and the B stands for Baron.'

Paolo nodded, as if that made perfect sense, but had the distinct impression George was lying to him. For some reason George found the name of his club humorous in a way he had no intention of sharing.

They said their goodbyes and headed back to the car park. As they got into the car, Paolo mulled over the way the world split into those with money and those without. A man like George Baron wouldn't have been given the time of day by his wealthy members if he was poor, but since he clearly had the funds to own the building and finance the club, that made him acceptable to them – at least as far as mixing at the club went. Paolo was willing to bet few of them would invite George to a private dinner party in their own homes.

'What did you make of him, Dave?'

'I'm not sure. He was almost too affable and obliging for my liking. I felt he had something to hide, but not to do with the plaque at the youth centre. You?'

Paolo thought for a moment. 'I got the same impression. I felt he didn't want us there, but went out of his way to give us the grand tour. It seemed as if he was trying too hard to show us how innocent the place was. I think he's involved in something dodgy, but I haven't a clue what it is. Oh well, until he breaks the law, Mr Baron is not our concern.' He smiled. 'Did you see the look his secretary gave him? No love lost there, that's for sure.'

Dave laughed. 'I'm surprised his suit jacket didn't catch fire the way she glared at his back.'

'The doorman looked more like a nightclub bouncer than a welcoming soul, didn't you think?'

Dave nodded. 'If I'm honest, the place gave me the creeps, but I don't know why.'

He started the car and reached out to key in the next destination into the SatNav.

'Where to now, sir?'

'Fletcher Simpson. Let's see what his reasons are for being in the youth centre. He was completely opposed to the renovations and tried everything he could to block funding for it, so it seems a bit odd that he just happened to drop in when he did.'

Chapter Six

Fletcher Simpson's offices were housed in a former warehouse next to the canal in the industrial complex. In Bradchester terms, Simpson was considered a magnate. In world terms, he ran a very small, but rapidly expanding, mini-empire.

As they got out of the car, Paolo's thoughts must have shown on his face, because Dave laughed.

'You don't think much of Mr Simpson, do you, sir?'

'Does it show?'

'I'm afraid so. It's that glacial look you get when we're going to see someone you don't approve of. You could freeze warts off with it.'

'Glacial? Nice one, Dave, very graphic.' Paolo pointed to the warehouse. 'Our Fletcher Simpson never shuts up about what he's done for Bradchester. If you give him half a second he's in and goes on about it as if he single-handedly saved the town from an economic crisis.'

Dave shrugged. 'He has provided lots of new jobs; you can't deny that, sir.'

'I don't deny it. I know he has. It's his attitude that grates. Everything he does is because it benefits him first and foremost. The fact that Bradchester does well out of it is secondary, but he promotes himself in that newspaper of his as the second Messiah – here to save the world one step at a time, starting right here, when in truth all he's really doing is building his bank balance.'

Paolo took a breath to stop himself from letting fly with a full-scale rant. The canal did need renovation, there was no question about that, but for Fletcher Simpson to put it across as if he was only interested in the improvements for the good of the community stuck in Paolo's throat.

He walked over to the canal edge, taking care to avoid tripping on the uneven paving. The last thing he needed was a fully dressed dip in the water. God knows what germs had bred in there.

While at school he'd learned the history of the canal and its importance to industry. In years gone by, the canal had been the lifeblood of Bradchester. Massive barges carrying raw materials to the factories and transporting finished products to other towns and cities had been a common sight. In one picture he recalled from those far off schooldays, the canal had been so congested with barges coming and going they had devised a traffic system to keep the waterway moving.

Now, the only barges in evidence were those that had been converted into houseboats. Paolo's eye was drawn further along the canal to the permanent moorings provided by the Simpson Holiday Accommodation and Travel Company. Brightly painted exteriors, with plants cascading from roof gardens, made him smile in spite of his objection to the man who'd made the burgeoning houseboat community possible. It must be nice, he thought, to wake to the feel of gently moving water and know that, if the urge was strong enough, you could start the engine and chug off to a different place every day.

Paolo shook his head and turned to Dave.

'You think I see people only in black and white?'

Dave nodded. 'Very few shades of grey in your world, sir.' He drew an imaginary line in the air. 'This side good guys, that side bad guys.'

Paolo shrugged. 'You think that's wrong?'

'Not if we're talking about villains, but when it's someone like Fletcher Simpson, I think we should give him the benefit of the doubt. You see it as making money for himself and the town benefitting as a side effect, which could well be the case, but is that so bad? The town still does well out of it.'

Paolo smiled. 'That's not what gets to me. It's the saint's halo he carries around with him that pisses me off. If he was honest and said, "I'm out to make money for me. If I do well, then so will Bradchester," I wouldn't have a problem with him. But he doesn't. He tries to appear as if he is running his various businesses as benevolent ventures and the fact that he makes money from his activities is something he had never anticipated nor wanted. In short, he's a hypocrite and that's what I can't stand—'

He heard the anger in his voice and stopped mid-sentence. He grinned at Dave, then turned and walked towards the buildings set back from the canal bank.

'You do it on purpose, don't you?' he said when Dave caught up with him.

'What, wind you up? Course I do, sir. It's so easy.'

'Bloody well stop it. I'm not here for your entertainment.'

'No, sir, whatever you say, sir,' Dave said, pulling a non-existent forelock.

Laughing, they reached the building and went inside. Although from the outside it still looked like a warehouse, from the moment they stepped over the threshold all traces of its previous incarnation disappeared. Their surroundings could have been photographed for an interior design magazine feature. Walls had been erected to segregate the previously open area into smaller self-contained office units. On the left as they entered, a wrought iron and stained wood spiral staircase led to the floors above. A mini waterfall cascaded down the wall to their right. Directly in front of them was a waiting area with three cream leather couches, a low metal and glass table was covered in glossy magazines, and against the far wall, a higher, but matching, metal and glass table holding the type of coffee machine Paolo had never quite got the hang of using. A wooden bowl contained capsules that he had been told he simply had to insert into the right slot for the coffee of his choice to appear from the spout. Jessica had one in her kitchen and it made Paolo look like a complete idiot every time he tried to use it. If he got the capsule in the right place, the water wouldn't come through. If the water came gushing out, it would be as clear as day because the capsule wouldn't have opened.

'This is all very nice,' Dave said, 'but are we supposed to wait here in the hope that someone will arrive?'

As he spoke, the waterfall slid to one side revealing an open plan office with three desks. The occupant of the desk nearest to them stood up and walked over.

'Hello, I'm Melissa Taylor. You must be Detective Inspector Sterling and Detective Sergeant Johnson. Mr Simpson is expecting you. If you take the stairs to the first floor, he will meet you there.'

'Thank you, Melissa, but how did you know we were waiting?' Paolo asked.

She smiled. 'One way mirror. The water is reflected on the lobby side, but we can see through from this side. Neat, huh?'

'Very,' Paolo agreed, enjoying her enthusiasm.

When he and Dave reached the floor above, Fletcher Simpson was there to meet them, as promised. At six feet five, he towered over them. His fair hair had been brushed into a style more suited to a teenager, but Paolo guessed that was more to hide the man's growing bald patches than for fashion.

'Welcome, Paolo. Let's go through to my office. Have you come to interrogate me about the vandalism? I'll be honest, it made my morning when I saw Montague's humiliation splashed across all the papers.'

He led the way along a corridor lined with photographs of his various businesses. Everything was represented, from the local dairy to his newspaper and radio interests. His office reflected the man perfectly. It was all cold colours, shades of silver, blue and grey, and sharp edges on modern furniture that looked unyielding, but turned out to be surprisingly comfortable when Paolo sat down.

'Would you like some coffee, or is this a flying visit?'

'Not a flying visit, but no coffee for me, thank you,' Paolo said. Dave, taking a seat opposite Fletcher, shook his head as well.

'Right then, down to business. Why are you here? I wasn't even at the ceremony, so don't see what you want to question me about.'

'The message was written at some point earlier in the day, or the day before. We know this because prior to that it hadn't been covered with the drape, so any vandalism would have been noticed.'

'Fair enough,' Fletcher said, 'but I repeat, what has that got to do with me?'

'You were seen at the centre during the day of the opening. Taking into account your animosity towards the place, I need to ask you why you went and what you did while there.'

Fletcher laughed. 'Do I look like the type to sneak a lipstick into a place to scrawl a badly spelled accusation?'

'I don't know,' Paolo said. 'Is there a type for that? I would have thought someone with reason to want to see Montague humiliated might think that was as good a way of doing it as any.'

'Not me,' Fletcher said. 'So you can just scratch my name off your list.'

Paolo nodded. 'I'll do that with pleasure, but you still need to tell me why you went to the centre.'

'I happened to be passing and decided to call in to see how public money had been used.'

'Really? You just happened to be passing and dropped in?'

Fletcher sighed. 'Yes. It was a spur of the moment decision. I told you, I wanted to see what had been done with the money I'd hoped would go into the canal restoration. Not that it matters now. I intend to fund the project myself as a gift to the community.'

Paolo caught Dave grinning at him and realised his face must have reflected how he felt on hearing Fletcher's predictable words.

'How exactly will it be a gift to the community when you are the one who will benefit from it the most?'

Fletcher looked at Paolo as if he couldn't believe what he'd heard. 'Business and tourism, Paolo. The two biggest money spinners for the town. Renovating the canal and opening it up to narrow boat holidays will improve tourism. The hotel further

44

along the canal, which I admit I own, will also benefit, but so will the town. The more businesses grow, the more jobs there are. It's a total win-win situation for everyone. The youth centre, on the other hand, doesn't provide jobs in the same way. Yes, you've taken on a few instructors, but in the main, you're simply encouraging young people to hang around waiting for things to happen.'

He finished by muttering something Paolo didn't quite catch, but it sounded derogatory towards Montague Mason.

'I'm sorry; you'll have to repeat that last comment.'

'I said and who knows what might happen with Montague let loose near impressionable teenagers.'

Paolo sat forward. 'What do you mean by that?'

'Do I really need to spell it out for you? I would have thought, having spent the last year in Montague's charming company, you would know exactly what I meant.'

'Yes, you do need to spell it out. If you think the young people at the centre are in any kind of danger, you need to tell me.'

Fletcher shook his head. 'I wasn't implying he likes them young, just that I wouldn't want my teenagers, if I had any, to use him as a role model. Why don't you dig into his private life a little? I'm sure there must be one or two who will have a tale to tell. Now, if there's nothing else I can do for you, I have a business to run and I'm sure you have criminals to catch.'

He stood up and held out his hand.

'Don't look on me as an enemy, Paolo. I don't like Montague Mason, but that doesn't make me a bad man.'

As they descended the stairs, the sound of the waterfall got louder, but overriding that was a voice in Paolo's head reminding him he hadn't yet asked Katy and Danny what they'd done to get on the wrong side of Montague. If he discovered the man had tried it on with Katy, Paolo wasn't sure the policeman in him would be able to control the father who'd want Montague's head on a plate.

45

Chapter Seven

Nemesis in Action Blog
Day Three – Jason Corbett

I keep getting this feeling I'm being watched. Maybe I'm imagining it, but the sensation is quite strong. I'm pretty sure I've not been careless enough to let anything slip, but maybe someone has found out who I am. If that is the case, I won't take any chances. I'll deal with the problem; grit my teeth and do it. My work is too important to allow any nosey bastards to stop me.

When I went into the punishment room to deliver Jason's final course of treatment, he was lying so still, I thought at first he was dead. Then I saw his body quiver. It was barely perceptible, but it showed he was alive. I went over and shook his shoulder, expecting another snarl of defiance, but he barely moved. I suppose I might have gone a bit overboard with the tazer the night before, but he'd been harder to break than the others. I'd managed it in the end, though. The marks on his flesh would heal soon enough. I knew from experience, the marks on his mind would last him a lifetime.

'Time for your final session, Jason. Come on, I need you to be awake for it.'

A groan was all I got in response, but that was enough to show he was still in the land of the living. Although, I suppose he was probably wishing he wasn't. There were times when death seemed preferable to life and the way I'd ridden Jason last night might well have pushed him to that point.

As I forced my way through his ruptured flesh, his scream of agony almost deafened me. I pushed in as deep as I could, whispering to remind him of the hold I had over him.

'I know where you live . . . I know where you work. I can pick you up any time I choose, day or night . . . I'll be watching your every move,' I warned, exertion making it hard to speak without gasping.

I had to wait until I'd finished before I delivered my final threat. I needed to make sure he was paying attention. I pulled out slowly, knowing each tiny movement would bring fresh agonies. When his final scream died down to broken whimpers, I leaned close to his ear.

'If you go to the police, I'll pick you up again. You can never hide from me, not even if you move to a different town. I'll find you and bring you back. The next time I'll keep you here for four days. Think you can handle what you've already gone through plus an extra day?'

Jason muttered something. It didn't matter what he said, he was mine to do with as I pleased. There was no way he would go to the police knowing I was watching him.

'This is what you have to remember, Jason. These are the new rules for the rest of your life. If you want sex, you stay home and play one-handed. If you feel the urge to terrorise someone, you stay home and remember what you've experienced here. If you even think about returning to your old ways, do yourself a favour and stay home because going out could cost you your life. I am Nemesis. Remember that I'll be tracking your every move. I will know if you step even an inch out of line and I *will* come for you. Don't ever doubt that. When you least expect it, I will capture you and bring you back here.'

Jason's face was turned away, but I knew he'd heard me from his quiet sobbing.

'Would you like a drink?'

'Yes.'

The word rasped out from a throat raw from screaming, begging for mercy I'd had no intention of supplying. Three days without water was supposed to be the limit of human endurance. He'd gone two and a half days and been tortured. That was probably beyond the limit of most people's endurance. He'd had his punishment. It was time to put Jason back where he'd committed his crimes.

I placed a straw next to his lips and watched as he greedily sucked down the water laced with Rophynol. In his weakened state, it wouldn't take long for the drug to work. The next part was the trickiest, but I'd done it so many times now, I didn't expect any problems.

I went out into the hallway to fetch the wheelbarrow and manoeuvred it into place next to the table. I cut through the string bonds and heaved him off the table. He fell with a thud into the wheelbarrow. I looked down and saw I'd need to change clothes before getting in the car.

As I wheeled him along the corridor and out through the door leading from the hall to the garage, I wondered if I'd gone too far with this one. The others had broken easily. Jason had been more of a challenge. I'd even found myself enjoying aspects of his torture, relishing what it took to reduce him to the wreck he now was. Did that make me as bad as him? No, surely not. What he'd done had been for his own foul ends, whereas I was making Bradchester a safer place.

I stopped the barrow next to the car and opened the boot. Hauling him out of the barrow into a fireman's lift, I tipped him into the car. His flesh slapped onto the protective plastic sheeting. I closed the boot and went to clean myself up. At this hour of the morning, it was unlikely I'd see anyone, but if I did, it wasn't a good idea to be covered in blood and skin fragments. That would take too much explaining and even I wouldn't be able to come up with a credible excuse.

When I reached the canal I drove past the industrial site and continued well beyond the houseboat moorings until I reached the lock where he'd attacked his last victim. I pulled off the road and parked as close to the tow path as I could. Hauling on the plastic sheet, I pulled him out and left him where he fell. I knew someone would find him in the morning and call an ambulance. My job was done. Nemesis in action.

Chapter Eight

Paolo was on the point of packing up and going home when his phone rang. He picked it up, hoping it would be Jessica, but was disappointed to hear a male voice instead.

'Have I been put through to D.I. Sterling?'

'Speaking.'

'This is Dr Brownlow at Bradchester Central. I have a patient who was admitted today. He is in intensive care post-surgery. Would it be possible for you to come over and discuss his situation with me?'

'Why? Is it someone I know?'

'No, I don't think so, but I wouldn't have called you if I didn't think it was important.'

'I'm sorry, Doctor, but I'm a bit confused. Why have you contacted me in particular?'

'I've seen you on various press conferences,' Dr Brownlow said. 'You come across as someone who nags away at things until you find answers. I don't want to go into details over the phone, but my patient has been the victim of a quite violent and sustained attack. Judging from the state of dehydration and other factors, I'd say he has been systematically tortured for at least two to three days.'

Paolo glanced at the files threatening to topple off the edge of his desk.

'I'll send someone over to take a statement from him.'

Dr Brownlow remained silent.

'Are you still there?' Paolo asked.

'I am, yes. I'm afraid a statement isn't possible at the moment as he is in a coma. Please, detective inspector, I really would like you to look into this. The man was found early this morning down by the canal by someone out walking with a dog. He's in a bad way, but the main reason for calling you is that I don't think this is a one-off. I had a similar case about two months ago, but the patient was in a better physical condition than today's victim. However, the trauma today matches exactly with that sustained by my earlier patient. I tried to get that patient to report the attack, but he broke down in tears and begged me not to call the police. I had no option but to treat him and let him go home when he had recovered sufficiently.' Paolo heard the doctor sigh. 'After surgery today, I looked into our records. It appears as though at least four other patients have been admitted with similar injuries. I didn't treat them, which is why I've only now picked up that you might have a disturbed individual out there. If I'm right, and I think I am, so far there are six known victims. The main trauma is, um, sexual in nature.'

He fell silent, but Paolo waited.

After a few seconds, the doctor cleared his throat. 'I am in a difficult position here,' he said, 'with patient confidentiality and all that, but I really feel you should come over and see my patient. You see he is definitely the victim of a crime and the trauma is such that I fear it won't be long before you will be dealing with a murder case, unless you can find out who is torturing these men and do something about it.'

Paolo promised to get to the hospital as soon as humanly possible. He put the phone down and headed for the main office.

'Dave, I want you to come with me. We're off to Bradchester Central. I'll fill you in on the whys and wherefores on the way. CC, what's the news from financial crimes?'

'They haven't got to the bottom of it yet, but are fairly sure that although there's no money missing, the funds haven't always been where they should be.'

'Did they say who they might be pointing the finger at?'

'No, sir, but surely it must be Montague Mason?'

51

Paolo frowned. 'Not necessarily. Let's look at things from a more devious angle for a moment. What if someone's plan all along was to cook the books in such a way that it appeared as if Montague was the culprit? What better way of making sure he takes the blame than proclaiming publically that he's a crook? I'm not saying he isn't. I just don't want to jump to conclusions.'

'Well, who else could it be?'

'His secretary for one. It wouldn't be the first time someone has pointed the finger in order to divert attention from their own wrong doing. Let's see what financial crimes comes up with when they've finished looking into it. Right, Dave, come on. We need to get going.'

By the time they arrived at the hospital Paolo had passed on everything Dr Brownlow had said.

As directed by Paolo, Dave pulled in the area reserved for the hospital administrators.

'One day they are going to complain about us parking in their bays,' Dave said.

'They already have – several times. Apparently we should park in the pay and display and claim the cost back later. As we are here on official business, I have no intention of doing any such thing. This parking area is the one closest to the building. It's even more convenient than the doctors' parking area. Let one of the people responsible for messing up the finances of this hospital cough up a couple of quid for parking for a change. I have no doubt they will get it back much quicker than we would.'

Dave grinned at Paolo over the roof of the car as he fumbled with the keys. 'Hospital admin not on your Christmas card list?'

'I don't have one, but if I did, these parasites wouldn't be on it. The doctors and nurses here work flat out, putting in far more hours than they should, and yet they get paid less than the administrators. How can that be right?'

Dave shrugged and dropped the keys into his pocket. 'I didn't realise you were so well informed.'

Paolo laughed. 'No one could be involved with Jessica and not be kept up to date on what goes on here. Come on, Dr Brownlow is waiting for us on the fourth floor.'

They crossed the short pedestrian area and entered the hospital. While waiting for the lift, Paolo wondered yet again why he hadn't heard from Jessica. It was four days now since they'd last spoken and that call hadn't exactly been all he'd hoped. He had the distinct impression Jessica was holding something back. He'd call again this evening, but he had a horrible feeling that when he finally spoke to her, he was going to hear something he'd rather not know.

He followed Dave into the lift and pressed the button for the fourth floor. As the doors closed, he glanced over at his young partner. Dave was marrying Rebecca later this year. Paolo had hoped he and Jessica might tread a similar path in the future, but at the moment he wasn't even sure there was a future to consider. He was relieved to have his dismal thoughts interrupted by the ping to signal they had reached their floor. As the lift doors opened, Paolo shrugged off his feelings of foreboding and strode out into the corridor and headed for the surgeon's office.

They found Dr Brownlow in the corridor talking to a nurse and waited while he gave instructions on the care of who Paolo assumed was the patient he'd come to see. From the treatment outlined, it seemed the patient was still on the critical list.

As the nurse set off towards the ward, the doctor looked up.

'It was good of you to come, Detective Inspector Sterling. You look younger in the flesh than you do on television and the pictures of you in the papers don't do you any favours.'

Paolo smiled. 'I try to avoid having my photo taken, but it seems I'm a favourite whenever there is a slow news day.'

Brownlow laughed. 'News must be very slow in that case. You seem to be a regular on our front pages just at the moment.'

'Sadly, that's true. But we haven't come to discuss my current notoriety. This is Detective Sergeant Dave Johnson. What can you tell us about your patient?'

'I think you'd better come with me. It will be easier if you see him.'

The doctor led the way to intensive care and stopped outside a glass-walled room. Paolo looked through and was amazed to see quite a large man occupying the bed. He'd assumed the victim would be of a much slighter build.

'Do you think there were several assailants?' he asked.

'I don't know,' the doctor answered. 'Are you thinking of his size in relation to being overpowered?'

Paolo nodded.

'I, too, wondered that and took some blood samples. The results came back a short time ago. His blood still showed a high concentration of Rohypnol, which means he must have been given it during the night, or early this morning. As I'm sure you know, this drug is commonly used in date rape cases. I would imagine that's how he was overpowered, but how he was moved from wherever he was tortured down to the canal, I have no idea. As you pointed out, he is a big man.'

Paolo looked again, but couldn't see any obvious injuries.

'How was he tortured? He doesn't look as if he's been beaten.'

Dr Brownlow pointed back the way they'd come. 'Shall we go to my office? I'll be able to answer more fully when I have his file in front of me.'

Once in Dr Brownlow's office, they settled down in the visitor's chairs and waited until he'd unearthed the right file from the pile on his desk. Paolo smiled. He wondered if he'd be able to put his hands on a particular file from the multitude on his own desk, if asked to do so. Probably not, but then he wasn't dealing with the health of patients. Most of his files were to do with reports and graphs on crime control.

Dr Brownlow opened the file. 'We don't know the victim's name, I'm afraid. As he was naked, he obviously had no means of identification on him when he was found.'

'I'll run a missing person's report when we get back,' Dave said, making a note.

'The patient has been repeatedly tortured on his back. There are multiple burns of what looks like the twin prongs of a tazer, but the front of his body is completely clear of any injuries, other than a straight line of bruising above his groin. His genitals have been subjected to several tazer attacks. He has wounds on his wrists and ankles, which makes me believe he was tied down over a surface so that his groin was pressed into the edge. That would have made it possible for him to be abused without being able to put up any resistance.'

Paolo waited until Dave had finished taking down the details.

'You said earlier the main trauma was sexual? From what you've said, he seems to have undergone more than just sexual trauma.'

Dr Brownlow nodded. 'Oh, yes, but he has also been repeatedly raped. Quite violently. It's almost as if the intention was to cause the maximum amount of pain. The anal trauma is extensive and required considerable reconstructive surgery. In addition to his many injuries, he was suffering from extreme dehydration. I think he had probably been deprived of water during the time of his captivity. He certainly hadn't eaten for some time. He was in a coma when he was brought in and hasn't yet shown any signs of coming out of it.'

Paolo nodded. 'What caused him to slip into a coma?'

'Acute renal failure. His kidneys couldn't cope with the toxins in his blood caused by the dehydration.'

'What's the prognosis? Will he recover?'

Dr Brownlow shrugged. 'If I could answer that question, they would erect a statue to me in every hospital. It's a piece of string question. It depends on the patient's general health, the level of trauma suffered, the level of toxicity in the blood prior to slipping into the coma. I wish I could give you a definitive answer, but I'm afraid the only honest answer I can give is to wait and see.'

Paolo nodded. 'I'll send over a constable to wait outside the room. If he wakes, we will need to talk to him. It's possible he might know who attacked him.'

'If he is anything like my earlier patient, who was positively glowing with health compared to this chap, he isn't going to tell you anything even if he knows the name of his assailant. My earlier patient was terrified. Not of me, or even of the police as such. He was terrified of letting anything slip because he was certain the person who'd attacked him would know about it. He'd been taught to keep his mouth shut and had no intention of opening it.'

Paolo knew what the answer would be, but had to ask the question anyway. 'Could you give us the name and address of your earlier patient?'

Dr Brownlow shook his head. 'I'm afraid not. I wish I could, because I am sure he could point you in the right direction, but my hands are tied. That's why I called you in while *this* patient is in a coma. As a physician, I can report a crime if my patient is unable to speak, but if I am sworn to silence by the patient, I cannot break that oath.'

'Pity, but if necessary I can get a court order for the information.'

The doctor smiled. 'I know. I wouldn't fight it too hard, but would need to put up a token resistance.'

'You'll let us know if anyone else arrives with similar injuries?' Paolo asked.

'If I can, I'll do that before speaking to the patient. That way there would be no conflict over confidentiality.'

Paolo and Dave stood and shook hands with the doctor.

'Thank you for calling us in.'

The doctor walked with them to the lift.

'One other thing,' he said. 'I don't know if it's relevant, but there seems to be a rumour going round about that new club in Bradchester. It's one of those places that everyone knows someone who knows someone who knows about it, but no one has actually been themselves. Are you aware of it?'

Paolo nodded. 'Are you talking about Triple B?'

The doctor nodded.

'I've not heard any rumours,' Paolo said. 'As far as I know it's simply a businessman's club. What makes you ask?'

'I don't know anything for definite,' Dr Brownlow said, 'but the whisper is that there are rooms upstairs where sadomasochism is taken to an extreme level. I wondered if there might be a connection.'

'If you don't mind my asking, where did you hear this?'

Dr Brownlow shrugged. 'I'd rather not give the person's name, obviously, but I was approached by a friend when he'd had more to drink than was wise. He is a member of the club and sounded me out to see if I wanted to join. When I made it clear my tastes didn't run in that direction, the subject was dropped, but he'd said enough to make me realise he wasn't referring to basic whips and bondage, but to much more punishing activities.'

Paolo nodded. 'Thank you for that. I'll look into it.'

He waited until the lift had reached ground floor level before speaking. 'It's too late to do anything productive this evening. Drop me back at the station. Tomorrow, I'll fill the team in on this development and find out what CC and Andrea have found out about the lipstick vandalism, if anything. Then it seems to me we need to pay another visit to the club. When we do, let's see if we can find out what goes on upstairs. Maybe one of their members was a little too enthusiastic.'

Chapter Nine

Paolo's mobile rang and he snatched it up as soon as he saw Jessica's name on the screen. At last!

'Hi, Paolo,' she said and her voice had never sounded sweeter to his ears.

'Hi, Jess,' he began, but she cut across his words.

'I can't stop on. There's lots going on here. Paolo, I'm coming home next weekend. Can you make sure you're off? We need to talk. It's important.'

Paolo felt his heart beating faster and his stomach lurched.

'That sounds ominous,' he said, hoping she'd laugh and disagree with him, but she didn't.

'It could be,' she said, so quietly he had to strain to hear her.

'Jess, tell me—'

'No, not over the phone. I've been offered an incredible opportunity. I need to discuss it with you. OK?'

She ended the call before he could answer, but he told himself it didn't sound like she'd found someone else down there in London. Or did it? No, she wouldn't have phrased it as an incredible opportunity. Or would she? No.

Paolo forced himself to put the call out of his mind. He'd find out what was going on when she came back at the weekend. Until then, he had an investigation to run – two investigations, in fact.

He stood up, put the phone in his pocket, and walked to the general office where his team were already waiting for him. When everyone was settled and paying attention, he outlined the visit he and Dave had made to the hospital the previous evening.

'Sounds like a nasty attack, sir,' CC said. 'Do we have any leads at all?'

'Unfortunately not. I've put a PC on duty outside the victim's room, so we should know as soon as he wakes up.'

'If he wakes up,' added Dave.

Paolo nodded. 'Yes, as you say. He's in a coma and may never come out of it. Andrea, is there any CCTV coverage of that part of the canal?'

'I'm not sure, sir. I'll look into it.'

'Is this going to be our main focus, sir? Or do we still concentrate on the lipstick scandal?' CC asked.

'I'd like to make it our prime concern, but we have nothing to go on at the moment. The victim has no identification and was found in a public place. The torrential rain yesterday will most probably have obliterated any evidence at the scene, but forensics went over there last night, just in case the perpetrator was kind enough to leave us a calling card. Sadly, that wasn't the case.'

He moved back and perched on the edge of the desk nearest to the board.

'In the meantime, let's see if we can discover who defaced the plaque and made the accusation about Montague Mason. CC, what did you and Andrea find out?'

She looked down at her notes. 'Starting with Clementine Towers – what a nut job she is!'

'CC!'

'Sorry, sir, but it's true. Apparently, she is at the centre every day, either bringing them more of her books from years gone by, or telling them how to run the place.'

'Who told you that?' Paolo asked.

'She did, sir! We called on her at her home and she went on and on about public morality and depravity in high and low places. According to her it would do the world good to bring back public flogging for minor offences and hanging for anything more serious than shoplifting.'

'So she had the opportunity to put up the lipstick scrawl?'

CC nodded. 'She did, but I can't see her doing it to be honest. She'd be more likely to stand in front of the plaque and make a public declaration. Clementine Towers is as mad as the proverbial hatter, but I can't see her sneaking in and making an anonymous accusation.'

Remembering Clementine Tower's visit to his office, Paolo was inclined to agree with CC's assessment.

'Fair enough. Who was next?'

'From there we went to William Coburn Electrical Contractors and spoke to the man himself. He says he was there on business. Apparently, April Greychurch found a discrepancy in his accounts and he was at the centre sorting it out so that he could get paid.'

Paolo nodded. 'And your impression of him?'

'Again, sir, I didn't feel he was our man.'

'But?' Paolo asked. 'I can hear a definite but in your voice.'

'You're right. There was something about the way he reacted that made me think he had something to hide. I don't mean the vandalism. Somehow, I can't see him up for that, but he really wasn't pleased to see us and acted as if he was being victimised over the account discrepancy. He even accused April of calling us in. Andrea and I got the distinct impression he might have been guilty of some creative accounting in his dealings with the centre and that April had found him out.'

Paolo smiled. 'Interesting, but not sure it's relevant to our investigation. OK, on to the people Dave and I saw. Derrick Walden is a bit of a fanatic about Chelsea and an evangelist about everyone learning to swim and keeping fit. I can't see him wanting to do anything that might cause problems for his hero.'

'Hero? Mason?' CC laughed. 'I wouldn't put him in that category, but it takes all sorts.'

Paolo grinned. 'He thinks the ground Mason walks on should be venerated because he gave him the swimming coach's job. He's also not a fan of April Greychurch, so that makes two of our interviewees.'

Paolo ticked Derrick's name on the board. 'He had the opportunity to deface the plaque, but no motive. On the other hand, if April did lose her lipstick, as she claims, Derrick might have picked it up and scrawled on the plaque to drop her in it, not expecting it to remain undiscovered until the unveiling.'

CC nodded. 'I'll tell you something odd; Clementine Towers loathes the sight of Derrick Walden.'

Paolo turned back to face CC. 'Really? Did she say why?'

'Towers says Walden doesn't stick to his place in the pool area. She says she always finds him in places where he has no right to be, completely oblivious to the fact that as an employee he probably has more right to go wherever he chooses than she does as a volunteer.'

'Maybe I should have asked Walden what he thought about Miss Towers, but I can imagine.' He told the team about Clementine Towers assertion that Derrick shouldn't be teaching girls to swim. 'Strict segregation for males and females is the way she feels it should be done.'

CC laughed. 'I told you, she's a fruit loop who should be locked away for her own good.'

'OK, everyone, Dave and I are going to pay a second visit to the Triple B club to see if we can sniff out any nasty doings that might be connected to the poor soul in the hospital. CC, if financial crimes come up with anything, tell them I'll return the call when I get back.'

He looked over to Dave, expecting him to be already reaching for his jacket, but Dave was engrossed in reading something.

'Dave!' Paolo said, raising his voice, but even that failed to draw his attention.

Paolo walked the few steps to Dave's desk. 'Did you not hear me? We're going back to the club.'

Dave jumped up, stuffing the piece of paper into his pocket, but didn't explain what was so engrossing he hadn't been listening to

61

the report from CC on her visits. By the look on his face, Paolo didn't think whatever it was had been pleasant to read.

Paolo waited until Dave had negotiated the traffic before raising the matter again.

'Bad news, Dave?'

'No, sir, what makes you think that?'

'I just wondered what was on the paper you were reading that upset you in there.'

Dave sighed. 'I wasn't upset, as such, just a bit pissed off.' He reached into his pocket and pulled out the scrap of paper, passing it to Paolo.

'*How to succeed in today's force. Step one, have a relative at the top. Step two, make DS without trying. Step three, repeat steps one and two until maximum rank achieved.* Nasty,' Paolo said. 'Where did you get this?'

'It was on my desk when I got in today.'

'Any ideas who the culprit might be?'

Dave shook his head. 'Not really. It's probably Jack Cummings, but it could be any of them. That's what makes me sick. No one has the guts to stand in front of me and spout that stuff to my face, but leaving it for me to find, that's OK. Fucking cowards.'

'I'd be willing to put money on it not being CC, if that's any consolation.'

Dave smiled. 'One thing's for sure, if CC had something to say she wouldn't do it anonymously. She'd spit it out for all to hear and damn the consequences.'

Paolo folded the piece of paper. 'Mind if I keep this?' he asked.

'Be my guest, but why do you want it?'

'No reason in particular, just a feeling I should hang on to it for you.'

The SatNav letting them know they'd arrived at their destination broke the pensive mood in the car, but Paolo made a silent vow to find out which idiot was tormenting Dave. As before, the car park bore testament to the high net worth of the club membership. Bentleys, Jaguars, even a Porsche and a Ferrari filled some of the bays, with a lone Ford Capri standing out like a beggar at a Hunt Ball. Paolo assumed it belonged to George Baron's secretary. Whoever owned it, Paolo was amazed to see Baron allowed it to be parked in the club members' private parking area.

For the second time in two days, they approached the grand building. This time the doors swung open before they reached them. Chaz stood at the top of the steps looking very like an immoveable object. Paolo smiled to himself. Chaz was about to meet an unstoppable force. It would be interesting to see which of them gave way. Without a warrant, there was no way they could force their way in, but Paolo was determined to get inside one way or another.

'Hello, you might remember us from yesterday. Is Mr Baron around?'

'Have you got an appointment? Mr Baron didn't mention it.'

Paolo smiled. 'No, not this time, but if you call Mr Baron, I'm sure he'll agree to see us for a few minutes.'

'What about?' Chaz demanded.

Paolo kept the smile fixed in place. 'That's between us and Mr Baron. Let him know we're here. He won't thank you for keeping us on the doorstep like this.'

Chaz looked them over, then turned on his heels and shut the doors.

'Do you think that means he's gone to confer with his boss, sir?'

'I have no idea. Possibly. We'll give him a minute or two, then start hammering on the doors. I'm sure Baron won't want the members inside disturbed during their tête-à-têtes.'

In the end, it was less than a minute before the doors opened again. Chaz came out, carefully shutting the doors behind him.

'Mr Baron is in conference at the moment. He says if you could come back in a couple of hours, he'll make time for you.'

Paolo got the distinct impression Chaz was uncomfortable about something. He decided to probe a bit to see if he could find out what it was that was making him sweat.

'No, I don't think we can do that. How about if we come in

and wait? We could sit in that nice comfortable lounge area. We promise not to talk to anyone.'

Chaz looked even more uneasy. 'I'll, er, I'll just go and see if Mr Baron can make time for you now.'

Once again, he turned around and went inside.

Dave laughed. 'What on earth is that all about?'

Paolo shrugged. 'Beats me. I think we might have interrupted something they don't want us to see.'

'You think it might be the type of activities Doctor Brownlow alluded to?' Dave asked.

Before Paolo could answer, the door opened and George Baron came down the steps, looking flustered and not at all pleased at being disturbed.

'Look, this is harassment. I answered your questions yesterday and certainly didn't have anything to do with the stupid bloody goings on at the opening ceremony.'

Paolo stepped forward. 'We're not here about that. We're here on another matter altogether. I was hoping to have a quiet word with you inside about what goes on in your club. I've been hearing some strange rumours,' he said, noticing a car pulling into the car park. 'However, if you like, I can ask questions out here in the open. Is that one of your members who's just arrived? Maybe he would like to join us.'

George opened his mouth, closed it again and shuffled on the spot. Paolo wondered what on earth was going on inside that made him so determined to keep them out.

The new arrival parked a few cars along from where they were standing. As the car door opened and a man's head appeared, Paolo saw George give a tiny shake of his head. The head dropped from sight and, within seconds, he heard the sound of the car's engine revving and gravel spraying as the car reversed out of the bay and drove off.

'Have we interrupted something? Your member seems in a terrible rush to get away considering he'd only just got here.'

The look George gave him was pure venom. 'No, you haven't

interrupted anything. What you have done is cause one of my bloody members to leave.'

'Why?' Paolo asked. 'Why would he leave just because we're standing here having a friendly chat?'

'Come off it, your attitude says this isn't a friendly chat. You must think I'm daft. You've come here with an agenda. I don't know what it is, and I don't want to know. We promise complete privacy for our members. They know they can come here and only other members will know who they are. With you two blocking the entrance, it was impossible for that member to enter without being seen. Let's get this over with. What do you want to know?'

'Are all your members so shy? What have they got to hide?' Paolo asked.

George laughed. 'Are you really that naïve? They aren't shy and don't have anything to hide, but more business gets done in social clubs such as these than takes place in boardrooms.'

'You mean insider trading?' Dave asked.

'What? No! Don't put words in my mouth.' He turned to Paolo. 'I'll ask again. What do you want?'

Paolo was about to frame his question when the doors to the club opened and Chaz looked out. The look of relief on George's face confirmed Paolo's suspicion. The club wasn't just a place for businessmen to have a chat and a pint.

'Let's go inside and discuss whatever it is like civilised people, shall we?' Paolo suggested.

George turned on his heel and sped up the steps. His jerky movements reminded Paolo of a mechanical hare he'd once seen set off for greyhounds to chase around a track. As they followed George into the club, Paolo tried to guess what had been going on inside.

He had a good look round when he reached the lobby, but there was no evidence of anything out of place. In fact, the only odd thing was the absence of sound. The last time they'd been in the club, there had been a faint murmuring of voices. This time there was absolute silence, which was strange considering the number of cars outside.

'Where is everyone today?' he asked, more to see George and Chaz's reaction than because he wanted to know, but the result was interesting.

Chaz looked down and shuffled his feet, as if he'd rather be anywhere than here. George avoided the question completely.

'Let's go through to my office, shall we?' he said. 'Chaz, I know you've got things to do.'

Remarkable, Paolo thought. It was amazing how often crimes were solved by no more than stumbling onto something by being in the right place at the right time. Even if the hospital victim had no connection to the club, it was clear activities were going on here they didn't want the police to know about, which meant, in Paolo's eyes, they were goings-on he *should* know about.

They followed George through Trudy Chappell's office and into his. George ignored his secretary, but Paolo paused to say hello. He was amused to see there was no offer of coffee today. George stood next to his office door and shut it behind them once they were in. He gestured to the chairs they'd sat in on their earlier visit.

'Take a seat. Now, what's this all about? You said it had nothing to do with that stupid business at the youth centre, so why are you here?'

He walked round his desk and sat down. Paolo noticed the man had regained his normal colour and demeanour, so decided to throw out a few random questions to see what reaction he got.

'Why were you so determined to keep us outside until Chaz gave the signal to say it was OK to let us in?'

Once again, the colour left George's face. 'Don't be ridiculous. I told you, our members are guaranteed privacy. I simply wanted to give Chaz time to let them know we would be having visitors. *Again*,' he added, with emphasis on the word.

Paolo nodded to Dave, who took a photograph from his inside pocket and slid it across the desk.

'Do you know this man? Is he one of your members?' Paolo asked.

George picked up the photo and glanced at it.

66

'No to both questions. Who is he? He looks in a bad way with all those tubes and things.'

Paolo nodded. 'He's in a coma. We're trying to find out who he is.'

George tossed the photo back towards Dave. 'Why on earth do you think I would know him?'

'Because of the type of sexual injuries he sustained during an attack. There's a rumour going round that your members like to engage in similar activities, so I wondered if this man had been a participant and things had got a little out of hand.'

Paolo hadn't thought it was possible for George to lose more colour, but he did. His face was now almost as pale as his shirt.

'What are you on about? I told you, this is a businessmen's club. Who told you otherwise? I'll sue them. There's nothing goes on upstairs of that nature.'

'Who said anything about upstairs?'

'What? You did.'

Paolo smiled. 'No, I didn't mention any area in particular. I simply said there was a rumour going round. So, tell me, what does go on upstairs? Any chance we could go up now and have a look round?'

George stood up. 'You can look upstairs with my blessing. All you need to do is come back with a warrant. I told you yesterday, we have private bedrooms up there for our members. There is no way I'm letting you lot loose in this club without a warrant and, as we haven't broken any laws, or given you reason to suspect we might have done, there's no way you'd get one. Now, if that's all, I'd like you to go about your business and let me get on with mine.'

He walked over to the door and opened it. 'Trudy, please show these gentlemen out the back way. I think our members have been inconvenienced enough for today.'

'Yes, Mr Baron,' she said. 'This way, please.'

Instead of going back into the lobby, she opened the door in the wall behind her desk.

Paolo raised his eyebrows. 'Servants' exit for us, Dave.'

Trudy led them along a dingy corridor, completely at odds

67

with the opulence of the main part of the building. They reached a small hallway with several doors leading off.

'Where do all these go?' Paolo asked.

Trudy pointed to each door in turn. 'That leads into the kitchens. That one into the wine cellars. That one goes into the main part of the building. That's just storage. I have to come in and go out this way when there are functions on in the club.'

'What sort of functions?' Paolo asked.

Trudy smiled. 'I have no idea. I'm not allowed in the main part of the club. It really is men only.'

'Aren't you curious?' Dave said. 'I'd be peeping at the keyholes if someone told me I wasn't allowed to see what was going on. What do you think they get up to?'

The smile left her face. 'I told you, I have no idea. I've no intention of trying to find out, either. I need this job and don't intend to lose it by sticking my nose in where it's not wanted. This leads to the back of the parking area.'

She opened the door and stood pointedly holding it for them.

Paolo smiled. 'Sorry, we didn't mean to upset you. Thank you for your time.'

Trudy continued to hold the door until they passed through and shut it behind them without answering.

They came out behind the club into an additional parking area not visible from the front of the building. It was fenced off with six foot high security panels with three strands of what looked like razor wire on top of that. Against the wall outside the door were three wheelie bins. Paolo lifted the lids, but they were empty.

'Must have been refuse collection day today,' he said.

Dave grinned at him. 'Don't tell me you were planning to rummage through their rubbish, sir.'

Paolo returned the smile. 'Nope, I was planning on making you do that, being as I'm the superior officer and all that. Seriously though, I thought there might be some paperwork to show what goes on in that place. To my mind, it stinks of something dodgy. I don't know what, but I'm going to find out.'

68

Chapter Ten

Paolo headed into the station bright and early the next day, determined to sort out the nastiness regarding Dave's situation once and for all. As he climbed the stairs, he was already working out exactly what to say without revealing he knew about the note Dave had received. Bringing that up would just serve to make it seem that Dave had gone running to Paolo like a schoolboy unable to stand up to his tormentors.

Paolo knew Dave wouldn't be in until later, as he'd sent him off to ask William Coburn what his dispute with the centre had been about. April's comment about discrepancies in the accounting had rankled overnight, so a quick call early this morning had solved both problems. It got Dave out the way so that Paolo could talk freely and it might just shed some light on what April had alluded to.

Paolo walked into the main office and stopped by the crime scene board.

'Listen up, everyone; I have something important to say.'

It took a while until phone calls were finished and files saved, but eventually he had everyone's attention.

'I've chosen this morning to talk to you because Dave isn't here.'

'Skiving off again.'

Although it had been whispered, the voice carried around the silent room. A few nervous laughs followed the words and then petered out.

Paolo forced himself to stay calm. Losing his temper wouldn't help Dave in any way.

'I don't suppose whoever said that has the guts to stand up and admit to it?'

He waited a few seconds, but there was no movement anywhere in the room. He was aware of CC's eyes on him and got the distinct impression she knew who'd spoken. Paolo had no intention of putting her on the spot by asking her to confirm it had been Jack Cummings. He looked around the room, making eye contact with each officer.

'There's no need to own up. I recognised the voice, as I'm sure you all did. That isn't the issue. The point is that one of you felt it was OK to malign a fellow officer who works bloody hard. Others found it funny. Maybe if you'd been on the receiving end, you might not have enjoyed the comment as much. Most of you are aware of the number of hours Dave puts in, without claiming overtime, let me tell you. The reason he isn't here is because I've sent him off on a job and I've done that because I'm sick to death of a room full of adults behaving like a kids in the playground. It needs to stop.'

He paused for breath and was pleased to see he still had everyone's attention.

'Yes, Dave is the Chief's nephew. While none of you knew about it I never heard a single word of complaint about Dave or his work ethic. The relationship made the press and suddenly some of you have taken it into your heads to see favouritism that isn't there. The person who leaked the information to the press was a bitter man. He was bloody good at his job, but thought Dave had been unfairly favoured by me because of his connections. I'm telling you now, that was crap then and it's crap now. You all know Dave. Stop acting like idiots and remember how you felt before you read the report in the papers!' He smiled. 'That's it. Lecture over.'

In the sullen silence which reigned over the room, Paolo turned to Andrea. Seeing as she was being mentored by CC, he was fairly sure Andrea wouldn't be harbouring resentment over imagined favouritism.

'Andrea, you were going to check on CCTV coverage of the canal area where the brutality victim was dumped. What have you found out?'

She pulled a file closer to her and opened it. 'Nothing of use to us, sir. There are cameras all along the canal, but the ones we needed are no longer functioning. Apparently, the cameras are still there, but they stopped using them when Fletcher Simpson started his renovation project.'

Paolo frowned. 'Did the council approve this, or did he do it without consulting with the other councillors?'

Andrea shook her head. 'I asked the spokesperson for Simpson Holdings and was told to contact the council directly for that information. I have it on my list for today, sir.'

'Leave it with me,' Paolo said. 'I have to speak to Montague Mason about youth centre matters at some point anyway. I'm quite sure if Fletcher Simpson acted without the backing of the council, Mason will be only too pleased to let me know.'

Andrea grinned. 'That reminds me. Did anyone listen to Radio Bradchester this morning? Clementine Towers has formed an action group and managed to get herself interviewed on that very subject.'

'Really? What's it got to do with her?' Paolo asked. 'I'd have thought she had her hands full making sure no deviant books get smuggled onto the shelves of the youth centre library.'

'She was making an appeal for people to join the Bradchester Brigade. They're protesting against Simpson's plans.'

Paolo laughed. 'Maybe I should volunteer my services. I'm not sure I approve of his renovation project.'

Andrea looked confused, but CC laughed. 'You've touched one of our beloved leader's sore spots. He likes the canal as it is.'

'What, all clogged up and dirty?'

'Of course I don't want that,' Paolo said. 'It has to be cleaned up, but I want it done for the benefit of Bradchester, not to line Simpson's pockets.'

'Blimey, are you on that soapbox again, sir?' Dave called out from the doorway.

'Always will be where greed gets in the way of the town, Dave. How did you get on with William Coburn? Come in and bring us all up to date. Andrea can fill you in on her findings afterwards.'

Dave walked over and stood next to Paolo.

'Coburn was there that day because one of his repeat invoices had been returned as already paid, but he hadn't actually received the funds in his account. Apparently, he was being given the run-around by April, so he went to the centre to have it out with her. She claimed Mason had insisted the account had been paid. According to Coburn, she made him feel like he was trying to pull a fast one, instead of simply getting the money owed to him. He wanted to see Mason, but even though he hung around for over an hour, he never got the opportunity. Funnily enough, he says the money was in his bank account the next day. He doesn't know whether it was Mason or his secretary who was playing games with his cash, but he insists one of them was.'

Paolo saw CC frown. 'Problem, CC?'

'Yeah, why didn't he tell us that when Andrea and I went to talk to him?'

Dave blushed. 'He, um, he . . . I don't know.'

'Rubbish,' CC said. 'What did he say that you don't want to tell us? Come on, Dave, spit it out. You couldn't lie to save your life.'

Dave looked as if he'd rather be anywhere than in the office. 'There's nothing, really.'

Paolo spotted CC winking at Andrea. 'Shall I tell you what I think he said? Andrea and I were talking about him this morning. I think he didn't trust a couple of girlies to get the facts straight. I bet he told you he was glad you came so that he could deal with it man to man.'

Dave's blush deepened. 'How the hell did you know that?'

'It was pretty obvious when we were there yesterday. You remember I said I thought he was holding something back? That's obviously what it was. He all but patted us on the head when we left. He didn't say the words, but the implication was to get back to the station and do the typing and leave the investigating to the men.'

'Sorry,' Dave said.

CC laughed. 'No need for you to apologise. It's not your fault he's an arsehole.'

'OK,' Paolo said, 'we've established he's a pillock, but that doesn't take away from the fact that he had to fight to get his money. That centre isn't exactly overburdened with cash, but there should be enough in the bank to cover all the invoices for work carried out. Dave, I want you to contact financial crimes and see if they've uncovered anything we can get our teeth into.'

He glanced back at the board. 'I take it there's been no news on the mystery patient?'

'No, sir,' Andrea said. 'I called in on my way to work this morning. There's no change at all in his condition.'

'Well, until we know who he is, it's going to be difficult to track down his assailant.'

'Right, Andrea, see if there are cameras on the approach roads to the canal. It's a long shot, but we've got nothing else to go on. CC, I need you to contact our local Rape Crisis and find out if there is a male equivalent service in Bradchester. If not, ask where the nearest one is. I know some towns and cities have them.'

'I can get the general information, sir, but you know they won't give any specifics, don't you?'

Paolo sighed. 'I know, CC, but I'm hoping if someone with injuries matching our victim in the hospital should get in touch, knowing there is a serial abuser out there might convince the counsellors to encourage a victim to talk to us. I know it's a long shot, but what else have we got?'

He left them to their allocated tasks and headed off to his own office to tackle the paperwork he never seemed to get on top of. The endless bloody forms and worksheets he had to fill in took more time than solving the crimes he was reporting on. And every government promised to cut back, but added to the paper trail as soon as they took office.

As he reached the doorway and put his hand out to push the door open, the phone in his pocket vibrated. He'd put it on silent while delivering his lecture, but fished it out now and flicked the switch to change from mute to ringing. He saw Katy's name on the screen and slid the bar across to answer the call.

'Hi, Katy, what's up?'

Kicking the door closed behind him, he walked over to his desk, trying not to look at the paper towers he'd constructed.

'Nothing's up, Dad. That's not nice, thinking I only call when something's wrong.'

He heard the laughter in her voice and relaxed. No matter what age she was, she would always be his baby and he'd never stop worrying that something bad would happen to her. She'd been through enough over the last couple of years to emotionally cripple most young people, but somehow she'd found a way to cope with the trauma and enjoy life again.

'OK, if there's nothing up, to what do I owe the pleasure of a call from you in the middle of the morning?'

'Oh, you know, just thought I'd ring for a chat.'

'Really?' Paolo said. 'No ulterior motive? Not even a tiny one?'

'Hmm, maybe a small one.'

'Financially small or emotionally small?'

She laughed. 'Can I go for the jackpot and have both?'

'That sounds worrying,' Paolo said. 'You'd better come round tonight and tell me your woes over takeaway pizza.'

'Great, see you about seven-ish,' she said.

'Whoa, hang on a minute. Pizza for two or for three?'

'Just two. Danny's volunteering at the shelter tonight. Besides, I need to talk to you on my own. I'll tell Mum I won't be home for dinner.'

Paolo ended the call not knowing whether to be worried or pleased Katy wanted to confide in him. A tiny voice told him whatever it was she had to say, her mind was already made up. He shrugged, whatever it was, he'd deal with it later. Right now, work called. He'd made considerable inroads into one pile when a tap on the door released him from his misery.

'Come in,' he called.

CC opened the door. 'Sorry to disturb you, sir.'

'Don't be, I'm not! Sit down and tell me what you've found out.'

'I spoke to a lovely lady at Rape Crisis who couldn't have been more helpful. I explained about our nameless victim and how we hoped she could help us prevent further attacks. She said that around half of the Rape Crisis Centres also offer a specific service to men and/or boys. We don't have one here, or in Leicester, but if a male, man or boy, contacted our local Rape Crisis Centre, he would be advised of the nearest appropriate services. There are two centres in Northampton I'm going to contact.'

'Northampton? Nothing closer?'

CC shook her head. 'Nope, not via Rape Crisis, but the person I was dealing with said there are other organisations that specialise in supporting male survivors and she's given me some info to follow up on.'

'Will you be able to contact the two Northampton centres? Although, to be honest, I think they are too far away, don't you?'

She nodded. 'Probably, but I'll call them anyway. One of them is primarily a telephone helpline support service, offering counselling and referrals for males and females over the age of thirteen. Even if they are in Northampton, they might still get a call from a victim of a similar attack.'

Paolo knew she was right, but wished there was somewhere closer. Probably victims of sexual abuse wished the same thing.

'Do what you can, CC. I doubt they will be able to persuade someone who's been subjected to that level of violence to come forward, but we have to at least try.'

'Right, sir, I'll get onto it straight away.' She stood up, but didn't move towards the door. Paolo could see she was debating whether or not to speak.

'Come on, CC, spit it out. What is it you don't want to say, but feel you must?'

She let out a long drawn out sigh. 'You meant well this morning, sir, but I'm not sure your talk had the right effect. The whisper now is that Dave's uncle leaned on you to lean on us.'

'Oh, for fuck's sake,' Paolo hissed, slapping his hand down on the desk and sending files sliding in all directions. 'What is wrong with people? Who is it?'

CC looked at him as if he'd lost his mind, which he probably had, asking her to grass on colleagues. She'd be more like to pull out her own fingernails than to split on anyone.

'I've nothing to say, sir, except, let things settle in their own good time. Dave's a good copper. You know that, I know it, and so do the idiots out there making the snide comments. Eventually it will all work itself out when they see that you really aren't playing favourites.'

She shrugged, as if to say sorry, and then left.

Paolo looked at the files now lying every which way on his desk. He needed to get out and do some proper police work instead of shutting himself up in here. He stood up, ready to sweep the whole lot off his desk when another tap on the door stopped him just as he'd raised his arm.

'Come in,' he snapped, then regretted it when he saw the wary look on Andrea's face. 'Sorry, ignore my bad mood. Come in. What have you found out?'

'There are CCTV cameras on three of the roads leading down to the canal, but not on another two. I've been in touch with the security firm who run the footage. I think it's worth calling in the DVDs and viewing them. You never know, we might strike lucky.'

Paolo smiled. 'I agree. Let me know if you find anything.'

As she was about to leave, Dave appeared in the doorway.

'Bloody hell, I'm popular this afternoon. CC, call Andrea in. We might as well all hear Dave's news together.'

Dave waited until everyone was settled and then opened his notebook.

'I spoke to Pat Byrne who is looking into the youth centre's books and asked him to pay particular attention to payments made to William Coburn. Pat has just called be back to say there are definite irregularities. There's evidence of funds being moved around, robbing Peter to pay Paul sort of thing. He is going to prepare a full report for you but said he's still looking back over past payments and money transfers.'

Paolo drummed his fingers on the desk. 'Did he give any indication as to who has been creative with the accounting? I know Mason controlled the centre's finances, but I believe April was involved with the bookkeeping as well.'

'Pat didn't say, sir. He said whoever was moving the money around was very careful and covered his or her tracks very well. If no one had raised a suspicion, the chances are it would never have been picked up. There doesn't appear to be money missing, but discrepancies could have been hidden in the ledgers under a different heading. To be honest, by the time Pat had finished explaining it all to me my brain had just about shut down, but he seemed to have a handle on it and said he'd put it into words of one syllable in his report so that even dummies like me could understand it.' Dave grinned. 'That last bit was my interpretation of what he actually said. His words were much more diplomatic.'

Paolo laughed. 'Let's hope we can follow the money trail when Pat lays it out for us. I'm going to call the centre and make an appointment for you and I to see Mason, Dave. Andrea, see if you can get a transcript of the minutes for the council meeting when the matter of the CCTV cameras was raised. I don't know why, but something is niggling at me that the person who dumped our victim knew those cameras were no longer functioning. See if it's on public record, would you?'

He picked up the receiver and dialled Mason's office.

'April Greychurch, how can I help you?'

'Hi, is Mason there?'

'Hello, Paolo. No, sorry, he's away until tomorrow. Anything I can help you with?'

'I don't think so. I need to talk to him about a council matter. Can you book me in to see him tomorrow morning?'

'Sure thing. How does ten suit you?'

'Perfect. See you then.'

He replaced the receiver and looked up at three puzzled faces.

'You didn't mention the financial report,' Dave said.

Paolo smiled. 'No, because it could be April who's behind the fraud. With a bit of luck neither of them will have any idea of the real reason we're going over. It looks like one of them has been doing some creative accounting; with a bit of luck we might surprise the guilty one into making a slip.'

Chapter Eleven

Paolo was overjoyed to see Katy that evening. They were still incredibly close, but since she'd been involved with Danny, the time he could spend alone with her was limited. Naturally so. Paolo wouldn't have had it any other way. Soon she would be going to university, moving out into the world to make her own way. But there was no denying he missed the long hours they used to spend playing video games, going to the movies, or just discussing anything and everything over a burger and fries in the dreadful places she used to love so much. Even that had changed recently. If he offered to take her out for a meal these days, it was more likely she'd choose an Italian restaurant over a plastic burger. Paolo grinned. That, at least, was a change for the better.

The pizza delivery arrived and they settled down on the couch. With the boxes open on their laps, they used the 'fingers before forks' school of eating, tucking into the steaming slices of food heaven before turning to the reason for Katy's visit.

As Paolo took the boxes through to the kitchen, he realised Katy looked more pensive than usual and his stomach lurched. He'd been hoping this wasn't a big deal, but the look on her face told him he probably wasn't going to like what was coming.

Taking more time than he needed to pour out the drinks, he knew he should get back into the lounge and face whatever it was head on, but he was a coward where Katy was concerned. What if she wanted to move in with Danny? His brain said fine, she's old enough to leave school this year, but his heart said no, no, no! She was his baby. Seventeen was too young. *Hypocrite!* his brain screamed. Seventeen was old enough for you and Lydia. Yeah, but times were different then, heart insisted.

Paolo smiled, remembering the years of happiness he and Lydia had shared. Then he lost all desire to smile as he thought about the hit and run, intended for him, that had taken the life of Sarah, their other daughter. He'd not only lost a daughter that day, but also his wife when he clammed up and couldn't share his grief.

Putting off the moment when Katy would tell him why she was there, Paolo decided now was as good a time as any to ask why Mason might imply she and Danny had defaced the plaque.

He walked back into the lounge and put the glasses onto coasters on the coffee table.

'Katy, I haven't had chance to talk to you since that night at the youth centre,' he said, sinking into his favourite armchair. 'Montague Mason seemed to think you and Danny should be considered suspects.'

Katy choked on a mouthful of lemonade. When she could finally speak, her eyes gleamed with anger.

'That slimy toad! After all the work we've put in over there? What did he say?'

'Nothing of any consequence. Just that you two shouldn't be left off the list of potential vandals.' He hesitated, but decided to plough on. 'Has he ever, you know, made a pass at you? I wondered if–'

He stopped when Katy burst out laughing.

'What? What did I say?'

Tears streaming from her eyes, Katy shook her head.

'Made a pass at *me*? Dad, what century are you living in? It's Danny he fancies. Not that I blame him. I fancy the pants off him myself. Thank goodness the feeling is mutual.'

Relief that Mason hadn't tried it on with Katy was quickly quenched by Katy's open statement of lust regarding Danny. Being a Dad sucked, Paolo decided. On the one hand he wanted Katy to be happy. On the other, he also wanted to rip Danny's head off and feed it to any ravenous animal he could find.

Fighting the urge to say something that would alienate Katy forever, Paolo forced out a smile.

'I realise that, Katy, but what is it young people say now? Too much information.'

She laughed. 'I know, but it's so easy to shock you. I couldn't resist it.'

'Tell me,' Paolo said, 'should I be worried about Montague with the younger boys who come to the centre?'

Katy shook her head, her smile fading. 'I don't think so. I mean Danny is legal age and looks even older than he really is, but Montague definitely fancies him. I haven't noticed him looking funny at any of the younger ones, but I'll keep my eyes open for you. OK,' she said, 'it's time to tell you why I'm really here tonight. It's partly to do with Danny and partly to do with my future.'

Paolo braced himself. 'Go on, fire away.'

'You know we do a lot of volunteering?'

Paolo nodded. It was one of the things about her that filled him with pride.

'Well, we want to take a year out and volunteer abroad. I've been looking into it and VSO have a youth scheme for eighteen to twenty-five-year-olds, which is perfect for me and Danny—'

'Whoa, just hold on a minute. Who or what is VSO?'

'It's a government funded set up. Just listen for a minute, Dad. Mum won't even give me chance to explain what I want to do. She just goes into one about university and not missing out on my place. I still want to go to uni, but I want to spend a gap year volunteering first. Dad, I really, really need your help.'

Paolo tried to take it in, but her words were so far removed from what he'd been expecting that he had difficulty processing it.

'OK, slow down a bit. Is this organisation on the level? Have you looked into how long they've been around and who is behind it?'

'Jesus, Dad, I *am* a policeman's daughter! Of course I have. The board are all big nobs in the city or important people, like judges. Half of them have titles.'

'Fair enough,' Paolo said, feeling his way into the conversation. 'What does it cost? I mean, if you're going to be abroad for a year doing voluntary work, how will you live?'

'The VSO provides living accommodation, meals and even pays us a small fee. Obviously, it would be great to have some money of my own, which is another reason I wanted to talk to you. I know you and Mum put money away for my uni fund, but can I use some of it? I can always get a student loan when I get back to cover whatever I spend.'

'Let's leave the money side of it for now, OK? Where will you go? Will you be safe? You're not thinking of going into war zones or kidnap areas, are you? If that's the case, it's a flat no from me.'

Katy threw up her hands. 'What is it with you and Mum? I'm not a child. No, I won't be going anywhere dangerous. At least, not more dangerous than living right here in Bradchester, or have you forgotten what happened a couple of years back?'

Paolo's stomach muscles contracted as if she'd punched him straight in the gut. Katy was right. She'd probably never be in more danger than she'd been back then.

His feelings of guilt must have shown on his face, because she put her hand on his arm and squeezed it.

'I'm sorry, Dad. I had to raise what happened because it puts things into perspective. Volunteering is something I really want to do. Please, help me talk Mum round.'

He could see by the look on Katy's face she wasn't going to give up her dream. Knowing her as he did, he could imagine her going anyway, with or without their approval and consent. Then what would happen? Lose contact with her for a whole year, not knowing where she was or what she was doing?

'I'll talk to your mum, but—'

He didn't get to finish. Katy launched herself at him. When he finally surfaced from the hug, he held up his hands to stop the flow of thanks.

'Listen to me, Katy. I'll talk to your mum, but I'm not sure any words of mine will help. In fact, it might be better for me to tell her I've forbidden you to go. There's more chance that way of her packing your bags for you.'

Katy laughed. 'She'll listen to you if you put on the charm.'

Paolo grinned. 'If I did that she'd know straight away something was up, but I'll see what I can do.'

Long after Katy had left, Paolo couldn't get the image out of his mind of his little girl travelling to a disease ridden place he'd probably never heard of to work with people who didn't even speak her language. Part of him was proud, but his overwhelming emotion was fear. If he felt like this, how the hell was he supposed to convince Lydia to let Katy have her way? Oh well, that was a problem for another day.

Realising he would just catch the local news, he reached out for the remote control. As the screen flickered to life, he was amused to see Clementine and about twenty supporters marching up and down the canal path waving 'Save Our Canal from Greed' placards. Simpson Holdings' vast warehouse office complex loomed in the background. Paolo wondered what Fletcher Simpson thought about having a protest on his doorstep. Probably thought it would help to bring awareness of his plans. He'd be likely to think all publicity was good publicity, especially if the person leading the objection to it was someone as offbeat as Clementine Towers.

Paolo settled back to listen as the interviewer pushed a microphone in Clementine's direction.

'Would you like to tell our audience why you are protesting the renovation of the canal? Surely its upgrade would be good for Bradchester?'

To Paolo's surprise and, he was ashamed to admit to himself, disappointment, Clementine the nutter was absent, leaving behind an articulate woman. She put forth all the arguments he had used earlier when explaining to Dave what his objections were to Simpson's scheme.

He was about to flick over to another channel, when a movement in the background caught his attention. A man, looking remarkably like Derrick Walden, was leaving the office block. Paolo sat forward, screwing up his eyes, trying to block out the figures in the foreground. As the man walked towards the car park at the side of the building, Paolo became more convinced than ever it was the swimming coach. Now what, he wondered, would someone who was such a fan of Montague Mason be doing visiting the offices of Mason's sworn enemy?

Chapter Twelve

Paolo and Dave arrived at the youth centre twenty minutes ahead of their appointment time with Montague. Paolo had filled Dave in on what he believed he'd seen the night before and planned to speak to the swimming coach before going upstairs to confront Mason about the finances.

'Are you one hundred per cent sure it was Walden you saw?' Dave asked as they walked from the car to the youth centre's main entrance.

Paolo almost said yes, but stopped himself. Was he one hundred percent certain? Almost, but not quite. The buildings had been in the background, made miniature by the camera angle and per-spective, which meant the man had been too out of focus for certainty, but the way he walked and his stance were pretty con-clusive in Paolo's mind.

'I could be wrong. Of course, I could, but it looked like him to me. Anyway, there could be a perfectly rational explanation for him being there. Maybe he's giving lessons to a member of staff, or something along those lines. We'll soon find out,' Paolo said as they passed through the double doors and into the lobby.

Following the signs to the swimming pool, they passed rooms buzzing with activities. Paolo felt a surge of pride at the way the young people of Bradchester had flocked to the centre to take up all the opportunities on offer. This was just what the town needed to get it up and running again. Yes, the canal renovations would provide some jobs and improve tourism, but here local young people were being trained, counselled and helped. The youngsters passing through this centre would at least have a fighting chance at making something of their lives.

As the thought entered his head, hard on its heels came the remembrance of his conversation with Katy. One of the delights in store for him today was a visit with Lydia to discuss Katy's plans. He almost shuddered. Whatever the outcome for Katy, it probably wouldn't go well for him.

They reached the pool area and turned towards Derrick Walden's tiny room. The door was closed, so Paolo knocked on it before turning the handle. As he opened the door, Arbnor came round from behind Derrick's desk.

'What are you doing in here?' Paolo asked, surprised at the look of guilt on the caretaker's face.

Before the man could answer, a voice from behind Paolo echoed his question, only Derrick Walden sounded more angry than surprised.

Arbnor looked down, seemingly fascinated by his feet. 'Nothing, I was doing nothing,' he whispered. 'Just making sure all is well in here. I go in all the rooms to check. Every day I do my rounds.'

Derrick pushed past Paolo into the room and strode behind his desk, almost knocking Arbnor to the floor as he did so. He scanned the effects neatly placed on the surface and seemed to be satisfied that nothing had been touched because he visibly relaxed.

'I touched nothing. I was just checking the room.'

'Well, in future, stay out of here unless I'm in the room. I don't want you poking around through my personal space. Get that?'

Arbnor nodded and scurried out. Paolo watched him disappear in the direction of the main hall before going in and sitting down next to Dave who was already settled with his notebook at the ready.

'Have you got a moment?' Paolo asked, promising himself he'd look into Arbnor's odd behaviour later.

86

Derrick smiled. 'Sure thing. What can I do for you today?'

'I just wondered what reason you had for visiting Fletcher Simpson yesterday?'

The smile wavered briefly, but then returned. 'I didn't. What makes you think I did?'

'I saw you on the news last night. While Clementine Towers and her friends were waving placards and enjoying their five minutes of fame, you left Simpson Holdings and headed for the car park.'

Derrick shook his head. 'Not me. You must have been mistaken. I've never been there in my life.'

'Hmm, it was certainly someone who looked remarkably like you. Even had a jacket just like the one over there,' Paolo said, pointing to the jacket Derrick had removed and hung on a peg before sitting down.

Derrick glanced at it and laughed. 'I think that jacket could be seen on any number of people. I bought it in the market and the guy selling them was doing a roaring trade.'

Paolo stood up and signalled to Dave to do the same. 'My mistake. I could have sworn it was you, but as you say, it couldn't have been.' He headed for the door, but turned back as if he'd just thought of something. 'In fact, I should have known it wasn't you. There's no way you'd have anything to do with someone so opposed to Montague, is there?'

He watched Derrick's face to see if there was any flicker of guilt, but not a muscle moved.

'Exactly,' he said. 'The man's a slime ball. What reason could I possibly have for going to see him?'

Paolo didn't answer, just smiled and said goodbye.

He waited until they were halfway up the stairs to Mason's office before speaking.

'What do you think, Dave? Lying or telling the truth?'

Dave laughed. 'Oh, lying, definitely, but why?'

Paolo shrugged. 'No idea, but we'll be keeping a closer watch on Derrick Walden from now on. If he'd admitted being there, but told me it was none of my business, that would be fair enough, but the fact that he felt the need to pretend it wasn't him tells me something is going on that he doesn't want us to know about.'

When they entered April Greychurch's office she looked up and nodded in the direction of Mason's closed door.

'I told him you were coming about council business. I should warn you, he's not a happy bunny this morning. Something's upset him, but I've no idea what. There are times when I think I'm working in a lunatic asylum. That bloody woman has been in here again this morning wanting to speak to Montague about joining her protest group. He refused to see her, said he was too busy, but she'll keep coming back until she gets her own way and who will have to deal with her? Me, that's who! I fall over her everywhere I go in this place. Honestly, if I didn't need the money, I'd stick to my volunteer phone counselling and never deal with anyone face to face.'

As she paused for breath, Paolo smiled in sympathy and moved towards Mason's door.

'We'll go in to see Montague and get out of your hair.'

She gave a whatever shrug and glared at her computer screen.

'As I said, he's expecting you.'

Paolo tapped on the door and then held it open for Dave to go in ahead of him. Closing the door behind him, Paolo grimaced at Montague.

'What's wound up April? I've never seen her like that before today.'

'How would I know?' Montague snapped. 'I thought you were here to ask questions about council matters, not the miserable, or otherwise, disposition of my staff.'

Paolo glanced at Dave who looked as bemused as Paolo felt. What was going on between Mason and his secretary? He would have thought it was a lovers' spat if it hadn't been for Katy telling him Mason's tastes didn't run to females.

'Montague, I need to ask you a few questions,' he said, sitting down next to Dave, who already had his notebook at the ready.

'Yes, so April said. Something to do with council matters. I'm sorry, Paolo, I can't see what council discussions have to do with you. It is privileged information, you know.'

Paolo nodded. 'I know that, and I'm sure I can find out what I want to know from public records, but you could make it easier for me by answering one question.'

Montague shrugged. 'If I can. What's the question?'

'Did Fletcher Simpson clear with the council his decision to disable the CCTV footage along the canal?'

'Yes, he did and I was completely opposed to it. I told him it was essential to the security of the people who used the canal path, but would he listen? No! Of course, he has most of the other councillors in his pocket, so he got his way on it. Why do you want to know?'

Paolo ignored that question to ask one of his own. 'Who would have known the cameras had been disabled, apart from council members?'

Montague looked as if Paolo was insane. 'The entire town, apart from you, it seems. Didn't you read the letters pages of the papers a few months back? Lots of residents, myself included, bombarded Simpson's rag of a paper with complaints, but he, of course, did nothing about it.'

Paolo looked over at Dave, who shook his head. Obviously, Dave didn't read the letters pages either, but whoever dumped the attack victim at the canal probably did. Great, the field was now narrowed down to several thousand.

'Is that all you wanted to know?' Montague asked. 'You could have picked up the phone to ask instead of traipsing all the way over here. I have a very busy day ahead and need to get on.'

Paolo leaned forward. 'Not quite everything. We've heard back from financial crimes and I'm afraid there is something very seriously wrong with the accounts here.'

The colour drained from Montague's face. 'That's not possible,' he said. 'I oversee the accounts myself. If there was something amiss, I would have spotted it.'

'Who else, apart from you, has access to the funds?'

'Are you accusing me? Who the hell do you think you are? I can tell you right now, there isn't a penny missing from the centre's funds. Not one single penny.'

'Calm down, Montague,' Paolo said. 'No one has been accused yet, but there are irregularities and we have to look into them. Now, I'll ask the question again. Who, apart from you, has access to the funds?'

Montague remained silent. He picked up a pen, fiddled with and then slung it back down onto the desk.

'Sorry, Montague, but I need an answer.'

'If I hand in my resignation from the council, can that be the end of the matter?'

'Are you admitting guilt?'

Mason nodded, but didn't speak. Paolo was amazed to see tears running silently down the man's face. As he watched, Mason's shoulders began to shake and then he fell forward, howling as if he was suffering more pain than he could bear.

The door flew open and April came in.

'What's that noise? Oh!' she said, moving towards the desk. 'What's happened? Can I help?'

She put her arm around Mason's heaving shoulders.

'What did you do?' she said, looking at Paolo as if he'd sprouted horns and a tail.

Paolo stood and walked over to April. Putting his hand on her arm, he nodded towards the door.

'I'm sorry. I'm afraid I have to ask you to leave.'

She glared at him. 'No way! If you think –'

He cut across her words. 'April, unless Montague asks you to stay, you need to go back to your office.'

She leant down so that her face was closer to the sobbing man. 'Montague,' she whispered, 'do you need me to stay?'

With a shudder, the sobs subsided and he shook his head.

'Do you want me to call anyone for you?'

He lifted his head and Paolo was shocked at the devastation

90

written on the man's face. Whatever his reason for fiddling with the finances, Montague's future was in tatters and he knew it.

'No, don't call anyone,' he said, his voice a shadow of its usual bluster. 'Leave me now, April. I'll talk to you later.'

'Are you sure?' she said, her arm tightening around his shoulders.

'Yes.' As she let go and took a step towards the door, he called out. 'April!'

She stopped and looked back.

'Thank you for caring,' he whispered, so low Paolo thought at first April hadn't heard him.

After a moment, she nodded, shot a look of venom at Paolo and Dave, and then left, shutting the door with enough force to make the point of how she felt about the scene she'd witnessed.

Paolo sighed. Another enemy gained from doing his job. He waited for Montague to finish blowing his nose. He seemed to have pulled himself together.

'I'll need you to come down to the station to make a statement about what you've done and why you did it,' Paolo said.

Montague shook his head. 'I don't have to tell you why.'

'No, but it might help you at trial if there was an extenuating circumstance for your actions.'

'Trial? No, there mustn't be a trial. I'll plead guilty to whatever you say, but no trial.'

'Montague, don't be daft. Of course there'll have to be a trial. This isn't some third world country where we sling you in prison and forget about you. Even if you plead guilty, there still has to be a trial to determine what sort of sentence you'll get.'

'You mean prison? I can't go to prison. I put all the money back. All of it. They can check. I only borrowed it until I could sell things to replace what I took. You have to believe me, Paolo. I moved cash around, yes, but I didn't steal anything.'

Paolo sighed. 'That's why there has to be a trial, Montague. If you're telling the truth, the chances are you won't get a custodial sentence. You might even get away with a rap over the knuckles,

91

but you must see that justice has to be done. You're in a position of trust and, for whatever reason, you abused that trust.'

'I've already said I'll resign. Please, I'm begging you, can't we just ignore this whole thing?'

'I can't. You know that.' A thought occurred to Paolo. 'Are you being blackmailed?'

Already ashen, Montague's face lost its remaining colour.

'You are, aren't you? Who are paying money to?'

He shook his head. 'No.'

'You are,' Paolo pressed. 'Come on, Montague, let me help you. Are you being blackmailed? Is that why you needed to produce cash in such a hurry you had to take it from the youth centre accounts?'

Montague hung his head, but his answer was clear. 'I'll be ruined when this comes out. The newspapers will splash it all over the front pages. Isn't that enough for you? Please, Paolo, I'm begging you, don't dig into why I did it.'

'I have to. It's my job. I can't sit by and allow blackmailers to ruin lives. Whatever you've done, paying someone to keep quiet about it won't hide the facts forever.'

Montague looked up. 'I haven't done anything illegal.'

'Apart from borrowing from public finances, you mean?'

He looked as if he'd been slapped and Paolo was surprised to find he felt bad.

Montague raised his shoulders and let them drop in defeat. 'I know taking the money was wrong, but I told you, I put it back. I'm not a thief. What I did, what the blackmailer found out about, it isn't illegal, but it's just . . . I . . . go away, Paolo, please. As of this moment, you can consider I've resigned. I'll get April to send out a press release and I'll come to the station later today to give a statement.'

Paolo stood. Looking across the desk he felt more sympathy for Montague than he'd considered possible. He didn't like the man, but to see him broken like this wasn't a sight Paolo could rejoice in.

'I give you my word, nothing will reach the press from me or any member of my team. It will come out eventually, but not via my office.'

'Thank you for that,' Montague whispered, his voice wavering as his tears broke through once again.

Paolo nodded and went to open the door. As he and Dave walked into the outer office, Derrick Walden made a sudden move away from April's desk.

'Right, April, I'll see you later, then,' he said and sauntered out.

April turned to Paolo. 'That bloody man is worse than any woman when it comes to spreading gossip. I hope you realise you've ruined Montague's reputation. By the time Derrick leaves today, everyone will know you've been here and reduced Montague to tears. I hope you're pleased with yourself!'

Paolo opened his mouth to justify his actions, realised he couldn't without compromising his position, so shut it again without saying a word.

'See! You know you've ruined that man and you won't even apologise.'

'April, it was partly through your nudge in that direction that we . . . sorry, I can't comment on an ongoing investigation.'

'Well, I didn't mean for you to come and persecute the poor man. I just thought you'd find out what was going on and help him. There's no money missing, that I do know.'

Paolo sat down. 'You're going to have to explain. I'm completely lost.'

She grimaced. 'I knew there was something not quite right with the books, but each time I thought there was money missing, it reappeared, so I knew Montague wasn't stealing. At first I thought it was my imagination, but now I think someone is blackmailing him. He's a nervous wreck these days and he's been selling off his stuff. He reckons it's to downsize, but you don't sell paintings and sculptures to downsize until you know what size place you're moving to and can work out what to keep and what to ditch. And that's another thing; he's put his house on the market. He loves that place. No way would he sell it unless he'd been forced to. Someone is bleeding him dry. I thought if I nudged you in the right direction you'd look into it and find out who it was.'

Paolo was aware of the scratching of Dave's pen as he scribbled down the notes of April's furious tirade.

'So was it you who scrawled on the plaque?'

She looked disgusted. 'How many times do I have to tell you? No, it wasn't me, but it might have been my lipstick. I lost it and haven't seen it since. I wanted to help Montague. I'd never publically humiliate him, but that's what's going to happen isn't it? I feel sick to think I'm responsible.'

Paolo stood up. 'You're not to blame. We'd have reached this point anyway.'

She gave a bitter laugh. 'That's easy for you say, but I've got to face that poor man when he comes out of there.'

Chapter Thirteen

I knew I was being watched. I've had the feeling of someone spying on me for weeks. It started with a tingle in my spine, a growing awareness of no longer being invisible. Now the sensation has deepened to the certainty someone is interested in my every move. There's no point in taking chances. I'll simply keep low for a while. Nemesis will have to go into hibernation for a few weeks. With all the bastards out there in need of punishment, it's going to be hard to ignore my calling, but I have to think of the longer term.

There are still so many truly evil people who need to be shown the error of their ways, but if I get caught, and forced to stop dealing retribution, it's the innocent women of the future who will suffer. If I don't stop these men from raping again and again, who will? The police don't care and the courts are useless. Even when rapists are convicted they get no more than a slapped wrist. How can that be right? Where is the justice in that?

My way works, though. I've proved it time and time again. Not one of the men who've been through my reconditioning programme has ever reoffended. Not one!

An eye for an eye, a tooth for a tooth, a rape for a rape. Nemesis in action.

Paolo turned to peer at the bedside clock. God, it was only six in the morning. Why did his internal alarm insist on waking him at this bloody ridiculous hour at weekends? Every Friday night he promised himself a lie-in. Every Saturday his eyes opened to the unwelcome sight of his clock telling him he could have slept for another couple of hours at least.

He squeezed his eyes shut and tried to force his mind to relax, but it was no good, his brain had already started processing the events of the week. Sighing, he sat up and switched on his bedside light. His thoughts drifted back to the day before when Montague had come into the station to make his statement.

The man was a wreck, a shadow of the bluster and bombast that had always been part of his basic personality. April had come in with him as support. Now that woman was a constant source of surprise to Paolo. He couldn't make her out at all. She seemed to veer between being a mindless flirt and a compassionate friend in need. He shrugged. Scratch the surface of most people and you'd find they had more facets to them than you'd ever dream were hiding there.

So far the press hadn't caught wind of Montague's disgrace, but it was only a matter of time before it became public knowledge. Paolo wondered how Montague would handle being headline news for all the wrong reasons.

Paolo knew he was dwelling on work to take his mind off Jessica's visit this weekend. Had she found someone else? Is that what she needed to discuss with him? She'd sounded very serious, so whatever it was, did not bode well for a joyful reunion. He tried to work out when they'd last spent a full uninterrupted weekend together and couldn't think of one during the past six months at least.

It was almost as if the criminal element of Bradchester knew when he was planning a relaxing couple of days with Jessica. The moment she arrived, the phone would ring on a case he couldn't ignore. Maybe that was the problem. Maybe she was just fed up with him being called out all the time.

He stretched and got out of bed. If he was going to stay awake, he might just as well get a caffeine fix. As he padded through to the kitchen, he thought about the other two women in his life, because he had to consider Katy in that way now. She was no longer a child, even if he'd have preferred her to remain one for a few years longer. He'd tried to discuss Katy's plans with Lydia over the phone, but she'd refused to talk to him about it until after this weekend. She and Katy were going to have a heart to heart and try to see each other's point of view.

Must be something in the air, he thought, as he filled the kettle. It seemed to be a weekend for heavy conversations and life changing decisions. As he reached into the cupboard for the coffee, a memory flashed into his mind. The last time Jessica had been here, she'd said something had changed for her. Something to do with her work. They'd been about to discuss it when his phone had interrupted her. Maybe she hadn't found someone else. Maybe it was work related. Now he was clutching at straws for sure.

He spooned coffee into the cafetière and poured the boiling water on top. As he replaced the lid and plunger, he tried to imagine life without Jessica and realised, with some shock, that's exactly what he'd been living for the last six months. The last time he'd cleared his work load so that they could go away for a few days, even planning to leave his phone behind so that no one could find him and drag him back to work, Jessica had cancelled a couple of days before. She'd had to go off somewhere work related.

Stop it, he told himself. Stop trying to overanalyse everything. Jessica will be here in a few hours. He poured a cup of perfect coffee and took it through to the bedroom. Just because he was awake, didn't mean he had to get up. A couple of hours with his favourite author would help to pass the time.

Four hours later, Paolo was pacing up and down at the train station, still trying to second guess Jessica's intentions. As the train flashed by, he spotted her standing next to the doors, ready to alight. He moved along the platform as the train slowed and eventually stopped, so that he was level with her carriage.

She came off the train, dropped her overnight bag at his feet, and hugged him.

'God, I've missed you,' she said.

All his fears and anxiety fled as he returned her embrace.

'I've missed you, too.'

'Good! I'm hoping . . . never mind. Let's go back to your place. We can talk there.'

Paolo picked up her bag and carried it to the car. He wanted to ask questions, but knew there was no point. If Jessica wanted to keep her news until they got home, no amount of probing on his part would prise information out of her. He smiled. Some of the criminals he interviewed could learn from Jessica about when to speak and when to keep quiet. A sudden vision of her coaching some of the harder nuts he needed to crack came into his mind. That really would be the ultimate nightmare scenario!

'So, how's London?' he asked, as he manoeuvred the car into the Saturday morning traffic.

'Busy. Noisy. Exciting. All the usual adjectives, but I won't be there for much longer.'

'Really?' he said, turning off the main road. 'I thought you were going to be there for another year.'

She laughed. 'We aren't supposed to be discussing this until you've made me coffee at your place. No more questions, OK?'

He agreed, but his heart soared. So this was the big discussion point. She was coming back to Bradchester. Maybe she wanted to discuss moving in with him – or him moving into her place. As he drove, he tried to analyse how he felt about that. Was he ready for a more permanent relationship? He smiled. Yes, he thought, that's exactly what he was ready for.

To avoid any awkward silences, he told her about Katy's plan to go overseas as a volunteer for a year.

'I've made a rash promise to talk to Lydia on Katy's behalf. I'm not sure how much good it will do. Maybe I should forbid Lydia to let Katy go, that might do the trick. She'd be booking Katy's air tickets before I'd even left the house.'

Jessica laughed. 'You do your ex-wife an injustice. She just wants what's best for her daughter.'

'I know, so do I, but I also know Katy. She's seventeen now, but will soon be old enough not to need our permission. If we stop her from going, the day she turns eighteen, she'll be off without so much as a backward glance. I'd rather she left with our blessing and kept in touch. God knows, it will be hard enough when she leaves without driving myself insane with worry because I don't know where she is or what she's doing.'

Out of the corner of his eye, he saw Jessica nodding in agreement.

'Everything changes. If you have exciting things going on in your own life, you might not miss her as much as you think.'

'I get quite enough excitement in my day to day existence, thank you very much. I don't think I want to search out any more.'

'Really?' she said. 'You might change your mind when you hear what I've got to tell you.'

Pulling up outside his home, he glanced over at her. She looked as if she was bursting with news. He opened the door, climbed out and walked to the rear of the car to grab Jessica's suitcase.

'You are so old-fashioned, Paolo,' she said as he insisted on carrying it from the car into the flat. 'How do you think I manage when you're not around?'

He flicked the door closed with his foot, put the case down in the hallway and walked into the kitchen to prepare some coffee. Jessica followed him in and perched on one of the bar stools flanking the breakfast bar.

'We women are capable of carrying our own bags, you know.'

Paolo grinned at her. 'I know and I also know lots of women who are much stronger, tougher and fitter than I am, CC for one, but I like doing things for you. It's the way I was raised. It's no big deal. I'm not trying to put you in box marked helpless.'

She laughed. 'Such a fine line between chauvinism and chivalry. I'll forgive you, though, because you do make a wonderful pot of coffee,' she said as he put the cafetière down in front of her.

Placing two cups next to it, Paolo smiled. 'Now, if I said you be mother and expected you to pour the coffee, that would be sexist, but if I said, I've made it, you pour it, that wouldn't be sexist, right?'

'You're learning, Paolo. It's not just in the words we use, but the hidden meaning behind them. Equal distribution of tasks is fine, but distribution because of gender expectations, regardless of whether or not it's a fair distribution, is not. However, to show there are no hard feelings, I *will* pour the coffee.'

'Thank you,' he said, as meekly as he dared.

She laughed, picked up the tea towel and flicked it at him.

'That's brutality,' he said, 'but I won't arrest you – yet! OK, now we've got the coffee, what's your big news?'

The smile left her face and she became so serious that Paolo's emotions once again took a dip.

'You remember the weekend we were due to go away to the Lake District and I had to let you down at the last minute?'

Paolo nodded. It had seemed to him at the time as if she hadn't told him the real reason for backing out of a trip they'd both been looking forward to for several weeks. He hadn't been able to get hold of her for a few days afterwards. When they finally made contact again, she claimed she'd been sick and not answering her phone. It was since that time that he'd felt the gap between them was widening.

'I flew to Canada for a week.'

'Canada? Why?'

She reached across for his hand and held it. 'I've been offered a post in a teaching hospital in British Columbia. I went over for an interview and also to see if it was something I wanted to take up.'

Paolo stomach lurched. Canada? Such a long way away and British Columbia must be about the furthest west you could get without falling off the North American continent. He tried to think of a rational response, but offering congratulations didn't tie in with how he was feeling.

'You lied to me,' he said, pulling his hand from hers. 'Why didn't you tell me the truth?'

She shrugged. 'Because I wasn't sure if I was going to accept.'

'No,' he said, 'there's more to it than that. If it was just a case of not being sure if you wanted the job, you could have told me about it, but you deliberately kept it from me. Why?'

'Aren't you going to ask me if I'm going to take up the position?' she asked.

Paolo noted how she'd avoided answering his question. Presumably she had her reasons, but he wasn't sure he wanted to hear them.

'Well, are you?' he asked, aware of the resentment in his voice filling the space between them.

She nodded. 'But one of the reasons for not telling you before was so that I could make some enquiries and present you with some information you might like.'

'You're planning to live God knows how many thousand miles away, but you think there's something I might like about it? You must have found out something truly amazing if that's the case.'

She smiled and reached for his hand again. 'What I found out is that the Canadian Police Force welcomes British detectives with open arms and wonderful financial packages. You could come with me. Katy's going off on her own adventures, you could as well.'

Paolo wanted to believe he'd misheard Jessica, but there was no point in pretending. He'd heard and understood exactly what she'd said.

'But my life is here. Why would I want to up sticks and move to a different country?'

Jessica shrugged. 'Well, one reason would be to live with me, but I can understand that idea has come as a shock to you.'

'No, that's not a shock at all. In fact, I've been thinking about us moving in together and I really like the thought of it. I just don't see why we would need to move to Canada to do it.'

'Because, Paolo, I've been offered the chance of a lifetime and I want to take it. I've looked into things over there and you, too, could rise up the promotion ladder much faster than you would here. They are crying out for officers with your experience. You'd really be in demand.'

He shook his head. 'I don't want to be in demand. I want to stay here where I belong.'

She laughed. 'How can you say that? You have no social life apart from our relationship. No friends to speak of outside of work. You don't see family members other than Katy and, as you pointed out earlier, she is going abroad for a year anyway.'

'But when she comes back,' Paolo said, 'I need to be here.'

'*If* she comes back,' Jessica amended. 'Usually, once young adults have lived abroad for any length of time, they can't settle back in the UK. She may never come home again.'

She smiled and shrugged.

'You know, Paolo, it's not that long ago that wherever a man was transferred, his wife and family were expected to give up everything and relocate for the sake of his career. I'm not asking you to give up your job, just do it in a new place with different challenges to overcome.'

'Jessica, firstly, we're not married, but even if we were, you haven't been transferred, you've applied for, and been awarded, a new position. Secondly, you did it without even discussing it with me and now you expect me to jump at an opportunity I hadn't even realised was on the table.'

'If I'd spoken to you about it before I went to Canada, would that have made any difference? Be honest, Paolo, you'd have done all you could to persuade me not to go.'

Paolo wanted to argue. To tell her she was talking nonsense, but he knew she was at least partly right. He would have tried to convince her there were more reasons to stay in the UK than to leave. His phone rang, sounding like a band playing full blast in the silence of the kitchen. Recognising Dave's ringtone, he snatched it up. Paolo was usually angry if interrupted during one of Jessica's visits, but today, even if it was just a traffic violation, he was going to be there in person.

'Sterling,' he said,. 'What's up?'

'I'm at Montague Mason's place, sir. It looks like he's committed suicide.'

Chapter Fourteen

Paolo parked in the street outside Montague's house, his mind in turmoil. He had to put all thoughts of Jessica and her bombshell to one side until he'd dealt with Montague's suicide. The driveway was full of police cars, with an ambulance parked outside the front door, obscuring much of the house from view. Lack of anything to photograph didn't seem to deter the crowd of reporters already gathered outside in the street. Flashbulbs flickered continuously as Paolo left his car and walked the few yards to the drive entrance.

The reporters were being held back by crime scene tape strung across the road, but that didn't prevent their voices from reaching him.

'Is it murder?'

'Do you have any suspects?'

'Is this to do with the accusation on the plaque at the youth centre?'

'How did he die?'

'What's the official position?'

Paolo ignored them all; shaking his head as he passed the vehicles on the drive blocking his route, he made his way towards the detached mock Georgian house Montague had loved so much. Negotiating the congestion in the drive, Paolo realised, when the ambulance was ready to leave, it would either have to drive across the miniature manicured lawn, or all the other cars would have to reverse out to make room. Either way, there wouldn't be any reason to rush. Montague was dead and couldn't get deader if it took an extra few minutes for the ambulance to edge its way down the drive and out into the street.

Inside, he found the entrance deserted and made his way to where he could hear voices. He came to the room Montague had grandly referred to as the drawing room. Paolo would have called it front room, but then he had been raised in a terraced house in a much poorer part of Bradchester than this estate of identical, but expensive, houses. Dave, CC and Dr Barbara Royston, the forensic pathologist, formed a semi-circle around Montague's body.

Paolo was aware of a strong chemical smell, but couldn't quite place it in his mind. Whatever it was, it was definitely out of place in a room such as this. He looked down; the dead man's face was contorted in such a way that Paolo could only assume he had died in agony. Whatever his feelings had been for Montague in life, Paolo would never wish that sort of death on anyone, far less someone he knew.

Paolo nodded to Barbara, who returned his greeting before kneeling down to next to the body. She pointed at a plastic bottle, the contents of which had spilled over onto a patch of the carpet next to the body, removing all colour. The smell was so strong it masked the other, more unpleasant, odour of death.

'Until I do the post mortem, it's unofficial, but I'd say it's fairly certain he died as a result of drinking bleach.'

'Dear God, no wonder his face looks like that.'

He shuddered and turned his attention to Dave and CC.

'Who found him?'

CC stepped forward. 'His sister, sir. She's in the dining room at the end of the hallway, being comforted by a family liaison officer. I'll show you the way.'

Paolo shook his head. 'It's OK. I've been here before,' he said. 'Montague held an open drinks evening when we were fundraising for the centre. I'd like you to come with me, though. His sister might respond more easily to another female. Dave, you stay here with Dr Royston.'

His last conversation with Jessica still fresh in his mind, he tried to put it out of his head, with only limited success. As he walked next to CC, Paolo wondered if Jessica would have seen sexist motives in his allocation of tasks. It was just common sense, surely, to take a female to interview another female? But then again, would he take Dave and leave CC behind if he was going to interview a male? Probably not, as CC was one of the best when it came to wheedling information out of people who didn't want to give any.

He was going to ask CC if he came across as chauvinistic, but pulled himself up. This wasn't the time or the place. Concentrate on the job on hand, he ordered his wayward mind. He could speak to CC later, though he dreaded to hear what she might have to say on the subject.

Paolo had met Gwendolyn Mason on two previous occasions. The first time when she'd played hostess here at the fundraising event and the second time had been the day before the opening of the youth centre. Although he knew, because Montague had told him many, many times, that his sister had been working tirelessly behind the scenes, she hadn't been able to attend the night of the opening. At the time Paolo had been glad she'd been spared the humiliation heaped on Montague that night, but given a choice, he'd rather she'd seen that than been the one to find her brother's dead body.

He and CC entered the dining room to find a WPC sitting at the table with Gwendolyn. They were talking too quietly for him to hear the words, but the feeling in the room came over loud and clear. Disbelief and horror on the one part, sympathy tinged with professional curiosity on the other. Paolo would find out later if the WPC had uncovered anything he needed to know while comforting the distressed woman.

Gwendolyn was considerably older than Montague, but the resemblance between them was strong. There could be no doubting the family relationship. He nodded to the WPC before sitting opposite Gwendolyn at the table.

'I'm sorry for your loss, Gwendolyn. I know how close you and Montague were. I hope this won't add too much to your distress, but I have to ask you some questions.'

She nodded mutely, her grey hair falling over her face in untidy waves. Tears filled her eyes and threatened to fall. Paolo waited while she pushed the hair behind her ears and rubbed at eyes reddened from earlier attempts to stem the flow.

'Can you take me through what happened this morning?'

'I was going to Wales for a few days to visit my friend, but she fell over yesterday and broke her leg. She's in the hospital and said not to come as she'd all her family round her. You see, I wasn't supposed to be here,' she said. 'I think that's why he did it this weekend; so that I wouldn't get to see him like that, but I opened the door and I could smell . . . I knew something wasn't right. I came in and . . .'

She put her hands over her face and sobbed.

That at least answered one question for Paolo. He knew Montague had gone out of his way to protect his sister, so arranging things so that she would be the one to find him hadn't made sense.

'Gwendolyn, I'm sorry, but we know Montague was being blackmailed. Do you have any idea why or by whom?'

She stopped rubbing at her eyes with the sodden tissue and looked up. Her face was a picture of horror.

'Blackmail?'

Paolo nodded. 'Montague didn't tell you?'

She shook her head. 'No, he never said a word. How do you know?'

'He admitted it when he gave his statement about manipulating the youth centre's funds, but wouldn't say what it was he was paying someone to keep secret.'

'Oh no, someone must have found out. Did he kill himself to protect me? Why didn't he tell me? I'd have said it didn't matter. Things are different today. No one would have cared, would they?'

'Gwendolyn, I'm sorry, you've lost me. What is it that no one would have cared about?'

106

A fresh burst of tears meant Paolo had to wait for her answer.

'I'm not Montague's sister. I'm his mother.'

Paolo stood in front of his hastily assembled team and apologised for bringing them in yet again on a Saturday.

'I promise you, at some point in the future you'll get an entire weekend to yourselves, but obviously it won't be this one. Barbara Royston is going to conduct the PM on Tuesday, but it seems pretty clear from the evidence at the scene that cause of death was directly related to his ingestion of bleach. We know Montague Mason was being blackmailed, what we don't know is why, how long it's been going on, or who was turning the screw on him.'

CC looked up from the notes she'd been writing.

'You don't think it was about Gwendolyn being his mother?'

Paolo shook his head. 'I could be wrong, but that doesn't seem to fit for me. I'm just not convinced fear of the mother/son relationship coming out is enough. Personally, I wouldn't have thought so, especially as Gwendolyn said Montague had known for several years. The only reason they kept it quiet was to protect her reputation, not his. Apparently, he was raised believing she was his elder sister, but guessed from various things that were said as he grew up that she might be his mother. There was only fifteen years between them. She was involved with someone who ran as soon as he heard she was pregnant.'

'So why did he continue to say she was his sister after he knew the truth?' Dave asked.

'For the sake of her parents. They kept up the pretence with their friends and neighbours and forced Gwendolyn to do the same. By the time her parents died, it would have been difficult to come out and tell the truth, but even so, had it come out, it wouldn't have been bad enough to warrant suicide. You've got to be bloody desperate to swallow bleach. Would he do that to cover up his mother's so-called shame? I don't think so. There has to be more to it. Andrea has Montague's laptop and is going to go through the files and emails this weekend. If she can't find

107

anything pointing to motive for him to take his own life, we'll hand it over to the IT guys to search for hidden files or fragments left behind after wiping.'

'Could he have topped himself because he couldn't face the music over the youth centre finances?' Dave asked.

Paolo nodded. 'Again, it's possible, but it feels like too extreme an action just to avoid bad publicity. He'd likely not even have been given a custodial sentence as there was no actual money missing. He'd misappropriated it, yes, but always put it back once he'd sold something. The chances of a judge sending him to prison were pretty remote and he must have known that. No, there's something in Montague's life he knew would come out because his source of funding to pay the blackmailer was drying up. Did you notice the bare walls and places where statues should have been? I think he'd reached the end of the line when it came to selling off his possessions.'

Tired of standing, Paolo leaned back to rest against a desk.

'April Greychurch said as much when we were there. Selling his house was the only option left open to him and, with the market as depressed as it is, the chances are he wouldn't get a taker for it for some considerable time.'

Andrea stood up clutching Montague's laptop. 'I'm going to take this home with me, if that's OK with you, sir. I'll work better without distractions.'

Paolo nodded. 'Of course, but call me the moment you uncover anything, no matter how small. I know we're dealing with suicide, but in my eyes, driving someone to kill themselves because they can no longer pay up is tantamount to murder. The courts might not see it that way, but I do. I want to know who was draining Montague and why.' He waved an arm around the room. 'The rest of you can get off home as well. There's not much we can do until we get more information. See you all on Monday.'

Dave stood up. 'You haven't forgotten I'll be in late on Monday, sir? The only time the wedding organiser has free is nine o'clock, but I'll get in as soon as I can.'

Paolo heard the whispered jibes coming from the back of the room and glanced in that direction, only to be met with a sea of innocent faces. Looking back at Dave, he saw from his pained expression that he too had heard the comments.

'That's not a problem, Dave. You're generally the first in and last out so being an hour or so late from time to time isn't going to impact on your work,' he said, raising his voice so that it was certain to carry across the babble of conversations.

Dave flushed bright red. Paolo couldn't be sure whether it was as a result of his words, or those of the idiot who'd commented on nepotism, but if *he* was getting sick to death of the jibes and innuendoes, and he was, how must Dave be feeling as the target of them?

Chapter Fifteen

The first thing Paolo noticed as he entered his flat was the absence of Jessica's suitcase by the door. The second thing was the silence. He didn't know whether to be pleased or annoyed that she'd left while he was away. On the one hand, some time for reflection on his own was probably a good thing; on the other hand, it would be good to get any difficult conversations out of the way as soon as possible.

He went into the kitchen and there, propped against the cafetière, was a note. He smiled. Jessica knew his first port of call on arriving home would always be the kitchen for a caffeine fix. He tore the envelope open and pulled out the contents.

Hi, I wasn't sure how long you'd be, so I've decided to go over to my place. I'll fix us dinner. See you about eight unless you're caught up in work and can't make it. Send me a text to let me know you've received this.

Love,
Jessica x

He pulled out his phone and sent her a see you later message, then went about making the coffee. As he moved around the kitchen, he tried to work out how he felt about living in another country. In truth, it wasn't something he'd ever contemplated, so had no idea where to start. Actually, that wasn't true. The best place to start would be to ask himself if he wanted to lose Jessica from his life. If she was determined to go, the only way to continue the relationship was by going with her.

As he poured the coffee, he wondered if making a pros and cons list would help him to sort out his thoughts, but kept coming back to the question: did he want to move country? Left to his own devices, the answer would be a resounding no. He rummaged through the drawer where he kept all the stuff that had no other home, moving aside bits of cardboard, string, scissors and sellotape. As he did so, he smiled, thinking of his childhood and Blue Peter days. He had all the items necessary to make something from one of those programmes: cardboard, string, scissors and stickyback plastic. God, life was certainly easier back then.

Eventually locating a pad and pencil, he sat down to draw up his list for and against going with Jessica. He was still sitting there half an hour later when his phone rang. So far all he'd put down were two words – the headings: Pros and Cons. Throwing down the pencil in defeat, he picked up his phone.

'Sterling.'

'Hi, sir, it's Andrea. I just wanted to let you know I couldn't find anything on Montague's laptop to give us any clues regarding motive, but there are files that have been deleted. Emails as well. Getting them back is beyond my capabilities, so I'm going to take the laptop into the station this afternoon. I've already called Mike from Leicester IT and he's going to meet me in the office to pick it up.'

'Did he give any idea of when he'd be able to get to it?'

'Not for a few days, I'm afraid. He said they are inundated with work. It seems more crimes are planned and even executed on computers than out in the real world. That's his words, not mine, by the way. It seems to me we get our fair share of face to face crimes committed.'

Paolo laughed. 'Agreed, more than our fair share sometimes. Thanks for bringing me up to speed. Enjoy the rest of your weekend.'

'Will do, sir. You too.'

Paolo ended the call and thought about Andrea's contribution to the team. She'd slipped into place so seamlessly, it felt as if she'd always been there. Dave, CC and now Andrea, he couldn't imagine working without them.

He picked up the pencil and under Cons wrote: not being able to take my best people with me.

Paolo arrived at Jessica's a few minutes early. He'd spent the afternoon thinking to such an extent, his head was aching. As he put the key in the lock, he thought again how close they'd become since their relationship had started and yet neither of them had suggested moving in together. They each had a key to the other's homes, but had kept those homes separate. They hadn't even lived together here in Bradchester, how would they manage sharing a home in a strange environment?

He sighed. That had featured heavily on the Cons side of his list.

'Hi, Jess, I'm here,' he called, using his foot to close the front door.

Following the wonderful aromas of garlic and herbs, he found Jessica in the kitchen. She'd laid the table, complete with candles already burning in their holders.

'Right on time. Good man,' she said as he kissed her cheek. 'Take a seat. I've just got to pop this into the oven to finish off and I'll be with you.'

Paolo pulled out a chair. 'Smells divine. What are we having?'

'Smoked salmon and cream cheese parcels to start and rack of lamb for the main. For dessert I thought you could take over and make some of those delicious pancakes I had at your place a couple of months back.'

Realising they were speaking with the careful constraint that had disappeared after their first few dates, Paolo followed her choice of neutral topic to avoid bringing up the big issue, at least until after they'd eaten.

'I'll have to see if I can get the mix right. Katy says my pancakes are either a delight or inedible.'

'Fingers crossed. So, how was your day?' she asked.

Paolo nearly burst out laughing, although tears might have been a better option. He shook his head

'This isn't good, Jess. We're making small talk. Skirting around the elephant.'

She sighed. 'I know, but I was kind of hoping we could ignore it for a few hours.'

'Let's do that,' he said.

By the time they were settled on the sofa with coffee, they'd slipped back into their old, more relaxed, routine. Paolo pulled her into his arms and kissed the top of her head.

'I wish we could stay like this forever,' he said.

Jessica laughed. 'No you don't, you'd be bored to tears within a day. Climbing the walls within two and breaking down the door to escape within three.'

'Not fair,' he said. 'True, but not fair to know me so well.'

Realising the moment had arrived, he pulled away a little and looked down at her.

'So, you've accepted the position?'

She nodded.

'When do you leave?'

'Just under two months. I'm going to sell this flat fully furnished, but obviously that won't happen before I go unless I'm really lucky. I'll leave the key with an estate agent.'

'What about your personal effects?'

She sat up, moving out of his arms. 'I'm getting in a few removal companies to give me quotes. I'll have to be quite ruthless and only take things that really matter. I may leave some stuff here in storage, though. I can always send for it if I decide not to come back again.'

'How long is the contract for?'

'Well, initially, for two years, but open to extend indefinitely.'

Paolo stared into his coffee cup as if it would provide the answers he sought. Putting it down on the table, he turned to face Jessica.

'You've just said you're not certain you won't come back again.'

She frowned. 'I know I did. How can I know for absolute

113

certain that I'll stay there forever when I don't even know if I'm going to like it in Canada?'

'Jess, honey, you're asking me to give up my life here: my job, my team, my daughter—'

'Katy won't even be here for the first year.'

'I know. And I know you think she might stay away for longer than that, possibly forever, but there's also a chance she'll come back. I have to be here for her, Jessica. I'm sorry. I can't come with you. I love this country. I know I get pissed off with it at times, but that passes. I've never wanted to live anywhere other than right here.'

'But you could come with me for two years, couldn't you? I've looked into it, Paolo, you would love it over there. In no time at all you'd be right at the top of heap, commanding more than just a team.'

He took her hand. 'I'm not that ambitious. Yes, promotion would be good, but that's not why I joined the force. I thought you knew me better than that. I just want to catch and put away the bad guys. Lock up the ones who hurt innocent people. I don't need to have a higher rank than the one I have right now to be able to do that.'

Tears seeped from under her closed lids and Paolo wished he could have reached a different decision, but there was no point in wishing for the impossible. He was who he was and doubted he'd ever change.

She opened her eyes and the tears fell faster. 'Please, Paolo, don't make a final decision now.'

'Jess—'

'Ssh,' she said, putting her fingers on his lips. 'Don't say anything else. I'm not leaving for another two months. Just promise me you'll think about it. Promise!'

He nodded. 'But I know—'

'Ssh,' she said again, leaning forward to kiss him. 'You never know what the future might hold.'

Chapter Sixteen

Paolo was still trying to sort out his tangled emotions three days later when he arrived to witness the post mortem of Montague Mason.

'I would offer you a penny for them,' Barbara said, 'but it looks like they might be worth more than I could afford to pay.'

'Huh? Sorry, what did you say?' Paolo asked, coming back to earth after following yet another carousel of images chasing each other endlessly.

'Your thoughts . . . I was going to offer you a penny. Oh, never mind. The moment has passed.'

Paolo was relieved. The last thing he wanted to do was discuss his situation with Barbara. He'd never mentioned her declaration of love while under the influence of anaesthetic, and neither had she, but he was pretty sure she remembered what she'd said when he went to visit her in the hospital after her operation. He'd gone to see her the day afterwards and she hadn't been able to look him in the eye. There'd been a barrier between them ever since.

'I take it you were right about cause of death?'

Barbara shook her head. 'Not exactly, although the bleach was to blame for him dying, it wasn't the cause of death. He didn't drink very much, but it was enough to burn his throat and mouth. What killed him was the heart attack brought on by the agony of the burns to his mouth and throat. If an ambulance had been alerted and arrived within minutes of him ingesting the bleach, he might well have survived, although with severe, and possibly permanent, damage.'

'So still recorded as suicide?'

She shrugged. 'I'm going to put cardiac infarction caused by ingestion of bleach on the death certificate, but the coroner is the one who'll make the final decision about suicide.'

As Paolo walked into the main office he saw Andrea deep in conversation with a man. She interrupted their conversation and called Paolo over.

'Sir, this is Mike Carnot, the IT specialist from Leicester. He's found some interesting files and emails on Montague's laptop.'

Paolo held out his hand for Mike to shake. 'Sounds like good news for us. Would you like to take us through what you've found?'

With all the enthusiasm of Messiah given a roomful of potential converts to captivate, Mike started to explain the complicated process of retrieval. Paolo watched as most of the assembled faces shut down and lost interest.

'Sorry to interrupt, Mike, but most of that is going over my head. I'm sure you've included the route to discovery in your report but, for now, could you outline for us what you found?'

Paolo felt sorry for Mike. It was clear that the actual contents of the laptop held no interest for him; it was uncovering the secrets others had tried to erase that fascinated the IT expert.

'Yep, OK, I'll give it to you briefly, but all the details are in there,' he said, pointing to a sheaf of papers on Andrea's desk.

'Right, so I started with the emails, because Andrea had said it was likely the owner of this laptop was being blackmailed. I found shadows of deleted emails.'

'Shadows?' Paolo asked.

Mike looked reproachful. 'Well, that was what I was explaining when you stopped me.'

Paolo nodded. 'OK, in words of one syllable for those of us not au fait with computer jargon.'

Mike sighed. 'Basically, when emails are deleted they go into the deleted items folder. The next stage after that is to empty that folder, which brings up a prompt reminding you the process is irreversible. So most people think that anything permanently deleted means exactly that. They think they have covered their tracks completely.'

'But they haven't?' Paolo prompted, to avoid another lecture when he saw the evangelical light come back into Mike's eyes.

'Nope, not even close. If he'd reformatted his laptop, it would have been harder, but not impossible to retrieve data.'

Andrea had set up an overhead projector for Mike, which he now turned to.

'This first slide shows the initial threat of exposure, but doesn't give any details. The sender assumes the recipient knows exactly what's under discussion.'

Paolo stepped back from the screen to read the words.

I know where you go and what you do while you're there.

'It appears Mr Mason ignored that first email. Perhaps he thought it was a joke, or maybe he didn't know how to respond, but the next email contained instructions.'

He touched the switch for the image to change.

I've seen you at the club many times. If you don't want the press to find out, leave £1,000 in cash behind the bins in the car park on your next regular visit.

Paolo already had a good idea where this was leading, but needed confirmation.

'Were you able to find out who sent the emails?'

Mike shook his head. 'It's a free email address. You can sign up for one of those giving any details you care to make up, but I was able to trace the IP address used to send the messages.'

Paolo smiled. 'Let me guess, that led you to the Triple B Club?'

Mike looked crestfallen. 'If you knew that, what was the point in me spending time on retrieval?'

'Because, until you uncovered the emails, I didn't know Montague was a member. One thing is for sure, it proves there's more going on there than a simple businessman's meeting point. How many demands were made?'

'One a month going back over a year and a half. For the first six months he was leaving a thousand pounds at a time. Then the demands changed.' He flicked the switch several times to bring up the image he needed. 'As you can see, this one is more sinister than the others.'

You really embraced the club motto, didn't you! Bondage, Buggery, Brutality. I've seen you in action, you perverted bastard. Clear images with your face showing. The poor sod you're buggering's face is on show as well. He doesn't look like he's enjoying what's being done to him. £3,000 or I'll send the photos to the press.

'So that's what Triple B really stands for,' Paolo said. 'Bondage, buggery and brutality. No wonder Montague didn't want this to come out. I wonder if Fletcher Simpson knows and that's why he dropped his hint about Montague not being safe to head up the youth centre.'

Mike flicked the switch again.

Don't believe me about the photos? Can you take that chance? You've got 24 hours to pay up.

'For the last six months it appears he's been paying £3,000 each time.'

Paolo sighed. 'No wonder he was selling his possessions at whatever price he could get for them. No way would he have survived the humiliation of this coming out. Did the blackmailer send any images, or just the threats and demands?'

Mike shook his head. 'None that I could find. If there had been any, I'd have uncovered them. He wasn't a very sophisticated user. Like most people, he had no idea how to cover his tracks.'

Paolo jumped in before Mike could give them all a lecture on computer privacy.

'And all the emails were sent using the club's IP address?'

Mike nodded.

'At least that's a starting point,' Paolo said. 'Trouble is, the sender could be anyone. There's no way of knowing which computer was used?'

Mike shrugged. 'Well, yes, if I had access to the machines, I could probably find traces, but I'm not a magician. I can't wave a wand over the building and say it was the computer housed in that room. One thing I do know, the messages were sent from the internet, not from a land based email server.'

'Sorry,' Paolo said, 'what does that mean?'

'That's one of the things I would have explained if you'd let me,' Mike said, sighing. 'Most computer users have programmes designed to keep emails tidily in one place. Mr Mason, for example, was using Outlook.'

Paolo nodded. He used it as well, so felt on familiar ground for a change.

'Well, if you wanted to, you can access incoming emails and send outgoing messages via the internet without using such a programme. This means none of the emails would be stored on a computer. They would all be online and accessible from anywhere, such as internet cafes or friends' computers.'

'So how would you know if a computer had been used? I mean, if it was all done on the internet and not sent using Outlook or one of the other programmes?'

'If I had access to the machine, I could probably pick it up from the browsing history.'

'OK, but you don't have that access, so how do you know the emails were sent from inside the club?'

Again Mike sighed. Paolo was beginning to think he should have let him go through his talk in the first place.

'Because, as I explained earlier, Mr Mason's computer retained shadows of the emails he'd received. By accessing . . .' he stopped, as if searching for the right words. 'By looking behind the email itself, I could find the information on which server had been used and when.'

'And all that information is in your report?'

Mike nodded and grinned. 'To my mind, it's in layman's terms, but if there's anything you don't understand, or need additional information on, my number is on the first page.'

'I've got a horrible feeling I'll be calling you to ask about something I see as too complex to cope with, but what you'll think of as baby questions,' Paolo said. 'Still, I'll try to get to grips with it and not show myself up too much.'

Paolo walked down with Mike, feeling bad that he hadn't allowed him to give the lecture he'd so clearly prepared and looked forward to giving.

'I hope you don't mind that I stopped you mid-flow at the beginning. It's just that I could see my team had switched off. We're not very good with the behind the scenes techy stuff, but really appreciate what you guys can do.'

Mike smiled. 'Most of my friends are in the same line of work as me, so we all tend to think everyone is as interested in the nuts and bolts as we are. If there is a next time, I'll keep it to the facts and leave out the way I uncovered them. I come from Bradchester, you know. Grew up here. Any chance of being taken on by you guys on a permanent basis?'

'I wish there was,' Paolo said. 'I'd love to have someone with your abilities on my team, but I know there's no point in asking upstairs. Budget restrictions mean I can't even take another PC on to my team. But if that situation ever changes, I'll be in touch.'

He shook Mike's hand and turned to go back upstairs. As he went past the desk, he heard his name being called. Turning back, he went to find out what the duty sergeant wanted.

'Fella came in to see you last night, sir. Wouldn't leave his name. Said he had information to do with the youth centre. Tall bloke, has a ponytail.'

An image of Derrick Walden came to mind.

'Did you get the impression it was urgent? Does he want me to call him?'

'Nah, I asked him that and he said it could wait until he came back again. Just that he had some info you could make use of.'

'Did he say when he planned to come back?'

The sergeant shook his head. 'No, but I said to call first to make sure you're here. No point in him cluttering up the place if you're out, is there? Anyway, he said he'll give you a ring later today to set up a time.'

'Thanks, John,' Paolo said, thinking that if Derrick didn't call today, he'd drop by and see him tomorrow. Whatever it was, it couldn't be urgent or he'd have said so.

Back in the main office, Paolo found a discussion about Montague well under way.

'I think that's our motive for suicide,' CC said. 'If his ability to pay had dried up and there was a chance of his private activities being discussed in the press, that would be enough for him to decide he had no other way out.'

Paolo nodded. 'I agree. If you add to that the chances of compromising photographs appearing in the papers, he couldn't have lived with the public disgrace.'

'So, not paying to cover his mother's shame, but his own,' Dave added.

'Exactly,' Paolo said. 'Come on, Dave, it's time for yet another visit to our favourite club. I wonder what they'll do to keep us out this time.'

Part of Paolo's mind had been running on his private life since Jessica had dropped her bombshell, but by the time Dave pulled in to the club's car park and switched off the ignition, he'd made a decision. He knew exactly what he was going to do.

'Do you mind if I ask you something, sir?' Dave asked, turning to face Paolo.

'I can't promise to answer, but you can ask.'

'Before you got married, in the lead up to it, did you ever wish you could just take off and tie the knot without anyone else being there?'

Paolo thought back to the early days with Lydia. God, they'd been so much in love. He nodded.

'I think every male who has ever contemplated marriage has felt that way. Probably quite a high percentage of the brides as well. What makes you ask?'

'Rebecca's mother,' Dave said with such a resigned look on his face that Paolo couldn't help but laugh.

'Tough going?'

Dave nodded. 'Every day there's something. It's either a rehearsal, or choosing stuff, or making lists. And I don't know why I even get included. Whatever I say is wrong. If I pick something, she ends up doing the exact opposite. I don't think my future mother-in-law is overjoyed with Rebecca's choice, to be honest.'

Remembering Lydia's mother's attitude to him, Paolo sighed.

'It's in the genes, Dave. You'll never be good enough for her daughter, but that shouldn't worry you. You're marrying Rebecca, not her mother. When the ceremony's over, it'll be just the two of you, so grit your teeth and put up with the nonsense. As they say, it's the bride's day and Rebecca's mother is just trying to make it all perfect for her little girl.'

'Fair enough,' Dave said, 'but if I end up murdering my future mother-in-law, I fully expect you to speak up on my behalf saying I did it while my mind was unbalanced due to extreme stress.'

'You're on,' Paolo said, opening his door. 'Come on, let's go and upset Mr Baron. Someone in this club caused Montague to kill himself and I want to know who.'

Chapter Seventeen

As they approached the building, it struck Paolo how very respectable it looked. The old saying about judging books by their cover could have been coined for exactly this situation. Montague, and presumably countless others, used the club as a place to gratify his particular sexual needs, but if the blackmailer was to be believed, the men on the receiving end weren't enjoying the attention. On the other hand, that wasn't for him to judge. Some people enjoyed masochism and good luck to them. As long as it was legal and by mutual consent, Paolo didn't have a problem with what people did to get their kicks. It was when people were coerced, or too young, that he had issues. Which way the club operated, legal or illegal, would come out in time, but there was a blackmailer in there and Paolo intended to find out who it was.

There were few cars in the car park, so presumably no special events were on for today. Knowing a bit more now about what went on upstairs, Paolo wondered exactly what sort of special event he'd interrupted last time. No wonder George and Chaz had been in such a state about their unannounced visit.

Oh well, time to find out what sort of reception they received this time. As they reached the top of the steps, the door swung open and Chaz appeared.

'Good day to you. Have you come to see Mr Baron?'

Taken aback by the warmth of the welcome and immediately on his guard, Paolo nodded. 'Yes, is he in?'

'He's in his office. If you could just wait here a moment, I'll call him for you.'

Less than a minute after Chaz put his phone back in his pocket, George Baron appeared. Walking briskly towards them across the vestibule, he nodded to Chaz, who disappeared through a doorway Paolo hadn't noticed on their previous visits. When the door closed, it blended in perfectly with the décor, hidden unless you knew where to look.

'That's how Chaz knew you were outside,' George said. 'It's a cubby hole with viewpoints into here and out to the car park. Chaz keeps an eye on things for me without anyone knowing he's there. I take it you've come to talk about Montague Mason?' he said.

'Now, why would you think that?' Paolo asked.

George shrugged. 'I read about his suicide in the papers. He was a member here, so I assumed you were following up on aspects of his life. I'm right, aren't I?'

'Yes and no,' Paolo said. 'Can we go through to your office?'

George nodded. 'Certainly, follow me.'

As they passed through Trudy's domain, George stopped. 'Coffee?' he asked.

'No, thank you. If we could go through to your office, I'd be happy. I've a number of questions to ask and would like to get them over with,' Paolo said.

'What about you, young man?' George said. 'Or do you have to follow the boss's lead?'

Dave shook his head. 'Not for me, thanks.'

George opened the door and stood back for them to enter. Taking up the same seats as the last time they'd been in the room, Paolo waited for George to settle before opening up with his first question.

'How do you advertise what goes on upstairs, George? We know there's a sex club operating up there, but it's not the kind of thing you can put an ad for in the paper. By the way, what tastes exactly do you cater for?'

Paolo thought George couldn't have looked any more innocent

had he been a new-born baby. The look of offended outrage was perfectly executed. Paolo guessed it was Baron's way of sticking two fingers up without actually raising his hand.

'I have no idea what you're talking about. I assumed you simply wanted confirmation that Montague was a member. The answer to that is yes, he was a very valued and well-liked member. This is a club for gentlemen to do business. It isn't a sex club and I have no idea why you would think such a thing.'

Paolo sat forward. 'We have proof Montague Mason was being blackmailed over what he got up to here. The person sending the blackmail emails did so from this club. Whoever that was seemed to think there were, shall we say, unpleasant sexual activities going on. Montague had been leaving a holdall full of cash outside behind your bins for more than a year and a half. Why would he have paid if there was nothing in the allegations the blackmailer made?'

This time Paolo would have sworn the look on George's face was genuine. He hadn't known about the blackmail. About the sex activities, definitely, but not about the blackmail.

'A blackmailer? That's not possible,' he said. 'My staff were handpicked by Chaz. They are trustworthy and would never . . .' His voice trailed off, almost as if he'd realised what he said confirmed the existence of the upstairs activities.

'What I mean is, there's nothing to blackmail anyone about. You must be mistaken.'

Paolo smiled. 'Not mistaken at all. We have email evidence that proves the emails were sent from inside this club. The contents of those emails are graphic enough to convince me, and probably a jury, that some of the participants in the activities are not necessarily willing to take part. I believe restraints are used to ensure compliance.'

George shrugged. 'If that were the case, and I'm not saying it is, what goes on between consenting adults in a private venue has nothing to do with the law. Times have changed, thank goodness. Those whose tastes run outside the so-called norms are now allowed by law to indulge.'

'Yes, as long as they are consenting adults. But it seems someone here decided to make some money out of those indulging their tastes. It might not even be a member of staff. It could be another member, or even one of those who have been used and abused and decided it was payback time. I take it you have a computer room here for your members?'

George nodded. 'And Wi-Fi downstairs.'

'Only downstairs?' Paolo said. 'Scared of what might get sent out if people had Wi-Fi upstairs?'

'Don't be ridiculous,' George said. 'I told you, this is a businessmen's club. Upstairs is not where business is conducted. There are private bedrooms for members to use.'

Paolo nodded. 'Yes, I know how they're used. By way, I discovered what the Triple B stands for and it has nothing to do with your name.'

George Baron laughed. 'You know more than I do, then. Come on, spit it out. What d'you think it stands for?'

Paolo leaned forward. 'I don't think, George, I *know*. Bondage, buggery and brutality, but not necessarily in that order.'

'You're making some pretty wild accusations. I could have you for police harassment.'

'I don't think so. Didn't I just tell you we've got proof? The blackmailer gave lots of interesting details to convince Montague to cough up. Why would he have paid if none of it was true? No, George, we'd like to take a look at your upstairs rooms. If you've got nothing to hide, why not show us around now?'

'I'd love to. All you need to do is show me the warrant and off we go.' He grinned. 'What? No warrant? Shame on you. You can't go poking around in private clubs without a warrant. Are you sure you wouldn't like a coffee before you go?'

'Quite sure,' Paolo said, standing up. 'My colleague and I are going to leave you in peace for now, but we will come back and, when we do, you can be sure I'll have a warrant firmly clutched in my hand.'

George rose as well and held out his hand. Paolo ignored it.

'Montague Mason wasn't a friend of mine, whatever the press might think, but he was driven to suicide by someone operating from these premises. I'm going to find out who. I'm also going to find out whether or not all the participants are here willingly, or being coerced into taking part in your sordid games. I haven't forgotten why you were at the youth centre. I've looked at your ad. You want young men of a certain age and they must be prepared to live in. You're not looking to help unfortunate young men into employment; you're looking for vulnerable people who can be exploited. Where do they stay, George, these young men you give jobs to? In the rooms upstairs, waiting to be serviced?'

'Get out! Get out and take your sidekick with you. You won't get back in without a warrant and you've got no chance of getting one. I've broken no laws, so just fuck off and don't bother coming back.'

Happy that his last barb had hit home, Paolo waited for Dave to leave before turning back to George.

'I'll get that warrant; you can bet your life on it.'

Paolo was still fuming when Dave pulled out of the car park and into the traffic.

'You really think we'll be able to get a warrant, sir?' Dave asked.

'I don't know, to be honest. I let him rile me, which was stupid. There's definitely something upstairs he doesn't want us to see, but a judge is not going to sign off on a warrant on the strength of my feelings. Even the blackmail angle, as Mike said, the emails were sent using the club's IP address, but not from an email programme, so it could have been another member. It could have been a cleaner, barman, anyone. Damn, I could have handled that better. Anyway, I'm going to try for a warrant. The blackmailer definitely used the club's premises.'

They drove in silence until they reached the station, then as Dave turned off the ignition, he turned to Paolo.

'I know it's none of my business, but you've been a bit preoccupied the last few days. Anything I can help with?'

127

Paolo shook his head. 'No, just a decision I had to make. I've made it. Now I've got to act on it and I know I'm not going to like the results.'

Dave raised an eyebrow in question.

'Not work related, Dave. Private life a mess, as usual.' Paolo laughed. 'I have no idea why you always ask me to help you sort out your personal life, I make a bloody mess of my own every chance I get.'

Dave grinned. 'That's why I ask you for advice, sir, to learn from your mistakes. I figure you've got so much experience of getting things wrong, you can tell me how to get things right.'

Paolo tidied his desk, ready to leave for the evening. Jessica was still in Bradchester and he'd arranged for her to come over to his place. It was his turn to cook and he was ready to tell her his decision. He looked around his office. Every item, from the pictures of his family to the police issue calendar, meant something to him. Leaving to go to Canada wasn't just a case of packing his bags; it would mean packing up his entire life.

He was about to switch off his office light when the phone rang. Sighing, he went back over to his desk to answer it.

'Sterling.'

'Am I through to Detective Inspector Sterling?'

'Yes, is that Derrick Walden?'

'It is, but how did you know?'

'Firstly, I've been expecting a call from you and secondly, you have a very distinctive London accent. Anyway, I believe you have some information for me?'

'Yes, I've got some info I think you might be interested in. I see a lot that goes on and, well, I think I should fill you in on what I know.'

Paolo sat down and pulled a pad towards him.

'Fire away, I'm ready.'

'Oh, I thought maybe I could come in to see you. I'd rather tell you in person, if that's OK with you.'

'Tonight?' Paolo said, thinking he was already cutting it fine to get home, shower and get a meal ready before Jessica arrived. 'I was about to leave, but if it's urgent you see me, I can stay on for a bit longer.'

'Nah, it's not urgent. Important yes, but not so urgent it can't wait until tomorrow. You'll be amazed at what I've got to tell you. Sometimes the ones who look the most innocent do things you just wouldn't believe. Listen, I can call by the station on my way to work. What time do you get in?'

'I'm generally here by half eight,' Paolo said, 'but I can get in earlier if you need me to.'

'Nah, you're all right. Half eight works for me. I'm telling you, you're gonna be shocked by what I know.'

'So you keep saying.' Irritated by the constant references without any real detail, Paolo's voice was sharper than he intended. 'Look, sorry, I didn't mean to snap. Are you sure you don't want to come over now?'

'No, I've got things that need doing tonight.'

'And you can't tell me over the phone?'

Derrick laughed. 'I wanna see your face when I tell you. You are gonna be so shocked.'

'Fine,' Paolo said. 'Tomorrow at half eight.'

He put down the phone and gave himself a mental shake. He'd cocked up his interview with George Baron and now come close to losing his temper with someone who just wanted to give him information. And was irritating with it, a little voice whispered. Paolo ignored the whisper. He needed to get his private life sorted once and for all to stop it intruding where it didn't belong.

Paolo put the finishing touches to the table and stood back to admire his efforts. He'd come a long way since his split with Lydia. Not only did he now cook for himself on a regular basis, but was confident enough in his skills to feed other people too. As long as he kept it simple that was. Smoked salmon and brown bread to start, with fillet steak and sauté potatoes as the main course. His limitations when it came to dessert were pancakes, pancakes or pancakes, so he'd bought in one of those fancy ice cream cakes to finish the meal.

Jessica arrived right on time and Paolo thought she'd never looked lovelier.

'Wow, you've really pulled out all the stops tonight. Candles as well!'

Paolo took her jacket and took it out to hang in the hall. By the time he came back into the kitchen, Jessica was seated at the table looking quizzically at him. She'd poured herself a glass of wine and raised it to him in salute.

'So, come on, Paolo, out with it. Is this in celebration of our exciting future, or a last supper to say goodbye?'

Chapter Eighteen

Paolo woke the next morning with a hangover to beat all hangovers. He didn't usually drink, but had polished off half a bottle of red wine the night before, followed by several brandies. God, how did regular drinkers cope? His mouth tasted too foul to even think of comparing it to anything rational. Maybe a sewer, but thankfully he had no experience of drinking sewer water, so couldn't be certain. Someone with a drum kit had moved into his head. As he went to sit up, his stomach heaved and threatened to empty its contents over the duvet. Paolo tried to make a dash for the bathroom, but had to settle for an unstable stagger. Thankfully, he reached the bathroom in time to throw up into the toilet bowl, instead of over the floor.

Why, oh, why had he been so stupid last night? But he knew the answer to that, so it was pointless dwelling on it. He forced himself upright and peered at his reflection in the mirror. The person staring back looked closer to a dead man than someone with a pulse. Right now, Paolo wasn't sure death wouldn't be preferable.

As he reached the bedroom door, his alarm clock decided to add its mite to what was the worst morning he'd faced in many years. Another stagger in the direction of the bed enabled him to smack the clock with enough force to shut it up. Hot shower and coffee, that's what he needed.

Half an hour later, he still felt like death, but no longer looked as if it was a distinct possibility in the near future. He dressed with care to avoid moving his head too much as his brain felt like it was sloshing around in a pool of liquid. Glancing at his watch, he remembered his early morning appointment with Derrick Walden. No way was he fit to drive. In fact, he wasn't at all certain he wasn't still drunk. Maybe not, but the alcohol would still be in his system.

Taking a deep breath, he hit Dave's number on speed dial and then held the phone away from his ear. The ringing tone pealed like thunder.

'Yes, sir, what can I do for you?' Dave's voice sounded too loud and too bloody cheerful to Paolo's sensitive ears.

'I need a lift into work today. I, er, I had a drop too much to drink last night and I don't think I should drive.'

'*You* got drunk?'

'Yes, but there's no need to shout. Can you pick me up or not?'

Dave's laughter fired bullets into a brain already under siege. 'Lucky for you my future mother-in-law has decided she doesn't need my participation after all this morning. I'll be there in twenty minutes. I'll bring a guaranteed hangover cure. You'll feel right as rain in no time.'

Paolo doubted that, but when Dave arrived with a box of capsules, he followed his advice and swallowed one of them.

'How long will it take to work?' Paolo asked. 'I've got a meeting with Derrick Walden at half eight. The way I feel now, I just want to fall down and die.'

Dave grinned and Paolo felt like strangling him. 'By the time we get there, you'll already start to feel better. You know when I was being an idiot and drinking too much last year?' Paolo nodded. 'One of my mates put me on to these things. It was the only way I could function for months.'

Paolo reached for his jacket. 'I hope you're right. Let's get going. Maybe I can rest my eyes for a few minutes before he arrives.'

During the drive, Paolo had to concentrate hard on controlling his wayward stomach, but Dave was right. By the time they reached the station he felt, if not cured, at least able to face the day ahead. He looked at his watch, still half an hour before Derrick

Walden was due to arrive. He could try to make a start on the reports while he was waiting.

He climbed out of the car and almost managed a smile.

'You were right, Dave. Those things are a bloody miracle. If I ever take up drinking seriously, I'll carry them around with me wherever I go.'

As they walked together into the station, Paolo's phone rang. He took it out to answer it, but the duty sergeant's voice stopped him.

'Don't bother, sir, it's me calling you. I hadn't realised you were on your way in. We've had a call from the youth centre and you're needed there straightaway. Dead body in the swimming pool.'

'Not an accident, I take it?'

'Don't think so, sir, the man was found by the cleaners at the bottom of the pool fully dressed. Apparently, he's the swimming instructor, so it's not likely he'd drown by accident.'

Paolo rocked on his heels. 'Bloody hell, I should have made him come in last night,' he muttered.

'What was that, sir?' Dave asked.

'I'll explain later,' Paolo said. He turned back to the sergeant. 'Have you alerted forensics?'

'Yes, sir, and the pathology department. Dr Royston is already on her way.'

'Right, come on, Dave. Let's get going. I've got a horrible feeling someone didn't want Derrick Walden talking to me this morning.'

When they reached the youth centre a crime scene tape was already in place, with constables keeping back not just the onlookers, but also those who wanted to get inside on legitimate business. One of them was April Greychurch, who called out to Paolo as he passed.

'What's going on, Paolo? Why aren't we allowed inside? He won't tell me anything,' she said, pointing to a young policeman a few yards away.

'I'm afraid I can't either until I've been in to find out for myself. Sorry about this, April. We'll let you back in as soon as we can.'

He and Dave continued into the centre and made their way to

the swimming pool. Barbara Royston was already there examining the body that had been retrieved from the bottom of the pool. Even from a distance, Paolo could see Derrick's features were bloated and swollen; he was almost beyond identification.

Paolo stopped by the young constable guarding the door. 'Who found the body?'

The constable pointed across to the other side of the pool to where an older woman dressed in cleaner's overalls was being comforted by a policewoman.

'Apparently her normal routine is to start in here, washing the pool surround and then moving into the changing rooms. She says she didn't notice the body until she'd worked her way along two thirds of the surround on this side of the pool. When she spotted him, she ran out screaming for help because she can't swim and thought maybe someone could still save him.'

Paolo nodded his thanks.

'Dave, you go over and see if she has anything more to add. I'm going to talk to Barbara Royston.'

He walked over to where Barbara was kneeling next to the body and dropped to his haunches. Although his hangover had all but gone, the queasiness in his stomach wasn't helped by the sight of Derrick's waterlogged body.

'Morning, Barbara,' he said, trying to concentrate on keeping his coffee from making a reappearance.

She glanced up. 'Morning, Paolo. You don't look at all well this morning. You OK?'

Paolo nodded. 'Think I might be coming down with something, but I'm fine. He's been in there for a few hours by the look of him.'

'Yes, he went into the water sometime last night. He was clutching that,' she said, pointing to a designer drinks container currently resting inside an evidence bag. 'I don't know if forensics will get anything from it after being in the water all night.'

'Are we looking at murder?'

'Possibly. Preliminary findings indicate there was no struggle and I wouldn't have thought he'd be an easy man to overcome unless drugged. There is an outside chance this was a successful suicide attempt.'

'Really?'

'Very much an outside chance. I would have thought drowning would be the last choice for such a competent swimmer, but who can guess what goes through people's minds when they are depressed enough to take their own lives? Maybe he drugged himself and then jumped in knowing he wouldn't be able to swim. Anyway, I'll know more after the PM.'

Paolo sighed. 'It's possible, I suppose, but the timing of it has me leaning towards murder. He was supposed to come to talk to me this morning. He rang me last night just before I left. Said he had information I'd find interesting. It looks like someone didn't want him to have the chance to pass on whatever it was he knew. I need to find out who was here last night. I know the pool shuts down for the evening, but there are lots of other activities taking place. Let's hope someone saw something useful for a change.'

Barbara turned back to the body, signalling loud and clear they'd reached the end of their conversation. Paolo missed the easy relationship they used to share, but it didn't look as if it was coming back any time soon.

He stood up; the chlorine in the atmosphere had brought back his thumping headache. Forcing himself to concentrate, he went to join Dave who was waiting for him at the end of the pool.

'Find out anything useful?' Paolo asked.

'Only that the place wasn't locked up when she arrived. She's the senior member of the cleaning staff and has a set of keys for all the doors. She normally has to unlock the pool to get in to clean, but the door was already unlocked. Shut, but not locked up. Other than that, she had nothing to say that we didn't already know.'

'Come on; let's find out who was here last night. I think it's time to bring April inside. She seems to know more about what goes on here than anyone else.'

*

135

Settled in April's office with a steaming mug of coffee in front of him, Paolo finally began to feel he might be able to cope with the day.

'I can't believe Derrick is dead,' April said. 'I just can't believe it. He was in my office only yesterday, poking around as usual, trying to pick up bits of information.'

Paolo took a sip of coffee, then put the mug down on a coaster on April's desk.

'What sort of information?'

She put her hands in the air. 'Who knew with Derrick? He was just one of those people who needed to know everything that was going on. Some people are like that. Digging into stuff that doesn't concern them because they can't bear to think they're being kept in the dark.'

'What time was that?'

'Mid-afternoon. About three, maybe four. I shooed him out and told him to keep his nose out of what didn't concern him. He laughed at me, said everything concerned him because you never knew when you picked up information you could use.' She sighed. 'That was the last time I saw him.'

'What time did you leave here last night?'

She put her head on one side, considering the question. 'I'm not really sure,' she said. 'It was quite late, maybe around nine, nine thirty.'

'What kept you here until that time?'

She smiled. 'Money. I was giving a private martial arts lesson.'

'I'll need to know the name of your client,' Paolo said. 'And anyone else you saw in this part of the centre.'

'Yes, of course,' she said. 'The client's a new one. Trudy Chappell. She'd called earlier in the day, begging me to fit her in. She said she needed to learn to defend herself. When I asked why, she said it was because she lived in a dangerous area and was scared of being mugged. I'm not sure I believed her, but it's not for me to judge. She must have had a reason, or she wouldn't have come. Anyway, she did well for a first lesson.'

136

Dave looked up from his notes. 'Trudy Chappell? Isn't she George Baron's secretary?'

April nodded. 'Yes, she mentioned she worked at the Triple B. In point of fact, as I left, I saw George Baron and another man in a car parked along the road from the centre. I assumed they were waiting to give Trudy a lift home. I thought that was nice, especially if she really did live in a rough area.'

'She didn't leave with you?' Paolo asked.

'No, she was still drying her hair when I'd finished my shower and was ready to go. I left her in the changing room.'

'Okay,' Paolo said, 'who else?'

'Well, there were loads of people in the other side of the centre. The canteen was open, as was the games room and the snooker room. I've no idea who was in there. You'd have to go and speak to the various people looking after the activities.'

'Yes, I realise that. Let's just concentrate on who you saw on this side.'

'Arbnor was doing his rounds. Checking the activity rooms were empty before locking them up for the night. Oh, and Clementine Towers was also in doing her usual. Now that Montague has gone she seems to think I'm the right person to buttonhole for complaints.' She rolled her eyes. 'This time it was the film we'd put on at the weekend for the younger age group. Subversive, violent and encouraging girls to act in a way that isn't conducive to feminine behaviour. Corrupting the morals of children too young to understand they were being brainwashed into accepting fantasy as part of their lives.'

Paolo heard Dave smother a laugh. He felt like doing the same himself.

'That sounds like a quote,' he said. 'What was the title of this dreadful film?'

'*Brave*. I ask you, how can anyone find that subversive? More to the point, and I asked her this, how can she know what the film is about if she hasn't watched it? Do you know what she said? She'd seen the poster and that was enough!'

137

April shook her head as if trying to rid her mind of the memory.

'I don't recall seeing anyone else.' She looked across at Paolo, a question in her eyes. 'Why do you need to know who was here? It was suicide, surely?'

Paolo shrugged. 'Possibly, but we're keeping an open mind until after the post mortem. Can you think of any reason why Derrick would kill himself?'

'He told me once he'd got into some trouble in London and that's why he came here. He wanted a fresh start. Maybe his past caught up with him and he decide to take the easy way out. After what happened with Montague, I no longer know what to think about anyone.'

'I can understand how you feel. If you remember anything from last night, anything at all, give me a call. What time does Arbnor come in?'

She looked at her watch. 'He should be here by now. That's if he's been allowed through the front door.'

'If he's still being kept outside, I'll go and vouch for him. Take care, April. The centre seems to be attracting a lot of bad vibes at the moment.'

She smiled, but it was a poor effort. 'I'm always careful.'

Paolo and Dave went downstairs to the caretaker's room, but there was no sign of him.

'You wait here, Dave. I'm going to have a look outside, see if he's being held back.'

Paolo looked out through the front doors and spotted Arbnor deep in conversation with one of the women Paolo recognised from the canteen. She was one of the cooks who'd been involved in the food preparation for the opening night's ceremony. What a lifetime ago that seemed.

He attracted the attention of a constable and asked him to let Arbnor through the cordon. As the caretaker ducked under the tape, Paolo could hear the cook's voice raised in complaint. As soon as everyone had finished their work around the pool and the body had been moved, Paolo would give the order to lift the tape, but until then only those he needed to speak to would be allowed in.

He greeted Arbnor and walked with him down to his room without explaining why he needed to speak to him. Better to ask the questions when Dave was there to record the answers. Paolo smiled to think how much he relied on Dave these days. They'd come a long, long way since their rocky start together.

When they were ensconced in the tiny room, Arbnor apologised for how cramped it was.

'I only have two chairs, as you can see. I can go and fetch another from . . .' He stopped, clearly not wanting to mention the fact that his room was next door to Derrick's and that had been where he intended to go for the third chair.

'It's OK,' Dave said. 'I'm happy to stand. No need to worry about me.'

'Tell me, Arbnor,' Paolo said, resting the ankle of his right leg on his left knee, 'was there anyone around last night you felt shouldn't have been here? Anyone out of the ordinary?'

Arbnor shook his head, more vehemently than Paolo felt the question warranted.

'No, no, I didn't see anyone or hear anyone. I was doing my rounds and didn't even know Derrick was still here.'

'But don't you normally lock the pool? Surely you must have looked inside to make sure there was no one there?'

Again, there was that over emphasised shake of the head.

'Not me. I have the keys to all the rooms on the ground floor, but not the ones for the pool and lockers. Mr Walden insisted on keeping those for safety reasons. He said it was his responsibility to make sure no one drowned. He always did his own last minute check of the locker rooms and the pool area before leaving.'

'So, when you left, was the pool locked up or not?'

'I don't know. I didn't try the door. I heard nothing and I saw nothing. I didn't go into Mr Walden's office.'

'Arbnor, I never mentioned you going into his office. Why did you say that?'

'Say what?'

Paolo sighed. Life was too short for this. 'Say you hadn't gone into his office?'

'Because I didn't.'

Paolo gave up. By the way Arbnor was protesting, Paolo was certain he was hiding something, but whether it was to do with Derrick Walden's death or not, only time would tell.

When he and Dave went outside there was the inevitable bank of reporters and photographers vying for attention and quotes. Paolo looked across to the other side of the road where Clementine Towers was, once again, holding forth for the cameras. He couldn't hear what she was saying, but guessed from her facial expression and arm gestures that she was worked up about something – no doubt saying the ungodly heathens at the youth centre had brought this new disaster on themselves. He made a mental note to avoid watching the news later. He really couldn't bear to listen to another of her tirades.

Paolo had never been more pleased to see the end of a working day. He let himself into his flat and kicked off his shoes. Shrugging off his jacket, he threw it across an armchair and flopped down onto the sofa. As he sprawled out, his gaze fell on the half-empty brandy bottle. A shudder ran through him at the memory of his hangover. God, he'd never felt so ill in his entire life. How on earth did people go out binge drinking knowing they'd be facing that sort of feeling the next morning? He'd hit the booze hard last night, but had no intention of chasing oblivion again. The consequences just wouldn't be worth it.

Somehow, he'd have to learn to live with his memory of Jessica's face when he'd told her he wasn't going to Canada. She'd tried again and again to make him change his mind, even finally pushing for a long-distance relationship.

Maybe she'd thought, with time, he would come over for a visit and end up staying for life. Paolo knew that wasn't going to happen, so had done what he felt was the right thing, even though it left him feeling like a monster. Jessica had left his flat in tears, refusing to stay the night. He'd called a taxi for her and seen her into it before coming back in and drinking himself to sleep.

He'd done the right thing. He knew that. Long distances relationships never worked out. Why prolong the agony? A clean break was better for both of them. He'd said all that last night and meant every word of it, so why did he feel as if he'd made the biggest mistake of his life in letting Jessica go?

Chapter Nineteen

Nemesis in Action Blog

The police seem to have been everywhere for the last week, but I don't think I have anything to worry about. I'm sure no one saw me with Derrick Walden that night. Murder has never been my intention. Never! Not even for those who deserve to die, but once I heard him talking, planning to visit the station the next morning, I couldn't take any chances. From what I overheard, I think he knew too much. I don't know what he'd found out, but it could have been my undoing. I had to act. I *had to*. I don't think he even knew what happened. I didn't want him to suffer and I don't think he did. I tried to make it a gentle passing for him. It was easy enough to slip some Rohypnol into his water bottle while he was on the phone. I thought he'd fall asleep and would have an accident while driving home, but he didn't leave when I expected him to. When I found him collapsed at the side of the pool, it left me with no other choice but to heave him into the water. I watched him sink to the bottom, ready to put on an act if anyone came in. If I'd had to, I'd have dived in and held him under while pretending to try to save his life, but luckily no one was about. I had nothing against Derrick personally, but I couldn't afford to let him live.

Is it really murder when you're forced to act?

Paolo put down the phone and punched the air. An entire bloody week it had taken, but he'd finally got the warrant he needed to gather in the computers from Triple B. He grabbed his jacket and rushed into the main office.

'CC, Dave, I want you two with me. We've got permission to get inside that bloody club at last. I've arranged for uniform to meet us at Triple B.'

Dave stood up. 'Full search warrant, sir? I thought you'd been told there was no chance of that.'

Paolo shook his head. 'No, but we've got the go ahead to bring in all the computers. To get those, we need to have a look in all the rooms. After all, who knows what might get left behind if we don't check every single room in the place,' he said, winking.

CC laughed. 'Good point, sir. They'll have to allow us full access, even if we can't take anything other than the computers with us, we'll get the chance to peer in all their dark corners. Pity Andrea went to the hospital to check on the coma patient this morning. It would have been good for her to get some experience on this type of search.'

Paolo stopped midway to the door and waited for CC and Dave to catch him up.

'Has she called in yet?'

CC nodded. 'Yes, she's just finished talking to the nursing staff and the constable on watch outside the patient's room. No change. The man hasn't shown any signs of coming out of the coma. As you requested, Andrea has been scouring missing persons, but there's been no one so far that matches the victim. He's been in a coma for weeks now. You'd think there must be someone out there concerned because a family member has dropped out of sight.'

Paolo led the way to the stairs. 'I agree, but have you thought that maybe someone might be glad to see the back of him? We're seeing him as a victim, but that doesn't necessarily mean he's a nice man. He could be a wife beater for all we know and the woman he's left in peace by being in the hospital is celebrating, not wondering where he might be so that she can get him back.'

CC laughed. 'That's a bit of a stretch, sir, if you don't mind me saying so.'

143

'I agree. I was just using that as an example of why some people don't get reported missing. There are times when the family members, work colleagues, whoever, are just glad the bastard has disappeared.'

By this time, they'd reached the car park. Dave went through the ritual of patting his pockets, looking for the keys Paolo knew would be in the last place he looked. When Dave finally located them, he looked up in triumph and pressed the button to release the central locking device.

'If my future mother-in-law disappeared,' he said, 'I'd make sure there was no search party sent out looking for her until *after* the wedding.'

'That bad?' CC asked, before climbing into the back of the car.

Dave grinned. 'Worse. I'm too traumatised to discuss it.'

As Dave manoeuvred the car into the car park outside the club, Paolo was pleased to see three uniform vehicles already waiting for them. I bet Chaz is not a happy bunny peering through his spyhole, Paolo thought. I wonder if he's already moving the members upstairs, out of our sight, to what he sees as a place of safety. Not that there could be many inside as there were very few cars in the parking area.

One of the cars missing was George Baron's silver Mercedes. Paolo hoped that didn't mean the man himself wasn't there either. He'd wanted to watch George's face while they ran the search. People gave more away by their involuntary expressions than they realised – and the most telling of all was when there was no expression to see. Paolo loved it when that happened because anyone who made such an effort to control their features showed there was something to hide.

With Dave on one side and CC on the other, backed up by a phalanx of uniformed officers, Paolo approached the steps. The door opened before he'd had chance to knock.

'This is a bit heavy handed, isn't it?' Chaz said, peering over Paolo's shoulder.

'Not at all, Chaz. Is George around?' Paolo said, flourishing a piece of paper under the man's nose. 'This is a warrant to remove all the computers from the premises.'

Chaz scanned it. 'George isn't here. You'll have to come back,' he said, attempting to close the door.

Paolo put out his hand to stop him. 'Oh no, you don't. We don't need George's permission to come in, or yours either. Stand back, please, and let my men enter.'

Chaz's expression was one of resignation, rather than the disquiet Paolo had expected.

'Feel free,' Chaz said, stepping back to let the uniformed officers pass by. 'Make yourselves at home, but if you come across any of our members, please leave them in peace. They pay a great deal of money to have the run of this place and I don't think they'd appreciate you bunch of clodhoppers disturbing them.'

Paolo let everyone else enter, but stayed by the door next to Chaz.

'So, where is George?'

Whatever he'd been expecting Chaz to answer, the words that came out weren't even close.

'Fucked if I know. He left here the night before last and I haven't seen him since.'

'He hasn't rung in?'

Chaz shook his head, for the first time looking uneasy. 'Hasn't called me and isn't answering his house phone or mobile. I've been round to his place. His car's parked outside, but he's not home. The bird what looks after his house said the car was there when she got to work yesterday morning, but his bed hadn't been slept in. She seemed to think he hadn't been inside the place since she'd been there the day before.'

'What made her think that?'

Chaz shifted his weight from foot to foot, clearly torn between not wanting to discuss his boss with the police, but at the same time worried that something had happened George Baron. Paolo could see the indecision written on his face as his expression underwent several changes. Eventually, he nodded as if he'd reached a decision.

'She said George had a routine. First thing he'd do when he got home was take a bath. Whether he was staying in or going out, he headed straight to the bathroom every night. She reckoned that none of the towels had been used. Normally there was stuff out of place, soap, shampoo, that sort of thing, but everything was where she'd put it the day before.'

'Where do you think he went?'

Chaz shrugged. 'I dunno, but, as I said, his car's outside the house. He wouldn't have gone for a walk, that's for fucking sure. Couldn't bear walking, George couldn't.'

'What about his secretary? Have you asked Trudy Chappell if she knows anything?'

An expression of alarm appeared so fleetingly on Chaz's face that Paolo wasn't even certain he'd seen it.

'She's off sick,' Chaz said. 'Been off work for four days.'

'But have you asked her? George might have told her something he'd forgotten to tell you.'

'Not fucking likely. Besides, he gave her the push before she went off sick. He's given her a decent final pay package, too, well over what he needed to pay, considering he gave her the elbow.'

'Really? She seemed to be settled here. What happened?'

Chaz looked away. 'No idea. Nothing to do with me, but I'm telling you she won't know nothing about where George is. If he didn't tell me he wouldn't have told her.'

'Why don't you come down to the station and put in a missing person's report? He might have gone for a walk after all, had an accident and be lying in a hospital bed somewhere,' Paolo said, thinking of the mysterious patient at Bradchester Central.

'Yeah, I might do that. Oi!' he shouted, catching sight of the officers climbing the marble staircase. 'Where d'you think you're going? There's no fucking computers up there.' He turned back to Paolo. 'You said that warrant was for computers. Tell them to come back down.'

Paolo stepped past him. 'But how will we know there are no

146

computers upstairs unless we go up to look?' he said, smiling at the look of fury on Chaz's face.

'Go on then, but you won't find any.'

Paolo headed for the stairs, waving his hand at Chaz as he went. 'Maybe not, but I'm dying to see what's so special about those upstairs rooms.'

The first ten bedrooms they entered were a disappointment. Beautifully furnished though they were, they didn't ring any bells as far as Paolo was concerned. No computers, nothing to indicate anyone did anything in them, other than sleep.

The eleventh looked to be even more innocuous, being considerably smaller than the others. Then one of the uniformed officers let out a shout from inside the fitted wardrobe which took up the entire wall on the left side of the room.

'I think you need to see this, sir.'

Paolo went over and peered inside. At the back of the wardrobe, hidden by a loose panel the officer had moved, was a concealed door.

'I tapped on the walls and it sounded too hollow to be solid. Then I found this bit here didn't quite meet with the wall in the corner, so dug my nails in. The panel came away quite easily.'

'Good work. Let's see where this leads.'

Paolo turned the handle, but the door wouldn't budge.

'Nip downstairs and bring Chaz up, would you?' he said to the constable. 'Don't tell him what we've found. I want to see his face when you bring him in here.'

Paolo stepped out of the wardrobe and closed the door in the hope that Chaz might not guess they had found the club's secret. The only thing he had to do now was find out exactly what the secret might be.

Chaz came into the bedroom looking wary, as well he might, thought Paolo.

'This room is much smaller than the others, why is that?'

He shrugged. 'Because that's all the space that was left after the other rooms were put in?' he suggested.

Paolo looked over at Dave and CC in mock inquiry. 'What do you think? Truth or lie?'

Dave shook his head. CC looked away, as if to hide her smile.

'No, I didn't think so, either,' Paolo said. 'If it wasn't for the fitted wardrobe, this room would be the same size as the others.'

'Well, there you go, then. What're you asking me for if you've already worked it out? I need to be downstairs looking after the place, not up here answering daft questions.'

'Yes, you're right. But before you go back down, do me a favour and unlock the concealed door in the wardrobe.'

The colour left Chaz's face, but Paolo was impressed with the man's reaction. He managed to look innocent, with just the right hint of confusion, as if the existence of such a door was news to him.

'I have no idea what you're on about,' he said.

'Fair enough,' Paolo said. 'Constable, go downstairs with this gentleman and search his room. Bring up every key you can find. But before you go, pat him down to see if he has any keys concealed about his person. Better strip him off and put some rubber gloves on. You never know where you might need to search.'

Chaz backed away. 'You can't do that. You're here for computers. You think I've got a fucking computer up my jacksy?'

Paolo shook his head. 'No, but it wouldn't surprise me to find a key tucked away up there. You're an ex-con, Chaz. Everything about you screams that at me, which means you know how to hide the things you don't want us to find. We have a warrant to take in all the computers. We've found a hidden door, which means we are within the remit of the warrant to search behind that door to make sure there are no computers concealed within.' He smiled. 'Now, are you going to hand over the key, or do you want to undergo the indignity of a strip search knowing whether we find the key or not, we *are* going to find out what's on the other side of the door?'

Chaz seemed to be debating with himself. 'Fuck you,' he spat. 'Why don't you knock the fucker down?'

'If we have to, we will, but I'd be remiss in my duty if I didn't have you searched first. I know a couple of officers who'll enjoy giving you a thorough examination. Much more thorough than this young constable. Do you want to wait for them, or are you going to be sensible and hand over the key?'

The look Chaz gave Paolo should have fried him on the spot, the amount of red hot venom it contained. Paolo stood his ground, smiling in a way he knew would infuriate Chaz even more.

'Even if I had the key I wouldn't give you the satisfaction.'

Paolo waited and then nodded to the officer to start patting him down. Within seconds he handed Paolo a large bunch of keys.

'Hmm,' Paolo said. 'This seems a bit too easy.'

He tried every key on the bunch, but none of them fit the lock. In the meantime, the constable had continued searching Chaz's pockets.

'Nothing, sir.'

'Right,' Paolo said, grinning at Chaz. 'Time to start stripping off. Put your clothes on the bed so that my young colleague can examine them thoroughly.'

Chaz glared at Paolo. 'I'm not taking my clothes off in front of *her*,' he spat.

CC laughed. 'You've not got anything I haven't seen before, but I'll spare your blushes. I'll go and search your office.'

'Am I under arrest?' Chaz demanded.

Paolo shook his head. 'Not yet, but you are impeding the execution of a warrant, so it's only a matter of time before you are. Why don't you do the sensible thing and give us the key? We're going to get the door open whether you cooperate or not.'

'If I had it and handed it over would you . . . but . . . I . . . look, I was just following orders, right?'

The claim of sadists and thugs through the ages, thought Paolo. I only tortured people because I was ordered to do it. He left the man to sweat a bit more.

'I can't go back inside. Not again,' Chaz said.

Paolo remained silent, watching the sweat appearing on Chaz's forehead, running down his face and dripping onto his collar.

'If I give you the key, will you put in a good word for me? Maybe get me a reduced sentence?'

Paolo nodded. 'I can't promise anything. You know that, but if you cooperate, I'll see what I can do for you.'

Chaz pulled off his belt and handed it to Paolo.

'Near the buckle there's a tab. Pull it,' he said.

The tiny tab opened to reveal a small pocket inset into the belt.

'Only the special members have duplicates of that key,' he said.

'Special members?'

Chaz nodded. 'They book in advance to use the additional facilities upstairs.'

Paolo lifted his eyebrows in question, but Chaz didn't explain.

'You'll see,' he said, closing his eyes as if in prayer.

Chapter Twenty

The door opened onto a staircase leading off to the right following the line of the wall. There was another door at the top, also locked, but it opened with the same key as the door in the wardrobe. Paolo opened it and stepped into a corridor similar to the one on the floor below. This, too, had doors leading off from it on either side, with a single door at the end facing them. Soft lighting illuminated the plush carpet and ivory walls, giving the impression of an extremely expensive hotel.

Each door had a plaque with a name on it instead of a number. The first one was named for the Marquis de Sade, followed in turn by Aleister Crowley, Caligula, Jean-Jacques Rousseau, A. N. Roquelaure, Leopold von Sacher-Masoch. Paolo didn't need to read any further to realise this was a haven for sadomasochists to indulge whichever sexual need they craved.

He opened the Marquis de Sade door. The palatial feeling of the corridor stopped at the entrance. This wasn't a room to make guests think of comfort, soft beds and chocolates left on the pillow each night when the sheets were turned down. This was a room designed to engender fear in one person and, presumably, sexual delight in another.

A table to the right of the door held an assortment of whips, some with spiked ends. Alongside the whips was a tazer. Hanging above the table was a rack with various hoods, whether for the victims to wear to increase their fear level, or for the sadists to wear for added kicks, Paolo had no idea and didn't really want to find out.

There was a bed of sorts against the far wall, but the interior designer had forgotten beds should have mattresses. This one was a basic plank of wood with leather restraints on either side to hold down the arms and legs of whoever was lying on the bed.

A tall cupboard stood in the corner beside the bed. Paolo opened it to find an array of metal gadgets that would have graced any museum devoted to torture techniques. Some of them were in the shape of extra-large penises with rough exteriors that would, presumably, add an extra level of pain to the experience. Paolo already felt sick and they'd only looked in this one room.

He backed out and gave instructions to the uniformed officers to search the other rooms on either side of the corridor.

'Dave, you and CC come with me. I want to see what's in the end room.'

They walked along the corridor, Paolo's feet felt too heavy to lift, as if they knew what his head was screaming – get the hell home and have a good hot scrub. He wasn't sure even that would make him feel clean again, but it would be a start.

There wasn't a sadist's name on the end door. The plaque simply read: Screening Room

Inside was a mini-theatre. Rows of velvet covered seats set out in curves faced a screen set up centrally on the far wall. To the right of the room was a well-stocked bar. The wall to the left had four doors, each marked Private Viewing. Paolo opened one of them. Inside was a couch and a smaller version of the main screen, with a DVD player underneath. Presumably so that the occupant could indulge his sexual urges while watching his choice of porn if whatever was being shown outside didn't appeal to him.

Paolo turned back into the main room.

'You know,' he said to Dave and CC, 'all of this turns my stomach, but none of it is illegal. So why keep it hidden? Why was Chaz so keen to try to get some sort of deal going before handing over the key. We're missing something here, but I don't know what it is.'

Dave pointed to the shelves to the right of the screen holding rows of DVD covers.

'Maybe the answer lies with those,' he said.

Paolo walked over and took out a few at random. They were all versions of the same type of film – hurt me and/or let me hurt you while I get off. Not nice, but not illegal either.

'Do you think the members took turns being whipper and whippee?' Paolo asked, more to himself than expecting an answer.

'Could be, sir,' CC said, 'but, as you say, that's not against the law.'

'What about the young men George Baron said he hired who had to live in?' Dave said. 'We haven't seen any sign of them.'

'Good point, Dave.' He looked around the room. 'Let's see if there's another concealed door in here. Start tapping on the walls.'

The search proved fruitless, none of the walls gave any hint of hidden chambers, but Paolo was convinced there had to be a reason Chaz reacted as he had. He stared at the screen. It was a large square housed in a box-like structure which reached from floor to ceiling. A memory was niggling in the recesses of his mind, but he couldn't quite grasp it. A thought nagged and refused to go away; something to do with the screen, so why was he thinking of waterfalls?

That's it, he thought. The waterfall at Fletcher Simpson's place had been encased in a similar structure which moved to allow a doorway to open. He strode across to the screen and tried to push it aside. It refused to budge, but he was certain now that he was right.

'Look for a remote control,' he ordered.

Dave held up two. 'I assumed these were for the DVD player,' he said.

Paolo took them both and examined them. 'This one is,' he said, 'but look at the buttons on here. It's only got three. The power button and arrows to left and right. I don't think this has anything to do with showing films, but I'm hoping it's to do with movies.'

He tried the on/off button, but nothing happened. Then he pressed the arrow pointing to the right, still no movement.

'Damn,' he said. 'I was sure this was the answer. Last chance.'

He pressed the arrow pointing to the left and the screen slid in that direction, revealing another door.

'This is like Hampton Court bloody Maze,' he said. 'Every time you think you've reached the end, another opening appears.'

The opening led to another set of stairs, more utilitarian than those they'd used so far. Paolo had the impression that club members didn't go up here. So, who did? And why? At the top was yet another door, but this time there was a key hanging from a hook on the wall. He reached up for it and saw that his hands were shaking. So far nothing he'd uncovered had been pleasant, but it had all been within the letter of the law, even if not within the spirit. He had a horrible feeling, he was about to uncover the part of the club that strayed outside the boundaries of legality.

Paolo turned the key, almost expecting creaking noises as the door swung inwards. Instead it moved on well-oiled hinges. They were now in the attic space above the club with yet more doors leading from another corridor. He opened the first door and ducked just in time as a shoe flew past his head.

'Fuck off. I was on last night. I can't do it again.'

Paolo stepped into the room. It was spartanly furnished. Bed, bedside table, desk, wardrobe with a skylight opening in the roof. A young man dressed only in boxer shorts, aged somewhere between sixteen and twenty, glared at him.

'Who the fuck are you? Oh, Jesus, fuck, you're the Bill.'

Paolo could hear the sound of other doors opening and a babble of noise behind him. He went back into the corridor to see nine other occupants, a couple of them looking more like boys than young men. They all bore the hungry look of addicts. None of them were fully dressed. The most clothing worn appeared to be tee-shirts over the boxers. All had manacle marks on ankles and wrists and most had whip marks across their bodies.

'Call for medical services, Dave. I want you to stay up here until they arrive. These poor bastards have to be taken care of. I'm going downstairs to have a stronger chat with Chaz. He'd better

154

have some answers for me or I'll kick him into the middle of next week to get them. CC, you come with me.'

He made his way back downstairs, through the video room and down again into the bedroom. Chaz was sitting on the bed with a constable standing on either side of him and one blocking the door.

'You,' Paolo snarled, pointing at Chaz, 'get the fuck downstairs to Baron's office. We're going to talk about what I've found upstairs. If you lie to me, or hold anything back, I'll make sure you end up in a cell with someone who likes to play the same sort of games as your sick fucking members do.'

The officers escorted Chaz from the room. Paolo was about to follow when he felt CC's hand on his arm.

'Calm down a bit before you go at him, sir. You're too het up.'

'Het up? *Het up?* Of course I bloody am. Did you not see those drugged up zombies upstairs? A couple of them are little more than kids.'

She held on to his arm. 'I know. That's why I want you to calm down a bit. You won't be doing them any favours if you lose it with Chaz.'

Paolo nodded. 'You're right.' He took a deep breath. 'OK, let's go.'

By the time he reached George Baron's office, his temper had cooled just enough to let his brain work properly, but not so much that he didn't still want to drag Chaz upstairs and manacle him to the wall of one of the torture rooms.

Chaz had been placed in one of the visitor chairs. CC sat next to him while Paolo walked around the desk and sat down in George's chair.

'Right, Chaz, start talking. I want to know everything there is to know about this place and its special members. Kidnap and false imprisonment are just two of the charges I've got on my list so far.'

'We didn't kidnap them,' Chaz said. 'They came to us.'

'Really? What did you do, put an ad in the wanted section of the paper? Good rates of pay, accommodation and meals provided for torture victims?'

Paolo was astounded to see Chaz nodding.

'What? You mean that's really what you did?'

A ghost of a smile flitted across Chaz's face as he nodded again. 'We didn't word it like that, of course, but when someone applied for the job we did a full interview. We knew straightaway the ones who would do anything for a regular supply of whatever they were already hooked on.'

Paolo nodded at CC. 'Add drug dealing to the list. Something tells me it's going to be a very long list by the time we're done here.'

Chaz sat up. 'We're not drug dealers.'

'No? I can't see how those boys can come down to buy their own, considering there are two locked doors and a sliding mechanism that only works by remote control between them and freedom.'

'It's a better life for them than being on the streets.'

Paolo felt the heat rising in his body and forced himself to stay calm. 'Is that how you justify it to yourself? Using those young men as objects to throw to your members to abuse is better for them than being on the streets? Let's get to the point. You said only special members have keys. I want the names of all of them.'

Chaz pointed to a ledger on the desk. 'That's our full membership list. We really are a businessmen's club. Only those members whose number starts with an x have access to the upstairs facilities. They pay triple the membership fee.'

Paolo banged his hand on the desk so hard Chaz jumped.

'Facilities being human punch bags?'

'No, we don't let them beat the boys. It's just, you know, bondage and so on.'

'So on? There are whips and tazers up there. Fucking manacles to hold the poor bastards down. But you think it's all OK because they aren't beaten? You are sick. Really and truly sick.'

Paolo opened the ledger and turned to the M section, not at all surprised to see Montague Mason's membership number started with an x. No wonder he'd committed suicide. If this had come out, he'd have been ruined.

And that question still remained. Who was the blackmailer? It had to be someone inside the club.

'What about staff? How many of your regular staff know what goes on upstairs through that hidden door?'

Chaz shook his head. 'None of them. They only know about the stuff that happens in the open areas. When we have special functions down here, like on the day you wanted to come in and we kept you outside, I work the bar and we have caterers who leave the food in the kitchen, ready for me to put out.'

'Special functions? What sort of special functions?'

Chaz looked as if he wished he'd bitten his tongue out.

'Come on, out with it,' Paolo said. 'You've gone this far. There's no point in holding back now.'

'We . . . we . . . sort of let the boys out and they have to hide in one of the downstairs rooms. The members . . .' He stopped and thinned his lips as if to prevent another word from escaping.

'You might just as well tell me,' Paolo said. 'If you don't, we'll get it from the boys themselves, I'm sure.'

'It only happens once a month,' Chaz said, eyes pleading for understanding.

'*What does?*' Paolo roared, hanging on to his temper by a thread finer than cobwebs.

'It's like a fox hunt. The first to be found has to service the group. The rest get to go back upstairs to have time off in their rooms.'

'And what exactly are you doing while this group rape is going on?'

Chaz looked up at the ceiling, then down at his feet. When he finally answered, Paolo couldn't make out what he'd said, but CC, sitting next to him, heard every word.

Her face a picture of disgusted outrage, she glared at Chaz before turning back to Paolo.

'He said he videos the proceedings, sir.'

157

Chapter Twenty-one

After taking Chaz to the station and leaving him there to cool his heels waiting for his solicitor to arrive, Paolo took Dave with him to call on Trudy Chappell. Even if, as Chaz insisted, she didn't know the whereabouts of her ex-boss, she might have seen or heard something to give them a clue of where to start looking.

As Dave pulled up outside a picturesque detached cottage on the outskirts of Bradchester, Paolo checked the address Chaz had given him for Trudy from the club's employment records.

'Are you sure we're in the right place, Dave? Your SatNav hasn't had one of its funny turns and taken us off to a surprise destination?'

Dave leaned over to look at the piece of paper in Paolo's hand and then back at the address he'd keyed into the SatNav.

'We're in the right place. This is the address.'

Paolo got out and looked up and down the street. Similar properties stood on both sides of the road. It was quaint without being over the top, but what it definitely wasn't was a rough area.

As Dave's head appeared on the other side of the car, Paolo glanced across.

'Do you remember when April said Trudy had asked for self-defence lessons? I'm sure she said it was because Trudy claimed to live in a rough neighbourhood.'

Dave nodded. 'You're right. That's exactly what April said. This is not my idea of rough, that's for sure.'

Paolo shrugged. 'Maybe April misheard or misunderstood. Anyway, let's see if Miss Chappell knows anything that can help us to find her missing ex-boss.'

A fragrant rose garden lined either side of a narrow path leading to a sapphire-blue front door. Paolo was able to appreciate the beauty of the place, but knew he would go insane if forced to live there. It was a bit too twee for his taste.

Dave lifted the heavy brass knocker and rapped a couple of times. A lace curtain twitched in one of the glass mullioned windows. Paolo held up his warrant card and waited. After a couple of minutes, he heard a chain being put on the door before it was opened just a few inches. He'd expected to see a face peering at him, but whoever was on the other side of the door remained hidden.

'Miss Chappell? Trudy? Remember us. We were at the club a few weeks back. Detective Inspector Paolo Sterling and Detective Sergeant Dave Johnson.'

'I know who you are,' she said. 'What do you want?'

'Could we come in to talk to you for a few minutes?'

'No. Who sent you? I'm not pressing charges, whatever you say.'

Paolo looked at Dave and shrugged.

'We've come to talk to you about George Baron,' Paolo said, but stopped when he heard Trudy whimper.

'Go away,' she whispered. 'I don't want to talk about what he did to me.'

'Trudy, we're not here to investigate anything that happened to you; unless you want us to, that is. We're here because George Baron is missing and we were hoping you might know where he might be found. As his secretary, we thought you could be aware of other properties he has, that perhaps no one else knows about. If that's the case, won't you please let us come in?'

To Paolo it seemed like hours before he heard the chain being moved. The door opened, but there was still no sign of Trudy.

'Come in,' she said, her voice coming from behind the door.

They stepped into a small lobby. The low ceiling beams made

Paolo want to duck, even though they were high enough to give him comfortable clearance.

As Trudy closed the door behind them, he couldn't help but gasp and was aware of Dave making a similar noise to his left. Trudy's face was a mass of bruises and there were finger marks showing around her throat where the collar of her dressing gown didn't quite cover them.

She gave a lopsided smile. 'If you ask questions, you have to leave,' she said. 'I'm not talking about what happened to me, so don't try to find out.'

She walked past them into a tiny sitting room. Again a claustrophobic feeling crept over Paolo. It wasn't so much the height of the heavily beamed ceiling this time, but the décor. Every spare space was taken up with dolls, teddies and other soft animals. It was like being in the stockroom of a Christmas Fayre. Paolo moved a giant panda to one side and perched next to it on a chintz covered armchair. He noticed that Dave had chosen to stand rather than move one of the occupants of the couch.

Trudy sat down opposite Paolo, every movement showing the pain she must be feeling. From the exaggerated way she inched herself down, it was obvious her bruises weren't confined to her neck and face.

'I'm sorry,' Paolo said, 'I know you said you don't want to talk about it, but because of what you said earlier, I have to ask. Did George Baron do this to you?'

She didn't answer, but her expression told him all he needed to know.

'I let you in,' she said, 'to tell you about his flat in Leicester. I don't think even Chaz knows about it.'

'But you do?'

She shrugged and winced at even that slight movement. 'I guess you could say I'm nosey. I like to know what's going on, so I pry in places I shouldn't.'

'Is that what got you fired?' Paolo asked.

She grimaced. 'You could say that.'

Paolo realised from her expression that he wasn't going to get any more details on what had passed between her and George Baron, but it was clear who'd come off worst from the encounter.

'Do you know the address of the flat in Leicester?'

She reached for her handbag, lying on the floor next to the chair, and rummaged around until she found a notebook. She flipped over several pages until she found the one she wanted and read out the address. Paolo waited for Dave to finish writing it down before turning back to Trudy.

'Have you seen a doctor? Some of your bruises look pretty severe.'

'No and I'm not going to. You've got what you wanted. I'd like you to leave now.'

'Before I go, Chaz seemed to think George had given you a special payment package. Was it because of this,' he said, indicating her injuries.

For the first time she seemed shaken by his words. Tears spilled from her eyes and ran unheeded over her bruised cheeks.

'Just go,' she said. 'Please, just go. I don't want to talk to you anymore.'

'I'm sorry. I didn't mean to upset you. Thank you for your information. It may help us to find George Baron.'

She drew a deep breath. 'If you do find him, tell him not to come within a mile of me. If I get the chance, I'll kill him.'

Back at the station, Paolo discovered Chaz's solicitor had arrived and was waiting for them in one of the interview rooms. When Paolo opened the door, the constable on duty left the room. Paolo and Dave sat opposite the two men. Reaching out to switch on the recorder, Paolo asked for the solicitor's name and then gave details of the time and date and who was in the room.

Paolo had dealt with Gordon Lightfoot in the past and was surprised to find him representing someone as far down the food chain as Chaz. He usually confined his client list to those who headed major corporations or were mentioned on the financial pages of broadsheets.

Before Paolo could ask any questions, Gordon spoke. 'I'd like to know why my client is being held, Inspector. He is an employee in a private establishment and has not broken any law in the execution of his duties.'

Paolo smiled. 'I think perhaps he hasn't yet told you of the young men we found locked up in the attic rooms.'

Gordon leaned back, clearly at his ease. 'He has, in fact, told me about them. I think you'll find they were there of their own free will and could have left at any time they chose.'

'Hardly,' Paolo said, 'unless they had Houdini capabilities. The doors were locked from the outside.'

Gordon nodded at Chaz, signalling for him to speak.

'None of them wanted to go back on the streets. All they had to do was say and we'd have let them go.' He shrugged. 'They chose to stay. I think they liked it up there.'

'And did they like it in the rooms below them?' Paolo asked, his temper flaring. 'Did they enjoy being used and abused?'

Chaz smiled. 'Yes.'

'Don't give me that,' Paolo said.

The smile never left Chaz's face. 'You've got no idea of what some people like. In the club George had in London there were politicians who paid good money to wear a nappy and be fed with a baby's bottle. Top businessmen would lie down for women in high heels to walk on them. There was a bishop who liked to be made to sit in a corner and be told he was a bad boy while he played with himself. Just because it doesn't suit you, doesn't mean it don't work for others.'

The solicitor leaned forward. 'Are you going to charge my client? If you're not, I suggest you let him go.'

'I have a few questions I'd like answers to before that's going to happen. What were you in prison for, Chaz?'

Gordon Lightfoot held up a hand to prevent Chaz from answering. 'I hardly see that as being relevant to today's interview.'

'Fair enough,' Paolo said. 'It's easy enough to find out for myself. How did you and George get together? It's clear you were involved in the London club, so your friendship must go back a long way.'

162

'I've been with George ever since I got out of the nick,' Chaz said. 'He'd just closed down his first club up north somewhere and was about to set up the London one. This is the third club he's opened. He's got a way of finding out what people want and providing it for them.'

'You sound as if you admire him,' Paolo suggested.

Chaz shrugged. 'He's been good to me. I've got no complaints.'

'Tell me, were you with George when he waited for Trudy Chappell to come out from the youth centre?'

He looked uneasy and glanced at his solicitor for guidance.

Gordon leaned forward. 'I cannot see the relevance here, Inspector.'

'Let's put it this way, Chaz. George was seen in his car by a reliable witness. Another man was in the car. I can easily show the witness a picture of you to find out if you were there. If you've nothing to hide, why not tell me if it was you?'

Chaz nodded. 'I was with George.'

'Was that the night Trudy was fired?'

He nodded again.

'The night she was so badly beaten she's covered from head to foot in bruises?'

'That was nothing to do with me. I never touched her.'

'But George did?' Paolo asked.

Chaz shrugged. 'I dunno. I told you. I never touched her.'

Gordon intervened. 'This doesn't seem to have anything to do with your reason for bringing my client to the station, so I must repeat my earlier question: are you going to charge my client?'

Paolo knew he needed one of the young men to admit being held against his will or he had no case against Chaz, or George Baron either for that matter. So far, all of them had told the same story and claimed they had the run of the place and the doors were not normally locked.

As much as he hated having to say the words, he knew he had no choice.

'Certainly, Chaz is free to leave. However, I would advise

against making any plans for holidays abroad at this stage. I would also like his assurance that he will remain in Bradchester. Should one of the young men change his story, we would like to be able to have another chat with your client.'

'Thank you, Inspector. My client will be available, should you have reason to question him further, but only when I am present to advise him.'

Paolo stood at the front of the office seething at the way things were going. As he brought the rest of the team up to date on Trudy's injuries, he couldn't help feeling Chaz knew far more about how she'd got them than he was letting on.

'From what Trudy Chappell said and, more to the point, what she didn't say, it seems pretty clear that George Baron gave her one hell of a beating. The inference was that she'd pried into matters that didn't concern her. Whether that's to do with George's personal life, or the goings on at the club, we don't know at this stage. Trudy has no intention of telling us anything, so, until we find George Baron, we're not going to know what caused him to lash out as he did.'

He turned to write on the board. 'Leicester police have already looked into the address Trudy gave us this morning. It does belong to George, but he hasn't been seen there for several months, so, although not a dead end as such, it doesn't help us to find him.'

Turning back, he perched on the edge of a desk.

'In addition to having to let Chaz go, we can't even proceed to investigate the events at the club. All the special club members contacted so far have elected to hide behind their solicitors. They all tell the same story – there were no boys, only men, and they were willing partners. There was never any coercion. None of them admit to the fox hunt games. Although we know there is video evidence somewhere, Chaz did admit to filming them, but said George held the copies of those sessions. Apparently, George was scared of them falling into the wrong hands.'

'I'm not surprised,' Andrea said. 'I'm amazed the club members allowed themselves to be filmed.'

Paolo shrugged. 'Most of them looked horrified when told of the existence of the videos, which leads me to suppose Chaz did the filming using hidden cameras in the various rooms. He, of course, claims the videos were made with the full consent of all participants, but I'm more inclined to think otherwise.'

'So,' Dave said, 'what have we actually got? A sordid set up, but unless some of the young men from upstairs are prepared to testify, we can't prove anything illegal took place?'

Paolo nodded. 'I'm afraid so and not one of them is willing to stand up in court to say what went on. We don't even know the names of most of them. The three who actually applied for jobs at the club say they were happy there. We've got a couple who are clearly under the age of sixteen, but claim to be twenty-one and all of them, without exception, are addicts. As far as we know, they're all victims and haven't broken any laws themselves, so we can't even keep them under lock and key while we look for George Baron.'

'Any news on the computers, sir?' Andrea asked.

'Your IT friend is doing his fancy finger work on the hard drives as we speak. He seemed to think it will take a few days to do whatever is necessary. He'll be in touch as soon as he finds anything worthwhile.'

He stood up. 'And we're no nearer to finding out who murdered Derrick Walden. We know George Baron was outside the youth centre with Chaz on the night Derrick drowned, but, as far as we can see, there's no link between Derrick Walden and the other two men. Any ideas?'

A sea of shaking heads greeted his question.

'I'm going to call it a day,' he said. 'Tomorrow we can have another go at the case, but for now I suggest we all get a good night's sleep and worry about developments as and when things change.'

Paolo pulled up outside the house he used to call home. To say he wasn't looking forward to his chat with Lydia was the understatement of the century, but he'd promised Katy he would try to talk her mother round. Knowing Katy was out with Danny tonight, he'd called Lydia to set up the meeting. She'd put him in the wrong before he'd even said a word. As soon as she'd heard his voice on the phone, lines had been drawn.

'You can come round,' she'd said, 'but you're wasting your time. I've already told Katy no and that's an end to it as far as I'm concerned.'

And yet, here he was, ready to plead Katy's cause. He sighed and got out of the car. He must be mad, but yet again he was going to set himself up for a verbal beating from his ex-wife. As always when walking to the front door, he felt weird not having a key to a house he still paid half the mortgage on. Maybe Lydia would finally agree to sell it once Katy left home.

He reached out and pressed the buzzer. Lydia must have been watching out for him because she opened the door almost immediately.

'I told you on the phone you were wasting your time,' she said by way of greeting.

Paolo grinned. 'And good evening to you, Lydia. My day has been fine. Thank you for asking. How was yours? Still enjoying the new job?'

He was pleased to see a reluctant answering smile as she stood back to let him in.

'Sorry, Paolo, but you and Katy wind me up with your tag team antics. You know that.'

Paolo dropped a kiss on her cheek as he passed. 'I promise you, this is not a tag team exercise. You think I want our daughter living God knows where in appalling conditions?'

She didn't answer, but led the way into the lounge.

'Sit down,' she said. 'I'll listen to what you've got to say, but my mind is pretty much made up. She's not going with my consent and that's final.'

'Fair enough,' Paolo said, collapsing onto the couch. 'That's how I felt until I gave it a bit more thought.'

He hesitated, wondering how best to get Lydia to see Katy would go without or without their blessing.

'You do know she will join this volunteer mob as soon as she's eighteen, don't you? But if she does it then, what do you think the chances are of her keeping in touch? Would you rather she was cut off from us completely? Because that's what would happen. She's going to go, Lydia, whether we like it or not.'

She shrugged. 'She wouldn't go if *you* asked her not to. She adores you, Paolo. She'd never do anything that would upset you. All you have to do is tell her it would break your heart and she'd stay.'

Paolo thought about it. Lydia was probably right. He could use emotional blackmail on Katy and she might cave in, but that was exactly why he'd never do it. He loved Katy too much to manipulate her feelings like that.

He shook his head. 'She'd hate me for it and I'd hate myself for doing it. I don't like the idea of her going off for a year, but I'm not going to stand in her way.'

'And me? Don't I get a say in this?'

'Of course you do. That's why I'm here.'

She laughed. 'To make me feel the same way you do? I don't think so.'

He leaned forward, his knees almost touching Lydia's who'd sat down on the armchair next to the couch.

'Lydia, we have to let her go. She'll keep in touch. We'll know where she is and what she's doing. Besides, it's not as if she's going all on her own. Danny's going with her.'

She drew back, moving her legs away from his.

'Don't you speak to me about that bloody boy.'

Paolo was surprised at the venom in her voice. 'I thought you liked Danny? I know you weren't that keen to start with, but I thought you'd got over that.'

She shook her head. 'I do like him, but it's all his fault Katy is so besotted with this crazy idea. He was the one who got her onto the volunteering craze. If she's not dishing out food in a shelter for the homeless, she's chatting to God knows who in that bloody youth centre. How do we know who she's mixing with there? It's full of drug addicts—'

'Ex-drug addicts,' Paolo interrupted. 'If they aren't in a programme, we don't allow them access. Part of the youth centre's aim is to help those kids turn their lives around. Katy is part of that with the volunteer work she does there.'

'You see! That's just like you, Paolo. Always seeing the bloody good in every situation. For you, it's cut and dried. Katy does good work, so it's OK if she's mixing with junkies . . . okay, *ex*-junkies.'

He grinned. 'Aren't you just a tiny bit proud of her? I am.'

She sighed. 'We're not going to see eye to eye on this, Paolo. Let it rest. You can tell Katy you did your best for her, but, for once, you failed.' She reached out and touched the back of his hand. 'Truce?'

He turned his hand over and grasped hers. 'Of course. I hate arguing with you. Always did.'

Paolo wished for a moment he could turn the clock back to the days when their marriage had been a success. Back to the days when they'd had two young daughters to care for and protect. Then Sarah had been killed and everything fell apart. He'd never stopped loving Lydia, not completely. He was fairly sure she felt the same way, but they'd given their marriage a second try and it hadn't worked out.

He became aware of tantalising aromas drifting through from the kitchen: garlic, herbs, tomatoes.

'Are you expecting someone for dinner? Sorry, you should have said.'

Lydia grinned. 'Idiot. It's for you if you feel like staying to eat. Don't worry if you've got somewhere else to go. It's only lasagne, so it will freeze for another time.'

Paolo didn't need a second invitation. Back in his flat it would either be a takeaway or a sandwich and he wasn't even sure the bread was still OK.

'I'd love some. Shall I come through and give you a hand?'

'Sure, why not?' Lydia said.

A couple of hours later, they sat side by side on the couch drinking coffee.

'That was an amazing meal. Thank you,' Paolo said.

'Thank you for not bringing up Katy's plans again,' Lydia said, turning to face him.

He reached out and touched the side of her face.

'I know when I'm fighting a losing battle,' he said, thinking how beautiful she looked in the soft glow of the table lamp. 'I should be going.'

He was never sure afterwards who moved first, but their lips met. Gently at first, then more demanding. He felt Lydia's arms around his neck, pulling him closer. Memories of other nights like this flooded his mind.

'Hello, I'm home!'

At Katy's voice calling through from the hallway, they sprang apart. Lydia glared at Paolo. He wasn't sure if it was because of the kiss, or a warning not to say anything to Katy.

She stood up, straightening her blouse. 'Time for you to go, Paolo.'

He nodded, wanting to say the right thing, but unable to think what that might be.

Katy opened the lounge door. 'There you are. I looked in the kitchen first, but all that's in there is a load of washing up. Want me to load the dishwasher for you, Mum?'

Lydia nodded and Katy disappeared. Within minutes, Paolo could hear the clatter of cutlery being dropped into the baskets in the machine. Neither of them had moved.

'I—' he began.

She shook her head. 'Don't say anything. Just go.'

Chapter Twenty-two

Paolo's hopes of finding George Baron had been high, but as each day came and went without any leads, he felt more frustrated. Ten days had now passed since George had disappeared and there was no sign of a breakthrough in finding him. How could someone so prominent simply walk away from his life? None of his bank accounts had been touched. The account connected to the club had been frozen, so that would have been closed to him anyway, but how could he survive with no money whatsoever?

One of Paolo's first questions had been to find out if George had made a sizeable withdrawal prior to doing a flit, but there had been no unusual activity on any of the accounts.

Another frustration for Paolo was not being able to make any headway with the sexual assault case. The hospital patient still showed no signs of waking up. Paolo had tried to get the doctor to give an estimate of how long the coma could last. Anything from another five minutes to fifty years had been the answer, which left Paolo no better off.

He sat, tapping a pen on his desk, thinking of all the things he hadn't been able to solve. The reason for Derrick Walden's death was still a mystery. It could have been George Baron, who then did a bunk, but why kill Walden?

The phone rang and he jumped, recognising his old home number on the LED screen. He'd left message after message for Lydia on her mobile since leaving the house a week ago, but she hadn't returned any of his calls. He had no idea what he wanted to say, but didn't feel he could leave things as they were. It was too awkward. With shaking hands, he picked up the receiver.

'Hi, good to hear from you at last, Lydia.'

'It's not Mum, it's me,' Katy's cheerful voice informed him.

Paolo wasn't sure if he was relieved or disappointed.

'Hi, kiddo, what can I do for you?'

'You've already done it. I'm just ringing to say thank you. Mum actually said yes!'

'Really? That's brilliant news.'

'I know,' she said, 'and I think it's all down to you. After you'd left last week, Mum said not to talk to her about the volunteer thing because she needed to think. Then, this morning, right out of the blue, she gave me her blessing. How about that!'

'I'm really pleased for you. Not so pleased for me or your mum, but pleased for you.' He glanced at the clock. 'Hey, I've just realised what the time is. What are you doing at home? Shouldn't you be at school?'

Katy laughed. 'If you were any sort of normal father you'd know I had an exam today. I only have to be at school in an hour's time. Anyway, I need to get ready. Just wanted to let you know and say thanks.'

Before Paolo could answer, the line went dead. Well done, Lydia, he thought. You made the right decision. He sat for a moment, imagining his life without Katy being a few minutes' drive away and didn't like the image at all. You'll just have to get used to it, he told himself, turning to pick up one of the files to work on.

He worked steadily for an hour before Dave disturbed him.

'Call's just come in, sir. There's a body at a fly tipping site just outside town.'

Paolo got up, only too happy to get away from the never-ending paperwork. 'What details have you got?'

'Naked man, body badly decomposed by the description. Nothing more than that.'

'Who found him?' Paolo asked, putting on his jacket.

'A local builder. According to the report, he just happened to be passing and spotted the body. In truth, I expect he was there to make an illegal dump of his rubbish.'

Paolo laughed. 'Most probably, but that's not our concern. Forensics on their way?'

Dave nodded. 'Dr Royston's been called out.'

Dave pulled up behind the builder's van. Judging by the way the rear window panels were obscured on the inside, Paolo guessed Dave's assessment of how the builder came to be there was probably correct.

He got out of the car and walked over to the constable on duty.

'Where's the man who called it in?' he asked, ducking under the tape and holding it up for Dave to follow.

The constable pointed along the roadside to where a man was leaning with his arm against a tree. Judging by the way the man's shoulders were heaving as his head rested on his arm, he'd been throwing up fairly recently.

As Paolo and Dave approached, the stench of vomit confirmed Paolo's suspicion. He stopped a little way from the tree and called out.

'I'm Detective Inspector Paolo Sterling and this is Detective Sergeant Dave Johnson. I'm sorry, I can see you're suffering a bit, but we need to ask you a few questions. Do you think you're up to answering them?'

The man turned an ashen face towards them and Paolo had a fleeting sensation of having met him before.

'As long as I don't have to go back over there,' the man said, pointing in the general direction of where lots of activity was taking place, 'I'll be fine.'

Paolo smiled. 'No problem, let's move along the road a little,' he said, wanting to get upwind of the man's vomit.

When he judged they were far enough away from the tree, Paolo stopped. The man swayed a bit, but seemed more under control of his emotions.

'Have we met before?' Paolo asked. 'Your face looks familiar.'

'If I was feeling better, I'd say on a wanted poster,' the man said with a forlorn attempt at humour. 'My name's Tom Cruise, same as the film star, except that I'm taller and he's richer.' He looked closely at Paolo. 'I've seen you on television,' he said, 'but I think you might have seen me when I was working on the youth centre a couple of months before it opened officially.'

Paolo nodded. 'Could be that's where I remember you from. What did you do there?'

'Some of the internal remodelling.'

'OK. Now can you tell us how you came to find the body? Please don't give me the line about just passing. From your van you wouldn't have been able to see down the bank.'

Tom hesitated. 'I don't think many of the other local builders know about this place,' he said. 'So that means it's not watched like some of the other fly tipping sites. I know we're not supposed to dump other than in the municipal recycling plant, but by the time the little Hitlers there make us wait for hours just to be able to tell us to put stuff in the same place we always do, it's easier to come here. I was just going to tip some rubble and planks. Nothing nasty.'

'If this place isn't common knowledge, how come you know about it?'

'I found out from someone at the youth centre.'

'Really? Who?'

Tom shook his head. 'I can't remember now. There were so many people around back then. Builders, painters, electricians, not to mention all the youth centre staff and volunteers getting under our feet when we were trying to get on. Any of them could have mentioned it.'

Paolo made a mental note to try to find out. As Tom had said, not many knew about this place, which meant the killer was definitely someone local. He would pass the information about the fly tipping site on to the council to deal with. His prime concern was the dead man.

'Tell me what happened when you got here,' Paolo said.

Tom swallowed a few times before answering. His face blanched as he spoke. 'I got out of the van and was about to unload my stuff when the smell hit me. I didn't know what it was, so went over to the bank to take a look and that's when I saw him . . . what was left of him. There were bloody great birds feeding on him.' He stopped and put a hand over his mouth as if to hold back another bout of vomiting.

'Take your time,' Paolo said. 'We can wait while you pull yourself together.'

Tom heaved a bit, but managed to control the urge to throw up.

'I'm OK now,' he said. 'There's not much more to tell. I ran back to the van, got my mobile and called you lot. The bloke I spoke to said I should wait here until I was told I could go, so I did.'

On the edge of his peripheral vision, Paolo saw Barbara Royston climb to the top of the bank and wave in his direction, indicating she needed him to come over.

'Give your full details to DS Johnson and then you can go,' he said. 'Dave, I'm going to see what Dr Royston has to say.'

Paolo joined Barbara at the top of the bank.

'You wanted to talk to me?' he said.

'Not talk to you, no. I want to show you something.'

She led him over to the stretcher where the body was resting in a black zipped bag.

'This should make it easier to identify the victim,' she said. 'A birthmark that is even more noticeable than mine.'

She reached out and pulled the zip, uncovering what was left of the man's face.

From the moment she'd mentioned the birthmark, Paolo had guessed what he was going to see. A glance confirmed his suspicion. They had finally found George Baron.

Chapter Twenty-three

'Cause of death?' Paolo asked.

'Difficult to say until I do the PM.'

Paolo sighed. 'I know that, Barbara, but what's your gut instinct?'

'I'm not trying to be difficult, Paolo. I honestly don't know at this stage. He has strangulation marks around his throat, but with half his face missing, including his tongue, it's not as easy as you would think to determine cause of death.' She must have sensed his frustration, because her face softened. 'I can tell you a few things that might help. He'd been tortured by someone with a tazer. More than once.'

Paolo thought back to what he'd seen in the club and been told in the hospital about the coma patient. 'Definitely a tazer?'

She nodded. 'Ja. The marks are clearly visible on his back and genital area. He's been the recipient of some violent sex acts, too. His rectum is torn ragged. He must have been in agony before he died.'

Once again, the doctor's words regarding his coma patient came rushing in to Paolo's mind. 'When are you going to be able to do the PM on this one?'

'Not for a couple of days.'

Paolo nodded. 'Let me know when you schedule it. I'd like to be there.'

She nodded and signalled that the body could be taken away.

Paolo said his goodbyes to Barbara and went to join Dave who was waiting by his car.

'We need to go to Bradchester Central to speak to Doctor

Brownlow.' He filled Dave in on the victim's identity and the similarity of injuries to that of the coma patient. 'If the same person killed George Baron as put that man into a coma, we might be getting somewhere at last.'

Paolo and Dave got into the lift. As Paolo pressed the button for their floor, he remembered the last time they had been here. Since then, Dave hadn't mentioned if he was still subject to snide comments. Paolo hoped not, but didn't want to ask in case it made Dave feel uncomfortable. He decided to ask CC when he got back to the office.

The lift doors opened and they walked along the corridor to Dr Brownlow's office. Dave tapped on the door and then opened it.

'Come in,' the doctor said. 'I'm sorry, I can't spare much time, but as you said it was urgent when you called, I've rearranged my ward visits to see you.'

'Thank you,' Paolo said, taking a seat opposite the doctor. 'This is about your coma patient.'

Dr Brownlow smiled. 'I guessed as much. I'm sorry; I have nothing to add to when you were last here. He hasn't shown any sign of coming out of it.'

'That's not exactly why I'm here. I need to tell you something that isn't yet generally known. We have just picked up a murder victim with almost identical injuries to that of your coma patient.'

The doctor sighed. 'I did tell you over a month ago that I feared that would happen one day.'

Paolo nodded. 'You did, which is why I'm hoping you'll help us to stop whoever is carrying out the attacks.'

'Me? How can I help?'

'You could give me the names of the other patients you found had suffered similar injuries. I'm not asking for details of their injuries or care, just names and addresses.'

The doctor was already shaking his head before Paolo finished speaking.

'You know I can't do that. Even if I wanted to break patient confidentiality, which I don't, I can't hand over hospital information. You'll need to get a court order. I'm sorry. I really wish I could help, but I can't.'

Paolo wanted to smack the desk with frustration. He understood the doctor's hands were tied, but unless he could speak to the earlier victims, more would be sure to follow. Possibly even more bodies.

'OK, one last question. With regard to your coma patient, you said there was severe anal trauma. Would you say it was in keeping with a sex game gone wrong?'

The doctor shook his head. 'No. I would say it was in keeping with someone wanting to inflict the maximum amount of pain and damage. No way was this a game, not even at the outset.'

Paolo thought of the instruments of torture back at the club. Could it be one of the members who'd moved on from games and needed greater thrills? Had George Baron been tortured and murdered by someone he knew?

They thanked the doctor for his time, but left no wiser than they'd arrived. In the lift Paolo shared his thoughts with Dave.

'You could be right, sir. Do you think we should take a closer look at the special members?'

'I wish we could, but they are all so carefully protected by their legal advisors, it's doubtful we'd even get to speak to them without something a bit more concrete.'

As the lift doors opened for them to leave, Paolo's mobile rang. He stepped out, then swiped the screen to answer the call.

Andrea's voice resounded in his ear. 'We've finally got a breakthrough on the blackmail case, sir,' she said. 'I've just had a call from Mike the IT guy. He's managed to find traces of the emails on one of the computers from the Triple B club. You'll never guess whose computer, sir. Trudy Chappell's!'

Paolo moved to one side so that people waiting to enter the lift could do so.

'But that doesn't necessarily mean she sent the emails. George or Chaz could have used her computer.'

'That's the really exciting bit, sir. Apparently, it's easy to pick up on the style of words and sentence structure we use when sending emails. It's very individual, Mike says. He's been comparing the blackmail emails with others on her computer. He says he'd be prepared to swear in court his belief that the emails sent to Montague Mason were written by Trudy Chappell.'

Paolo ended the call and explained to Dave what Andrea had said.

'Next port of call is another visit to Trudy Chappell. Whether she wants to tell us or not, we're going to find out exactly what happened between her and George Baron.'

Pulling up outside Trudy's cottage, Dave switched off the ignition and turned to Paolo.

'I can't make head or tail of this, sir.'

Paolo sighed. 'That makes two of us. Trudy suddenly gets the need to learn self-defence. She gets fired and then beaten up by her ex-boss, or the other way round, she gets beaten up and then fired, but he then turns up dead. She didn't look capable of killing him, but maybe she did. I'm not certain of anything anymore. Come on; let's see what she's got to say about the blackmail emails.'

This time when Dave knocked, the door opened almost immediately, but still with the chain in place.

'What do you want this time? I can't help you with anything else regarding George Baron.'

Paolo watched her face carefully. 'No one can help him now, Trudy. He's dead.'

Her body sagged against the doorframe and Paolo was fairly sure the news came as a shock to her, but knew it could have been an act. He'd seen too many criminals put on a convincing show of innocence to accept anyone at face value.

'Are you sure it's him?' she asked.

He nodded. 'We recovered his body this morning. His birthmark is pretty distinctive.'

Trudy slipped the chain off and opened the door. She was still wearing the dressing gown she'd worn the last time they came to speak to her. Judging by her body odour, she hadn't taken a bath in that time either. Paolo recalled how smartly dressed she'd been at the club and wondered what had happened between her and George. Outwardly, her bruises had faded, but he was willing to bet the mental wounds hadn't yet begun to heal.

She slouched through to the over-crowded sitting room and flopped down onto an armchair.

'So, he's dead. Good. I don't see why you're here though.'

Paolo thought it was strange she hadn't asked how he died, but decided to leave that question until later. For now, he felt a direct attack about the blackmail would work better than trying to ease a confession from her.

'We're here, Trudy, because we have evidence you blackmailed Montague Mason over a long period of time. In the end he took his own life because he could no longer afford to pay you.'

He'd been expecting a denial, but she nodded.

'I know,' she whispered. 'I never expected that. That wasn't supposed to happen. I thought he'd find the money from somewhere. He always did.'

'You admit it? You admit blackmail?'

She nodded, her head barely moving, as if she couldn't be bothered to make any effort.

'What difference does it make now? I'm going to lose everything anyway.'

She opened her mouth to speak again, but Paolo stopped her.

'Trudy, I'm going to read you your rights. I'm also going to switch this on,' he said, showing her the small voice activated recorder he'd taken from his pocket. 'OK? I don't want you to say another word until I've finished. Is that clear?'

She gave the barest hint of a nod, so Paolo went ahead with the prepared words. Afterwards, Paolo asked her if she'd understood what he'd read out to her. Again, her head hardly moved.

'I need you to say it out loud this time, Trudy. Have you understood your rights?'

'Yes,' she said and Paolo thought he'd never heard a more resigned sound.

'You are entitled to legal representation. Would you like to call someone?'

She shook her head.

'Trudy, for the record, you have to say it.'

'I don't want to call anyone. Can we just get this over with?'

'Of course. Trudy, can you tell me how you came by the information you used to blackmail Montague Mason?'

'I told you when you came here last time. I like to know what's going on. I poke my nose in where it's not wanted. I get a thrill from learning everyone's little secrets.'

'And then you use those secrets to blackmail people?'

She shook her head. 'Not people. Just one. Just Montague Mason.'

'Why him?' Paolo asked. 'Why not one of the other members?'

She started pulling at a loose thread in the brocade of the armchair. 'It started as a crusade in a way. One day I walked into George's office as he was putting DVDs in his safe. I guessed he didn't want me to know about them, because he ordered me out and shouted at me to knock before entering in future. That made me curious, so I decided to find out what was on them. I'd long since found the code for the safe, so it was easy enough to go in and take one while he was out.'

She stared into space, as if caught by the memory. Still pulling at the thread as it unravelled the embroidery, she shook her head.

'You have no idea what depravity was on that DVD. Young men, naked as the day they were born, ran here there and everywhere, trying to find safe places to hide. A couple of minutes after the last one disappeared from view, a group of men dressed in red hunting outfits came through from the billiard room. One of them was blowing one of those horns they use for fox hunts and they were all yelling tally-ho and other stupid hunting cries. It didn't take them long to find one of the young men. They dragged him out from a cupboard. He was screaming. Begging them not to hurt him.'

Tears fell unheeded onto her dressing gown.

'George wasn't part of the pack, but he appeared from the top of the stairs and called all the others out of hiding. Told them they were safe for this month. They fled upstairs. George told the members to enjoy their prize and he went back to wherever he'd been before they found the boy.'

Paolo didn't want to know the answer, but had to ask the question.

'What happened next?'

'Can't you guess? They took it in turns to use him. He was bleeding by the time they'd finished. One of the first in the queue was Montague bloody Mason, the so-called social pioneer who was going to help all the young people in Bradchester to become better citizens.'

She brushed a hand roughly across her face as if her tears offended her.

'So you decided to blackmail him rather than take the DVD to the police? You could have used it to rescue the young men.'

'That's what I should have done. Do you think I don't know that?'

Paolo handed her a tissue. 'So why didn't you?'

'Debt. I was up to my eyes in debt. Still am. I thought I'd use the knowledge to get some money, clear my debts and then go to the police.'

She fell silent.

'But?' Paolo prompted.

'I gamble. I have an online account that somehow never seems to be in credit. I borrowed from one of those Pay Day loan companies to get through one month, but then needed to borrow from another one to make the payments on the first one. Before I knew where I was, I owed thousands and couldn't pay my mortgage on this place.'

The thread she'd been pulling finally came away from the

fabric. She looked at it wound round her fingers as if she couldn't work out where it had come from.

'It didn't seem fair. I've never hurt anyone, not like those revolting men, and I thought, why not make him pay? So that's what I did.'

'Do you still have the DVD?'

She shook her head. 'No, I put it back in the safe the first chance I got. I don't think George ever noticed it had been missing. There are loads of them in the safe at the club.'

'Weren't you worried he'd be on to you?'

She shook her head. 'Not until you lot came round. After that, I realised it was only a matter of time before he twigged the blackmailer might be me. I knew about his temper, so decided to learn how to protect myself.'

'You had a lesson with April Greychurch.'

She nodded. 'Just the one, but it didn't do me any good. When I came out of the youth centre, George and Chaz were sitting in George's parked car, waiting for me. He told me I was fired and to follow him to the club in my own car to collect my things. When I got to my office, Chaz went off somewhere, but George locked the door and told me he knew I'd been blackmailing Mason.'

'How did he know it was you?'

'He said it could only be me. No one else could have found out about Montague Mason. He told me he remembered me coming in when he was putting the DVDs away. I denied it all at first, but then he started punching and kicking me, calling me names. The next thing I knew, his hands were round my throat and I couldn't breathe.' As she took a breath, a look of venom passed across her face. 'I'm glad the bastard is dead. I hope he suffered. Did he?'

Paolo ignored the question. 'Is that why he gave you such a handsome payoff? So that you wouldn't file a complaint against him? Surely he must have realised you were in no position to do any such thing considering that would raise the blackmail issue?'

She shook her head. 'It wasn't that,' she whispered. 'The violence must have got him worked up because . . . because . . .'

Paolo watched as her composure crumpled. She began to shake. Her mouth moved soundlessly, as if she wanted to get the words out, but they turned to vapour before she could formulate them.

'Trudy, I'm sorry, I have to ask. What happened?'

She finally got the words out. 'He raped me.'

Chapter Twenty-four

Paolo stood in front of the board, wiping out the references to Montague Mason's suicide and blackmail. Over the last few days, Trudy had been charged and released on bail, pending a trial date. He'd taken no joy in charging her, but was pleased to be able to delete at least one of the many puzzles from the board. Montague's name remained up there, though, because they still had no idea who'd defaced the plaque.

It had been the catalyst for so much of the violence that followed that he couldn't simply put it down to a prank and ignore it, even though there were far more serious crimes still unsolved. He turned to his team, who were patiently waiting for a few words of wisdom. Paolo wished he had some to give.

'OK, we've cleared up the blackmail issue, but we're no nearer to finding out who murdered Derrick Walden. We know George Baron and Chaz were both at the youth centre that night, but we haven't yet uncovered a connection between them. That doesn't mean there isn't one, just that if there is, we haven't found it.'

He glanced over at Andrea.

'What's the situation with the online searches on the three of them? Any chat room activity? Are they Facebook friends? Members of the same online club or forum?'

Andrea shook her head. 'I've been through the links on hundreds of search engine pages and found nothing. I've only got three pages left to go through. If I don't find something on one of those, it's highly unlikely there's a connection to find.'

Paolo nodded. 'Stay with it.'

He looked across the room. 'As you all know, the DVDs are the key to being able to charge people over the club activities. If we could find those, Chaz would be back behind bars and the special club members would become likely cellmates. We've searched the club and George's house with no joy.' He sighed. 'It's possible they were destroyed when George discovered Trudy had used the contents to blackmail Montague, but they might still be hidden somewhere. I want you all to dig into every scrap of information you have. Is there anywhere we might have overlooked?'

He half-turned to tap on the board.

'And then there's Baron's murder. Don't forget, we have a sadist to find and whoever that is, the killer has to have a link of some kind to George Baron and, probably, other men who have been tortured in a similar fashion. If we can find out what that connection is, we can probably follow the trail back to George Baron's murderer.'

He noticed a lack of enthusiasm on a couple of faces. It was most marked on the face of Detective Constable Jack Cummings.

'Not keen to find a killer?' Paolo asked.

'It's not that, sir. It's hard to feel outrage on behalf of a victim like George Baron.'

Paolo looked hard at the DC. Jack was the one Paolo suspected of leaving those nasty messages on Dave's desk. He'd never caught him in the act, but knew the man mistakenly saw Dave as a blockage to his own advancement.

'I couldn't care less who the victim is or was. We can't pick and choose who we go after and who we don't. Do you want to live in a country where the government says some people are allowed to get away with murder because they're only killing off the scum? If that's the case, you may not be right for this job. If you honestly feel that way, you're definitely not right for my team. We go after the bad people, regardless of who their victims might be.'

He waited to make sure his words had hit home, pleased to see Jack could no longer look him in the eye.

'Right, I'm off to the PM on George Baron. Dave, I want you with me. The rest of you, keep digging.'

As always during a post mortem, Paolo wished he hadn't elected to attend. It was with some relief he watched Barbara move over to the wash basin to clean up.

'My office?' she said as she turned back towards them.

Paolo nodded and waited with Dave by the door for Barbara to join them. They walked together along the corridor in silence; Paolo forced himself not to ask questions until they were sitting down and Barbara was ready to talk.

'Coffee?' she asked.

Paolo and Dave both nodded.

'Your coffee is wonderful,' Dave said. 'Much better than the revolting stuff we get in the machines back at the station.'

Paolo watched as Barbara expertly manipulated her fancy coffee maker. Capsules in one end, delicious coffee out the other. The shorter hairstyle she'd kept since she'd finished chemo suited her. She looked on the road to recovery, he decided. Not yet back to her old self, but fine to people who didn't know her as well as he did.

As she placed the tray of coffee on her desk, Paolo noticed she was frowning.

'I recognise that look,' he said. 'What is it about this victim that's troubling you?'

'Cause of death,' she said, sitting down and lifting a cup to smell the aroma.

'But isn't that straightforward? You said he had strangulation marks around his throat. If that didn't kill him, what did?'

Barbara took a sip, then put her cup down and stared at them across her desk.

'Suffocation,' she said, 'probably with a pillow. I won't know for sure until I send the microscopic piece of feather I found in his bronchial tubes away for analysis, but it seems likely a feather pillow was the murder weapon.'

'So, let me get this straight,' Paolo said. 'He'd been burned with the tazer, anally raped, strangled, but what actually killed him was a feather pillow?'

She smiled. 'I said *probably* a feather pillow, but definitely suffocation. The rape is odd as well.'

Paolo raised his arms in surrender. 'Everything is odd about this one. Go on; tell me what's particularly odd about the rape?'

'The direction of the thrusts, for one thing. I've been trying to picture the angle in which he must have been held for the wounds to be inflicted and it just doesn't add up. If I place his body in one position, the angle of damage is wrong, but if I put his body into the right position for the angle of damage I can't see how the rapist could get himself into the right place for penetration.'

Paolo shook his head. 'Sorry, Barbara, you've lost me.'

She picked up her phone and opened the cover to form an L shape, then placed it face down on the edge of the desk with the flap hanging straight down towards the floor.

'Let's say George Baron had been tied to a structure, a table of some sort, which he was, judging by the marks on his wrists and ankles. That would leave him in this position, with his legs hanging down towards the floor like the flap of my phone. With me so far?'

Paolo and Dave both nodded.

'Right, well the angle of damage, the angle of thrust, if you like, should be along this trajectory.' She pointed with her finger in a line level with the back of the phone. 'But it isn't. The angle of damage follows a downward line. The only way to get that line would be to lift his rear end like this.'

She picked up the phone case by the join where it hung over the edge of the table and raised it so that the top of the phone was still touching the desk, but the corner of the L shape was in the air.

'I'm not saying it's impossible, but how would the rapist achieve that?'

Paolo smiled. 'I can hear in your voice you have an alternative suggestion.'

She nodded. 'Yes, and it's consistent with the extensive internal injuries inflicted. I think the main damage was caused by a very large penis-shaped solid object inserted by hand.'

'So no normal penetration?' Paolo asked. 'Please note, I'm using the word normal selectively here.'

Barbara shrugged. 'Impossible to say. I found traces of lubricant, which implies penile penetration, but obviously no semen to test for DNA.'

Paolo groaned.

'Now comes the good news,' Barbara said. 'I was able to lift traces of foreign matter from the depressions on his throat. I'll send them away for analysis.'

Paolo smiled. 'That's the most positive thing I've heard in ages. Can you give us an estimated time of death?'

She nodded. 'Judging by the state of decomposition, I'd say he'd been dead approximately a week when we found him.'

Paolo thought about the timing for a moment. 'So that would mean he died about three days after the last time anyone saw him. Thanks, Barbara, you've been a great help, as always. And thank you for the coffee.'

As Paolo waited for Dave to carry the tray back to the coffee machine, he had the feeling of being watched. He turned quickly to find Barbara looking at him as if she was sending a silent message.

He waited, but she shook her head and glanced in Dave's direction. Whatever it was, she obviously wasn't going to say it in front of an audience.

Paolo arrived back at his office still wondering what Barbara had wanted to get across to him. He had a strong suspicion it was to do with what she'd murmured when she was floating in and out of consciousness after her operation the previous year.

As he walked into the main room, Andrea stood up, a look of suppressed excitement on her face.

'I think we might finally have found something, sir.'

Paolo walked over to her desk. 'Really? I could do with some good news. What've you got for me?'

She turned a printed page towards him. 'This blog, Nemesis in Action, is encrypted. I've tried everything I know to get into it, but haven't been able to break the codes. I've sent a copy of the details over to Mike. I hope that's okay?'

Paolo lifted the page. 'I don't mind if it will help us solve the case, but why are you so excited about it? I don't see anything here that seems related to anything we're working on.'

'Sorry, sir, I should have explained, but I was so pleased with myself, I've told you the wrong way round. You know I was working on the searches? The Nemesis in Action link was the final one that came up when I searched under George Baron's name, but without any explanatory text. When I clicked on the link, I found I couldn't get access. It could turn out to be nothing, but in there somewhere must be a mention of George's name, otherwise why would it come up on a search? Also the title of the site is pretty telling, don't you think? Sounds to me like someone with a mission.'

Paolo wondered for a moment what she meant, then made the connection. 'Nemesis! Ah, you think this is the site of someone dishing out retribution? It could be, but don't get your hopes up too much. It could equally be some weird bondage club members' list.'

'I hadn't thought of that. You're right; I've jumped to a conclusion that might not be there.'

He saw the deflated slump of her shoulders and wished he'd kept that thought to himself.

'But you could be right. All I'm saying is, don't pin all your hopes on this. Let's see what Mike can find out before we celebrate.' He smiled. 'Good work, though, Andrea. I'd have given up long before, but you kept at it and I hope you're going to get your reward. Talking of research, what have you found out about Chaz's prison record?'

'He's only been inside the once, sir. That was for GBH, section eighteen, not twenty.'

189

'He intended to cause harm? That's interesting. How long did he get?'

Andrea checked her notes. 'He put in a guilty plea and was handed down ten years, but was out in five. The interesting thing for me was who he shared a cell with for part of his term. Frank Baron.'

'Yes, very interesting,' Paolo said. 'The same Frank Baron we've been unable to locate to inform him of his younger brother's death?'

She nodded. 'One and the same, sir.'

'Well, as Frank is abroad, destination unknown, we're not going to find out anything about Chaz from that source. We can only assume that's how George and Chaz found each other, via Frank. Who did Chaz hurt so badly with intent?'

'I've got the victim's name, but not the back story. I'm waiting for more information to come through, but from what I have so far, I think Chaz is fortunate he wasn't up on a murder charge. He very nearly killed the man.'

Chapter Twenty-five

Paolo was busy collating crime figures when he heard a knock on his office door. He looked up to find Andrea, Dave and CC waiting.

'By the looks on your faces, we've got some news at last. Don't stand there, come in and share it with me.'

Dave walked over to pull up a third chair, while Andrea and CC moved the ones in front of Paolo's desk to make room for him.

'Judging by the fact that all three of you are here, I take it the news is outstanding.'

Andrea nodded. 'CC and Dave haven't heard it yet, sir. I've just received a file from Mike and thought it would save time if I read it out to all of you at the same time.'

Paolo nodded. 'That makes sense. What has our friendly IT man found for us?'

'You remember that Nemesis in Action site I found but couldn't access?'

Paolo nodded.

'Mike has managed to unencrypt some of the pages.'

'Why not all of them?' Dave asked.

Andrea turned to answer him. 'It's a blog and each page has been individually encrypted to stop search engine bots running over them to pick up key words.'

'But then how did Google pick up George Baron's name? If the page was encrypted, the bots shouldn't have been able to get into the site,' said CC, sitting on the other side of Andrea.

Paolo had the bizarre feeling of watching a tennis match as Andrea turned in the opposite direction to answer CC.

'Mike seems to think Nemesis either forgot to encrypt the page and did it later, giving the bot time to find the site. Or, and he thinks this is less likely but still possible, it was a complete fluke that the bot ran over the site before Nemesis had time to put the encryption in place. He says the fact that it was the very last entry on all the searches I pulled on George Baron's name would have been because there were no backlinks or—'

Seeing in Andrea's eyes the zeal he'd last spotted in Mike's, Paolo interrupted her. 'So does he think there is much more to find, other than the pages he's unencrypted so far?'

Andrea nodded. 'He says there are loads more, but thought he should get this information to us as soon as possible. It's a pity we couldn't have him here with us permanently, sir.'

Remembering Mike's comment to him as he was leaving, Paolo wondered if Mike had been working on Andrea to plead his case for him.

'Unfortunately, our budget doesn't run to our own IT department. Not even if it only consists of one man.'

'I know, sir. Shall I read the last entry on the site?'

'We're all ears,' he said.

Nemesis in Action Blog
Day Two – George Baron

I entered the room to find the coward still whimpering and begging to be released. He hadn't shown any such mercy to Trudy Chappell, so why he thought I'd extend any to him was beyond me.

I picked up the tazer and ran it over his back. I hadn't even fired it before he pissed himself with fear. Of them all, this one was the weakest.

I placed the tazer between his legs and he began thrashing his head from side to side.

'Don't,' he begged. 'I'll give you anything. Please, oh dear fucking God, please don't.'

Calling on God to help an animal like himself? That really made me mad, so I let him have a burst of pain. He screamed until his throat must have been raw. I toyed with the idea of a second blast, but decided against it. It was better to go for the real pain instead of playing with him.

As I prepared for another penetration, I heard him gasp, but didn't think anything of it until I looked up to find him looking back at me. In his thrashing, he'd managed to work the blindfold loose and one eye was exposed.

'You!' he said.

I knew then he had to die, but didn't feel bad about it. Vermin should be eradicated.

I've never tried to strangle a man before and was surprised at how difficult it was. I found in the end that I simply couldn't do it, but neither could I let him live. I left him wheezing and gasping on the table and went to find a pillow.

When I returned and lifted his head to put the pillow underneath his face, he smiled and thanked me. The piece of garbage actually smiled at me because he thought I was making him more comfortable.

'Let me go,' he said. 'Let me go home and I promise I won't give you away. I could use you in one of my clubs.'

How dare he? How dare he put my vocation on a par with his disgusting clubs? I took both sides of the pillow and pulled them taut behind his head, then pressed down with my body to suffocate him. He reared up and the pillow shifted enough for him to be able to breathe, so I put pulled the edges of the pillow even tighter and smothered him until he was completely still. Even then, I didn't move until I was certain he was dead.

I usually put them back where they'd committed their crimes, but I could hardly dump him in the car park of his club and hope to get away with it. Not with all the police activity there. I had to think hard about the right place to leave him and then

I remembered about the illegal dump site on the way out of Bradchester.

Garbage dumped in a fly tipping site. Perfect!

'Bloody hell,' Paolo breathed. 'Is that all we've got or is there more?'

'There's more, sir. Quite a few pages of it. Obviously, I haven't had time to read all of the stuff Mike sent me, but I've pulled out all the names I could find. The one before George Baron is Jason Corbett. The online diary says his body was dumped at the canal, so I think that might be the coma patient. I haven't had chance yet to check for certain, but I'd be amazed it if wasn't him. It says in the diary that he'd given a false name in the club where Nemesis picked him up. But then Nemesis goes on to say lots of rapists do that.'

'Excellent work, Andrea. I agree with you about the man in hospital. What other names have you come up with?'

She referred to her notes. 'Only another two so far, sir: Colin Jameson and Glen Scott.'

Paolo wrote down the two names. 'Andrea, I want you to stick with the online diary. Read through the pages as and when Mike sends them to you. Make a list of any other names you uncover. Also, find out from Mike if there is any way of tracing who is behind the blog. It would be great if there was a nice big sign in cyber space saying the killer lives here, but I don't suppose it's going to be that easy.'

Andrea shook her head. 'I'd already asked that question, sir. Mike is doing his best to trace the originator of the blog, but as all the information is encrypted, it's going to take a while.'

Paolo nodded to show he'd understood, then looked across at CC. 'While Andrea is trawling through the Nemesis blog, I'd like you to take over researching the background of these three men, plus any others Andrea turns up. Look into their lives and history. Find out what they've done, or seem to have done to raise the ire of this Nemesis character.'

Paolo stood up. 'Dave, call Dr Brownlow and find out if the two patients he knows about are Colin Jameson and Glen Scott.

If the answer is yes, get their addresses. If Dr Brownlow bleats, tell him this is now a murder investigation and that we would have no difficulty in getting the necessary permission to access the files. All we want are the addresses, so if he wants to preserve his patients' medical confidentiality, he'd be better off cooperating with us.'

He smiled. At last they had something concrete to go on.

'When you've got the addresses, we're going to pay them a visit to find out why they've never reported the attacks. If they underwent anything as bad as Jason Corbett and George Baron, they must have gone through hell. While you're finding out where they live, Dave, I'm going upstairs. The Chief has been giving me grief for weeks over this. It'll be a relief to tell him we finally have a breakthrough.'

In the car, on the way to visit the first of the two names uncovered on the Nemesis in Action blog, Paolo asked Dave if Dr Brownlow had put up much resistance to giving out the two addresses.

'He wasn't keen, sir, but once I pointed out to him that we would be able to get full access to the files in any event, he decided it was in his patients' interest to keep us sweet so that he could protect the contents of their medical records.'

Paolo nodded. 'I thought he'd see sense.' He hesitated, but had to ask. 'Have the idiots back at the station given up on baiting you?'

Dave's shoulders visibly tensed and Paolo felt the car judder slightly as Dave's grip on the steering wheel tightened.

'I'd rather not discuss it, if you don't mind, sir. I'm just going to have to prove my worth and that's all there is to it.'

'Don't think you've got anything to prove to me, Dave, because you haven't. You're one of my most valued team members.'

Dave laughed, but there was little humour in it. 'Maybe that's part of the problem, sir. A few of the others think you're giving me preferential treatment. Anyway, as I said, I don't want to talk about something that will only get me riled up when there's bugger all I can do about it.'

Paolo nodded. 'Fair enough. Where are we headed to first?'

'Tudor Close. It's part of that new development right on the outskirts of town. Funnily enough, we passed through it the other day going out to the fly tipping site where we found George Baron's body. Maybe that's how the killer knew about the site. Could be that Nemesis had been out this way before. Didn't Andrea say Nemesis dumped the torture victims back where they'd committed whatever crimes they were supposed to have committed?'

'She did say that. From what she'd read so far, what impression did you get of the victims?'

Dave shrugged. 'Just that Nemesis had decided to play judge and jury to rapists, or at least to people Nemesis believed were rapists.'

'My thoughts exactly. So, if that's the case, the next questions is this: how did Nemesis know?'

Dave turned into Tudor Close and slowed the car before answering. 'Know what, sir?'

'Know who to pick up and torture. How did this Nemesis character know that any of them were rapists? Most of the time, even *we* don't know who the rapists are on our patch, because so many rapes go unreported. If we don't have them on our radar, how can Nemesis be so certain of picking up the right people? Where is the information coming from?'

Dave pointed to a semi-detached house on the other side of the road. 'I can't answer any of those questions, sir, but that's the house we need. Number sixty-three Tudor Close,' he said as he pulled up opposite the property.

Paolo got out of the car, still mulling over the various ways someone outside the force could get access to information on rapists, or, more to the point, suspected rapists. Were the men guilty, or picked up on someone's whim?

They crossed the street and walked up the short drive to the house. As Dave rang the bell, Paolo had a look around. Tudor Close was typical of many of the newer housing estates. Semis, with small, but well-kept, gardens in front and probably a larger version behind. It didn't look like the type of street that saw much in the way of discord, other than the neighbourly type such as "his hedge is encroaching on my property". Mind you, Paolo thought, some of those disputes could turn very nasty.

Before he could follow this stray thought, the door opened to reveal a harassed woman with a toddler clinging to her leg.

'If it's religious, I don't believe, if you're selling I don't want any, if it's anything else, I don't have time,' she said, preparing to close the door.

Paolo held up his warrant card. 'I'm Detective Inspector Paolo Sterling and this is Detective Sergeant Dave Johnson. Is Colin Jameson in?'

She looked suspicious, but nodded. 'He is. What do you want with him?'

'If we could just have a few words with him in private, we promise not to disturb you for long.'

She remained blocking the way, but reached down to pick up the toddler who'd started to cry.

'What's it about?'

'Are you Mrs Jameson?'

She nodded.

Paolo smiled. 'I'm sorry, I can't tell you at the moment why we need to speak to him, but I can promise that he isn't in any trouble if that would put your mind at rest.'

She thought for a moment and then stood aside. 'He's in the back room, but please don't mention you're police officers. If you get him worked up, I won't be able to calm him down again. You'd have to take him to the psychiatric ward. I can't go through all that again.'

'All what?' Paolo asked.

She shook her head. 'Nothing. Just don't mention anything to do with the police or get him worked up, please. It upsets little Ben. Doesn't it, my darling?' she said, nuzzling into the child's neck.

Paolo and Dave walked along the short hall to the room that had probably been intended as a dining room by the builders, but was clearly in use as a family room. Opening onto the kitchen area, it was full of children's educational toys, building blocks, soft animals and the type of larger toy a child of Ben's age would be able to push around while learning to walk unaided. Against one of the walls was an old, but comfortable looking, sofa. Adjacent to it was a matching armchair. Slouched in the chair, eyes fixed on the flat screen television screwed to the wall, was a man, possibly a few years older than the woman who'd let them in but not come through with them.

'Colin Jameson?' Paolo said.

The man briefly took his eyes from the screen and nodded before turning back again.

'Mr Jameson, would you mind if I turned that off for a few minutes?'

'Why?'

'So that I can ask you a few questions.'

Colin muted the sound, but continued to watch the antics of two people on a confrontational chat show who'd been yelling at each other. A glance at the screen told Paolo the couple were still yelling, but at least he didn't now have to compete with the noise.

'Mr Jameson,' Paolo said, moving over to the sofa to sit down, 'it's important I have your full attention. I'm investigating a murder and I think you might be able to help me with my enquiries.'

Reluctantly, Colin picked up the remote again and flicked the off switch.

'Who are you?' he asked.

'My name's Paolo Sterling and this is Dave Johnson,' Paolo said, bearing in mind Mrs Jameson's request, he didn't mention their rank. 'I'm sorry if this is going to remind you of a distressing incident in your past, but does the name Nemesis—'

Colin sprang to his feet, shaking from head to foot. 'Get out!' he yelled, holding his arms tight around his body and rocking from side to side. 'Get out! Get out! Out! Get out! Now! Get out!'

His wife came running into the room, still holding her child.

She put him down and reached out for Colin, enclosing him in her arms.

'What did you do?' she yelled over the sound of her husband screaming for Paolo and Dave to leave. 'What did you say? He hasn't been like this for months.'

Paolo watched as she soothed the shattered man, admiring the way she talked him down from his emotionally distraught state. As she settled him into the armchair and switched on the television and sound, Colin began a different chant.

'Don't tell the police. Nemesis is watching. Nemesis will know. Don't tell the police. Nemesis is watching. Nemesis will know.'

Mrs Jameson smoothed the hair from her husband's brow. 'Nobody will tell the police. Don't worry, you're safe now.'

While she was calming him down, the little boy came and took hold of his father's hand.

'See, here's little Ben to keep you company while I show these gentlemen out,' she said, signalling with her head to Paolo and Dave they should move towards the door.

Colin lifted his son onto his lap and cuddled him. The boy put his arms around his father's neck and snuggled down to watch television with him. Paolo had difficulty believing this was a rapist, but knew that very often quite ordinary people were guilty of extraordinary crimes.

They didn't have to wait long by the front door before Mrs Jameson came out to join them, carefully closing the door to the family room as she did so.

'I need to know what you said to Colin,' she demanded, but so quietly Paolo had to lean forward to hear her. 'If he goes into one of his panic attacks, I need to know what brought it on so that I can deal with it.'

He kept his own voice low. 'I asked him what the name Nemesis meant to him.'

She nodded. 'I guessed it was that. If you'd told me what you wanted in the first place, we could have avoided all this. He was picked up one night in a club, he has no idea who by, and tortured for nearly three days. When he called me from the hospital he was so damaged, I couldn't recognise him.'

'He'd been beaten?' Paolo asked.

She shook her head. 'No, I don't mean I didn't recognise him physically. It was the mental change. Before the attack, he was outgoing and fun to be with. Afterwards, well, you've seen what he is now and this is a massive improvement on how he was when he first came home. He still has nightmares and screams out the name Nemesis sometimes, but not as often.'

'You say he doesn't know who attacked him, but he must have seen how many people there were. Your husband is not a small man. It would take more than one to overpower him.'

She scowled. 'You'd imagine so, wouldn't you? I think someone slipped him something in his drink. He'd gone with a group of friends from work, back when he had a job,' she added, the bitterness in her voice almost tangible. 'It was a stag do. They'd all had too much to drink. Colin remembers being in the club, then nothing until he woke up in some weirdo's torture chamber. I don't know what exactly happened to him while he was away, but whatever it was, it's destroyed him. He was dumped in Bradchester Park and now refuses to go anywhere near the place. It used to be where we went with Ben, every Sunday, but not anymore.'

Paolo hesitated. The family seemed to have suffered enough, but he had to ask.

'Mrs Jameson, has your husband ever been accused of rape?'

'Are you mad? No, never. Colin is the gentlest man. Even now, even after all he's been through, he'd never hurt another person. What made you ask such a stupid question?'

'We think there may be a connection between men accused of rape and these attacks. Your husband wasn't the first and there have been a few since.'

Paolo watched as her face changed.

'Oh my God, you don't think whoever did this to Colin was after Brent?'

'Brent?'

200

'Brent Harrison. He works, or rather worked, with Colin. He was on that stag do and they're about the same height and colouring. It would be easy to mix the two of them up in a dark club.'

Paolo waited until Dave has his notebook ready. 'And Brent Harrison was accused of rape?'

She nodded. 'Yes, but not convicted. I'm not sure what happened in court, but he was cleared of all charges.'

'From your tone of voice, you sound as if you have reservations.'

She looked at Dave before answering. 'Don't write this down. I've got enough on my plate without that bastard after me, but when he was accused, I was sure he was guilty. I would never allow myself to be alone in a room with him. He's one of those men who keeps making suggestive jokes, really unpleasant ones that make you feel dirty and just a bit scared, but then accuses you of having no sense of humour when you complain. He always feels me up as he goes past and then turns it back on me if I say anything.'

By this stage tears were streaming down her face. 'Are you telling me that my lovely husband's life was ruined because some nutter thought he was Brent bloody Harrison?'

Paolo had no answer to give other than the truth. 'I'm so sorry, but I think that could be the case.'

Paolo and Dave drove in silence to the next address. How cruel could life be? Someone who probably was guilty, even if cleared, of rape, gets off without any penalty. An innocent man, who just happens to have a passing resemblance, ends up mentally scarred for life. Whatever Nemesis was up to, surely ruining the lives of blameless people wasn't part of the plan. Paolo wondered if Nemesis had ever realised the error. Probably not, he thought, remembering what Andrea had mentioned about Nemesis never being surprised to find the victims had different names to the ones given in the clubs.

'We're here, sir,' Dave said, pulling up outside a dingy terraced house in one of Bradchester's less salubrious areas.

Paolo was glad to have his thoughts interrupted. It was pointless to speculate on Nemesis's thoughts and emotions. Whoever it was had to be stopped and brought to justice before any more lives were ruined.

Before Dave could knock, the door opened. In stark contrast to Mrs Jameson's quiet dignity, the woman before them looked ready to punch someone.

'What the fuck do you want? You're old Bill, ain't ya? Well, you're too fuckin' late, so you've wasted your time.'

Paolo showed his warrant card, not that it was necessary in the face of her conviction they were the police.

'Mrs Scott? We need to speak to your husband.'

She laughed. 'Then "old a fucking séance. That's the only way you'll get to talk to that bastard. 'E topped 'imself four months back an' good fuckin' riddance is what I say."'

Chapter Twenty-six

The frustration Paolo felt as every line of enquiry seemed to meet a dead end was growing day by day. Mike was still tracking down the site owner's details, but that was proving harder than he'd expected. The server provider was proving obstructive and quoting data protection. It was going to take a warrant to get the information from that source. In the meantime, Mike was working on hacking through the encryption to find out for himself who'd set up the blog.

Paolo had given Brent Harrison's name to CC in place of Colin Jameson's and she was looking into the rape trial. Until she or Mike came up with some new information, he was stuck in a corner.

And then there was Derrick Walden's murder still unsolved. Had he been killed to stop him from passing on information to do with the Nemesis case, or had Derrick wanted to tell him something totally unconnected? The lipstick on the plaque mystery was also still outstanding, but Paolo really couldn't bring himself to get overly worked up about that when so many other, more important, issues were screaming for his attention.

Thinking about Derrick reminded Paolo there were a few people at the centre he'd been meaning to follow up on. Arbnor, for one, had raised a few concerns in Paolo's mind. He turned up in strange places and definitely looked shifty at times. Then there was the weird atmosphere between Derrick and April. What had that been all about? Shutting the file of crime reports he was supposed to be working on, he decided to go to the youth centre and find out.

He went out to the main office to find Dave and then remembered he was off getting measured for a morning suit. Paolo had a mental image of Dave's face as his future mother-in-law marshalled him into obeying her latest orders. He could only hope for Dave and Rebecca's sake that she backed off after the wedding. If Rebecca's mother continued to interfere once they were married, Paolo couldn't see a happy future for the newlyweds.

Andrea was still deep into the unencrypted pages sent over daily by Mike, so Paolo didn't want to disturb her. CC, too, was hard at work reading through trial transcripts and trying to find links between the victims. Paolo shrugged, he had no choice but to request Detective Constable Jack Cummings' company. Maybe going out with Paolo would finally shut off the man's griping about nepotism and Paolo's supposed favouritism towards Dave.

'Jack, I'm going to the youth centre. I want you to come with me to take notes and keep your eyes and ears open.'

'Yes, sir, what am I looking for exactly, sir?'

Paolo smiled at the enthusiasm. Maybe he'd misjudged Jack and the man just wanted to be useful.

'You're not looking for anything in particular. Just keep an open mind and note down anything that strikes you as odd or out of place. You know, snippets of conversation, people where they shouldn't be, that sort of thing.'

Jack nodded. 'Shall I drive?'

Paolo shook his head. He'd heard from others how hair raising it could be as a passenger with Jack driving.

'No, we'll go in my car this time.'

As Paolo pulled into the youth centre car park, he swore this would be the first and last time he took Jack out with him. For the full twenty minutes of the journey the man had laughed so heartily at Paolo's jokes he'd almost choked, agreed with every word out of Paolo's mouth and generally done everything bar lick Paolo's shoes.

204

And he might even have done that, Paolo thought sourly, if he'd been able to get his head under the steering wheel. Twenty minutes spent in Jack's company was nineteen minutes too long.

The first sight that greeted Paolo as he parked the car was Clementine Towers striding towards him. He groaned. As if his day wasn't bad enough, he didn't think he could bear listening to a rant from her. Maybe he could palm her off on Jack. As the evil thought entered his head, he smiled.

'Jack, the woman bearing down on us is going to try to pin me in a corner. I want you to head her off.'

'Yes, sir!'

The response came back so smartly, Paolo missed Dave's irreverent sense of humour. He'd have come back with a witty quip about not wanting to steal Paolo's limelight, or upset one of his fan club. He strode on towards the youth centre's front doors, but whatever Jack had said to Clementine Towers clearly hadn't been successful because he heard her calling out to him.

'Detective Inspector! Detective Inspector Sterling!'

He couldn't ignore her without being rude, so turned round and forced a smile to his lips.

'Miss Towers, what can I do for you today?'

She tottered towards him on heels so high she was in danger of breaking an ankle. Today's outfit consisted of a mid-calf purple skirt topped by a bright orange V-neck jersey. Paolo wondered if he could get away with putting on sunglasses to minimise the glare.

'It's what I can do for you, Detective Inspector. There has been more wickedness –'

'Miss Towers, I have to go inside to speak to some people. Perhaps you could tell my Detective Constable all about it?'

She shook her head, sending her grey hair flying in all directions. 'No, no, no! The information I have is far too important. It needs your attention. It would be better going to someone even higher up, but –'

Paolo smiled. 'I would love to give you my full attention, but not right at this moment. Perhaps you could come to the station with your information?'

'No, I'll wait here for you. How long will you be?'

Resisting the urge to shout at her, Paolo shrugged. 'I'm not sure. I have to interview a couple of people.'

'Who?' she demanded.

'Miss Towers, that is none of your business,' Paolo said, finally losing patience.

He spun on his heels and headed towards the centre, closely followed by Jack. When they were inside, Paolo turned to Jack.

'Miss Towers is the self-appointed guardian of Bradchester's reading material. Left to her, Enid Blyton would be the only choice of books for everyone aged between eight and eighty – and even then she'd want to take out the racier bits.'

'I don't think there are any racy bits in her stories, sir.'

Paolo smiled. 'Believe me, Miss Towers could find some. Right, let's go and have a chat to April.'

Halfway up the stairs, they met Arbnor coming down. As they exchanged greetings, Paolo recalled April saying Arbnor only oversaw the rooms downstairs. He was about to call him back to ask where he'd been, but decided to find him after he'd spoken to April. Maybe Arbnor had been to see her, which meant he was fully entitled to be up there.

The door to her office was open and April was behind her desk, head down and oblivious to the world. Tapping on the door frame to get her attention, Paolo waited for her to look up. When she did, he went in and introduced Jack.

She grinned. 'What have you done with the handsome one? Hiding him away from temptation?'

Paolo laughed and decided to keep that gem to share with Dave.

'No, he's busy doing something else today.'

Hearing what sounded like a snort, he turned to glare at Jack, who looked too guiltless to be innocent.

Bringing his attention back to April, Paolo concentrated on the reason for being there, but promised himself he'd have a stronger word with Jack later.

'April, on previous occasions you've mentioned Derrick Walden poking his nose into things that didn't concern him. I know he used to come up here and irritate you by trying to find out snippets of information. He was due to come to the station on the morning his body was discovered. Any idea what that might have been about?'

She shook her head. 'I wish I could help you, but it could have been anything. I've never known anyone as nosey as Derrick was. I caught him rummaging in Montague's desk once, but when I called him on it, he laughed and said he just liked to know what was going on.' She shrugged. 'For all I know, he could have gone through my desk as well without my knowledge.'

Paolo glanced over to make sure Jack was taking notes and then felt bad for doubting him. The man was a trained police officer, after all.

'Do you think Derrick did that to anyone else?'

April laughed. 'I don't know for sure, but I would imagine so. I don't think he could help himself. For him, it wasn't snooping, it was gathering ammunition to use if he needed it.'

'Blackmail?'

She put her head on one side, clearly thinking about it. 'No,' she said, 'I wouldn't say that. More to use as leverage. He wanted to know people's secrets so that he knew how their minds worked. If he knew that, he could play them to his advantage.' She laughed again. 'He was always grateful to anyone who helped him, even if they only did it because he'd manipulated them into doing it. I've made him sound more calculating than he probably was.'

Paolo smiled. 'It sounds to me like you've understood him. Tell me, he was very grateful to Montague for giving him the coach's position here. Do you think he manipulated that situation.'

She shrugged. 'I have no idea and the only two people who can answer that are both dead. I miss Montague, but life moves on. If there's nothing else I can do for you, Paolo, I need to get back to work. I'll have a new boss once the council sort out who is going to take over here and I want to make sure everything is in place for whoever it might be.'

'One last thing before I leave you in peace, did Arbnor come up to visit you?'

'No,' she said. 'Should he? Is there something I should know about?'

Paolo stood up. 'No, nothing really. I passed Arbnor on the stairs and remembered you telling me he didn't have any duties up here.'

She made to rise, but Paolo waved her back down again.

'Don't worry. I'll go and find out what he's up to. If it's something you need to know about, I'll come up and tell you.'

She smiled. 'Thanks, Paolo. With everything that's gone on here, I'm up to my eyes in work.'

Paolo signalled to Jack to get up, said goodbye to April, and went in search of the caretaker. On the way downstairs, Paolo decided not to pussyfoot around with Arbnor. He'd arranged the job for him and felt responsible for his conduct. If he was doing anything wrong, which seemed likely, given that his job requirements ended at the foot of the stairs, then Paolo wanted to put a stop to it. He found him in his tiny room, next door to the empty swimming coach's office. The job had been advertised since Derrick's untimely demise, but so far there hadn't been any takers. With a suicide and a murder connected to the place, it wasn't surprising that word had got round this wasn't a healthy place to work.

Arbnor looked up when Paolo and Jack came in. If guilt had a definite expression, Paolo thought, then Arbnor was displaying it. Paolo went straight on the attack.

'What were you doing upstairs? And don't give me some line about looking after the rooms, or visiting April, because I know you were doing neither of those things.'

Arbnor didn't answer. Dropping his head, he wrung his hands as if by doing so he could wipe away whatever secret he was hiding.

208

Paolo sat down and waved his hand at Jack to do the same.

'Arbnor, stop standing there looking the picture of shame. Sit down and tell me what it is you've been doing. I know you're up to something.'

Keeping his eyes firmly on the floor, Arbnor shuffled over to his chair and collapsed into it.

'I'm sorry,' he said.

'You might well be sorry, Arbnor, but I need to know what it is you're sorry about.'

'I've betrayed your trust in me. When you arranged for me to work here, I was so very, very grateful and now I've let you down.'

Resisting an urge to shake Arbnor till his teeth rattled, Paolo waited for more to come. He didn't have to wait long.

'It is because my child is sick. My baby in Albania.'

Paolo glanced over at Jack. He looked as confused as Paolo felt.

'Sorry, Arbnor, you're going to have to explain. You've lost me there.'

'I send all my money home to my wife. I keep very little for myself, but my daughter is very sick and I need to talk to my wife. How can I do this when I have no money for phone calls to Albania?'

A light bulb lit up in Paolo's mind. 'You've been using the youth centre's phones to call home.'

Arbnor nodded. 'Please, I beg you, don't tell anyone. I need this job to keep a roof over the head of my wife and daughter. My wife cannot work because we have no one to look after Besjana.'

'That's your daughter's name? It's pretty,' Paolo said, when Arbnor nodded. 'Look, I can see your dilemma, but you can't just use the centre's telephone system without permission. That's theft.'

Arbnor's head shot up. 'No! I would never steal. Never! You cannot think that of me.'

Paolo knew Arbnor would feel that way, most people seemed to. It wasn't stealing if it was just a phone call, even though that was taking money out of a business. That was the same as saying it wasn't stealing if you took paperclips, elastic bands, toilet rolls, reams of

209

paper or envelopes home from work. It was amazing how people could delude themselves into thinking such things didn't count, while at the same time condemning others for robbing banks.

Looking at the distraught man in front of him, Paolo knew he wouldn't report his misuse of the telephone system, but he couldn't allow it to continue either. He reached into his pocket and pulled out his wallet.

'Arbnor, here's twenty pounds. I want you to go and get a pay as you go card that allows cheap overseas call rates. Until your daughter is well again, come to me each time the credit is getting low. I'll fund your phone calls until Besjana is on her feet again. OK?'

Tears filled Arbnor's eyes as he reached out to take the money. 'You are a good man. A very good man. I can never thank you enough.'

'You could say thank you by telling me who drowned Derrick Walden,' Paolo said.

'But I don't know!' Arbnor replied, a hunted look on his face.

Paolo smiled. 'I know. I was being flippant.' Seeing a look of confusion on Arbnor's face, Paolo explained what flippant meant. 'I wish someone did know something though. We've come to a dead-end with that enquiry.'

'Then why not ask Mr Fletcher Simpson?'

Paolo thought he'd misheard, but Arbnor looked serious and repeated the name when asked.

'Why would I ask him?'

'Because he was here earlier that day. I could hear through the wall, he was having a big, big argument with Derrick.'

'What about?' Paolo said, sitting forward.

Arbnor shook his head. 'I don't know. I tried not to listen, but Mr Simpson was very angry. When the argument went on for a long time, I became very embarrassed and went to do my rounds.'

Paolo stood up. 'Thank you, Arbnor. You've been very helpful. Don't forget, when you need more credit for the phone, come to me. Don't use the phones here.'

'Thank you. I am sorry I let you down.'

Paolo grinned. 'Just don't do it again. Come on, Jack. We've got another visit to make.'

As they left the youth centre, Paolo saw Clementine was still outside. He tried to make it to the car unobserved, but she looked up and spotted him. As she tottered across, Paolo was already formulating what he needed to say, so spoke before she had chance to.

'Miss Towers, I'm really sorry, but I have to rush to interview someone. Really, it's better if you call the station and speak to someone there.'

'But, it's important. I have to speak to you about the licentious behaviour I've observed.'

'Call the station. Someone there will attend to your concerns,' he said, getting into the car and barely waiting for Jack to fasten his seatbelt before pulling away.

Chapter Twenty-seven

During the drive to Fletcher Simpson's office, Paolo was struck by the difference in Jack's attitude. From being fawning and over anxious to please, he was silent and almost surly in his only response when addressed. Paolo decided he preferred the silent sulk to the effusive toadying, but wondered what had caused the change in him.

As he pulled into the car park, Jack had the car door open before Paolo had brought the car to a stop.

'Have you got a problem with something, Jack?'

'Well, since you've asked, yes. You let that man get away with running up international call charges and then rewarded him by giving him money to get a prepaid phone!'

Paolo smiled. 'Did you not listen to his story? His little girl is seriously ill and he sends all his money home. I know what he did was wrong, but I'll pay the phone charges at the centre so that no one loses out by it.'

'Why? What's Arbnor to you?'

Paolo shook his head. 'He's a fellow human being in difficulties. Isn't that enough?'

Jack shrugged. 'He could always go back to Albania if he needed to be close to his family.'

'Where there's no work for people like him? Like you, I have a good job and a roof over my head. I happen to know Arbnor is dossing down on the floor with half a dozen others who are doing all they can to look after their families back home.' Paolo paused for breath, determined to calm down before he began yelling. In a more measured tone, he continued, 'I can afford to be generous. It's only a few quid. Come on, we're not going to see eye to eye on this, so let's put it to one side.'

And please, God, thought Paolo, don't let me put myself in the position of having to take Jack out with me ever again!

By the time they were standing next to the waterfall wall, Paolo had his temper back under control. He shouldn't have lost it with Jack as he did, but the man would try the patience of a . . . Paolo laughed inwardly. No way was he a saint. Determined to make amends, he pointed to the waterfall feature as it began to slide across.

'Pretty spectacular, isn't it.'

Jack nodded, but didn't speak. Oh well, Paolo thought, at least I tried. When the same woman appeared who'd helped Paolo and Dave on the previous visit, he smiled and asked to speak to Fletcher Simpson.

'I'll just call up and ask him if he has any time free, but I think he has meetings all afternoon.'

Paolo smiled. 'Perhaps you could let him know it is in connection with a murder enquiry and I'm prepared to stay here until he can spare me a few minutes.'

He watched the woman's eyes grow large at the words murder enquiry. She hurried back to her sanctuary on the far side of the waterfall and picked up the phone. Paolo couldn't hear the words, but from her body language he could tell she had first been told to tell them to come back at some other time and then she must have repeated Paolo's words, because she listened, nodded and put the phone down. By the smile on her face, Paolo knew what she was going to say before she got the words out.

'Mr Simpson can spare you a few minutes if you would like to go up,' she said.

When they reached the top of the stairs, Fletcher Simpson was already waiting for them.

'Come into the boardroom,' he said. 'I'm expecting visitors at any moment and I'm not sure how they would react to having police in my office when they arrived.'

He held the door open for Paolo and Jack to pass through and then closed it.

'Now,' he said. 'What's all this nonsense about helping you with a murder enquiry? I don't know any murder victims and I certainly don't know any murderers.'

Paolo pulled out a chair from the polished mahogany board-room table and sat down before answering.

'But you do know a murder victim, Fletcher. You know, or rather knew, Derrick Walden.'

Paolo had expected Fletcher to deny knowledge of the dead man, but that wasn't what happened. To his amazement, Simpson laughed.

'You find his murder amusing?'

'Not that, no. What I find amusing is you trying to turn a suicide into a murder. The papers have only reported it as a suicide.'

'Do you still believe everything you read in the press, Fletcher? And you the owner of one of our very own gutter rags that couldn't print the truth even by accident?'

Fletcher's smile slipped just enough to let Paolo know he'd scored a hit.

'We deliberately allowed the press to think it was an accident. The fact that it was reported as a suicide was something over which we had no control. However, there is no doubt in my mind, Derrick Walden was murdered.'

A wary look settled on Fletcher's face. 'And you've come to me about this why?'

Paolo put his arms on the polished wood and leaned forward. 'Because, it seems you might have been one of the last people to see him alive. Would you like to tell us about your trip to the youth centre where you were heard arguing with Derrick Walden? While you're at it, you can also tell me why Derrick came here to your office.'

'But he didn't!'

'You'll have to try better than that, Fletcher. I saw him leaving

214

here. It was on the news footage the night that Clementine Towers held her protest out the front.'

'If he was here, and I'm sure you wouldn't lie about it, I certainly didn't see him. Hold on a moment, I'll ask the girls downstairs.'

He picked up his phone and pressed a few buttons. After a brief chat, he ended the call.

'It seems someone did come here on that night, demanding to see me, but he didn't leave his name. Judging from the description I've just been given, it was Derrick Walden. As you've no doubt realised by now, if someone arrives without an appointment, they don't get to see me. Present company not included in that restriction, of course.'

'If you didn't meet with Derrick here, why did you go to the youth centre to see him?'

'Because he somehow got hold of my direct line number. I have no idea how. He insisted I went to see him.'

Paolo felt like shaking the man. 'For the Lord's sake, spit it out, Fletcher. What did you and Derrick Walden argue about?'

For the first time since they'd sat down, Fletcher looked uncomfortable.

'I should have told you before. God knows, I've come close enough times, but, well, I'm not exactly proud of what I did.'

An inkling of the truth entered Paolo's mind, but he couldn't quite bring himself to believe it.

'Don't tell me it was you with the lipstick?'

Fletcher nodded. 'I told you the truth about why I was at the centre. I'd gone there to see how the funding I'd hoped would come to the canal restoration project had been wasted. There was no one around in the main hall, but I saw everything set up for the big unveiling.' He sighed. 'I went over to the plaque and lifted the cover to see what had been engraved. I swear to you, I had no thoughts of vandalism in my mind, but when I stepped back, I nearly fell when my foot slipped on something. I looked down and there was the lipstick. I have no idea what came over me, but I lifted the cover again and scrawled the accusation.'

Paolo was amazed at what he was being told, but knew Simpson was telling the truth.

'Why did you use those words?' Paolo asked.

Simpson shrugged. 'I'd heard rumours about the youth centre funds being misused.'

'And yet you didn't report that to the police or print it in your paper? I find that hard to believe.'

Simpson smiled. 'Contrary to what you think, we don't actually print accusations without proof to back them up.'

'Fair enough,' Paolo said, hoping his voice betrayed his scepticism. 'Why did you spell the words as you did?'

'Why do you think? To make it look as if one of the yobs hanging round the place had done it. Then I left. As far as I know, no one saw me do it.'

'Apart from Derrick Walden?' Paolo asked.

Fletcher shook his head. 'No, he didn't see me. I passed him as I was leaving. When the plaque was unveiled he put two and two together. I think he believed he could bleed me for a few thousand, but I had no intention of allowing that to happen. Blackmailers never stop.'

'So you killed him?' Jack said.

Paolo jumped. He'd been so taken up with Fletcher's story that he'd forgotten Jack was even there. No, he didn't think Jack was right, but he wanted to see what Fletcher had to say.

'Don't be ridiculous! Kill a man over something so stupid? I might be made to look a fool, but it's hardly on a par with what I hear Montague was getting up to.'

'And how would you know what he'd been doing?' Paolo asked.

Fletcher laughed. 'My gutter rag newspaper, as you called it. We have ways of finding out things in the public interest.'

'You mean things the public are interested in,' Paolo said. 'There is a big difference between the two. Let's get back to your altercation with Derrick. You went to the centre, as asked. Why, if you had no intention of paying up?'

'I wanted him to see my face when I told him to go to the police. I wanted him to realise I meant what I said. You can't tell when someone is sincere over the phone.' He stood up. 'I'll face the public humiliation of my idiotic act. It was stupid and childish. I'll hold my hand up to that. You can charge me with vandalism, but you sure as hell can't pin a murder charge on me. That man was alive and well when I left the youth centre.'

Chapter Twenty-eight

The following morning, Paolo sat at his desk staring into space. The early edition of Simpson's rag was spread over his desk with the headline proclaiming *My Moment of Madness!* Fletcher had taken the opportunity to turn his confession into an attack on the youth centre, making it seem as if he'd deliberately cast suspicion on Montague Mason for no other reason than to make the public aware of how their money had been misused. The following paragraphs all dealt with the benefit to the town which would come as a result of the canal renovations.

Paolo felt like punching something. He'd gone to Fletcher Simpson's believing he was on the right track, but from the moment Fletcher had begun his tale, Paolo had seen there was no way he would have murdered Derrick Walden to keep the matter quiet. It just wasn't a big enough deal to kill over. As was proved by today's newspaper spread.

If it wasn't Fletcher Simpson and it wasn't Arbnor, who did that leave? It could have been Chaz, or even George Baron, as both of them were seen outside the centre that night, but what possible connection could there be between the two clubmen and the swimming coach? They were all originally from London. Is that where the answer would be found? It was possible, but Paolo had a strong feeling the reasons were closer to home.

Paolo knew he was missing something. Derrick and George appeared not to be connected, but he felt sure they were, even if the connection was tenuous. He was almost certain something he'd seen or heard recently to do with George Baron would help solve the mystery of Derrick Walden's murder, if he could only grasp it. Why did he have a feeling it was to do with George Baron's autopsy? What had been said there that he should have paid more attention to? There was definitely a clue hiding in the recesses of his mind. He closed his eyes and tried to tease it out.

A tap on his door stopped the thoughts from swirling to the surface. It didn't matter. Now that he knew there was something to recall, he would find it.

He looked up to find CC standing in the doorway.

'I'm sorry to disturb you, sir,' she said, entering the room and closing the door behind her. 'I could see you were deep in thought, but you asked me to dig deeper to try to find a connection between the known victims, plus the one we believe Colin Jameson was mistaken for.'

Paolo pointed to the chairs in front of his desk.

'Take a seat, CC.' He waited until she'd settled herself and opened a file on the desk. 'So, I take it you've found a definite connection?'

She sighed. 'It appears so. All three of them have been arrested in connection with rape. The first one, Jason Corbett, who we've now positively identified as the coma patient, was released without charge. The second, Glen Scott, who you discovered killed himself, was also arrested and released without charge. That's why those two didn't show up immediately on our system when I first ran a search. The third on the list, Brent Harrison, the one we think was the true target when poor Colin Jameson was taken, did go to trial but the case against him collapsed. His barrister was able to convince the jury that the rapist—'

'Alleged rapist,' Paolo interrupted. 'If the trial collapsed, he was never convicted.'

CC looked as though her mouth was full of lemon juice. 'As you say, sir, *alleged* rapist . . . you know, sir, I read the trial transcript, it's pretty obvious he was as guilty as hell. He kept the poor woman trapped in her home for over twenty-four hours. He admitted being with her for that length of time, but claimed she had invited him in after a date and they had a consensual relationship. He even said in court he didn't hold a grudge and was looking forward to seeing her again! How's that for a veiled threat? The victim wasn't in court that day, but members of her family were. You can be certain the message was passed on.'

Paolo could see by the way CC was flexing her hands that she would like to offer up a few threats of her own. He'd be prepared to put money on the outcome if she ever followed through on it.

'Calm down, CC. Justice stinks at times, but we have to roll with whatever happens. Why did the trial collapse?'

'Two reasons, sir. His confession wasn't considered valid evidence. He'd boasted about what he'd done to the victim before the arresting officer had time to read him his rights. As soon as his rights *had* been read, he changed his tune completely. The bastard claimed he was innocent and the woman had enticed him from a nightclub with promises of a good time and only screamed rape when she realised he wasn't up for a long-term relationship.'

Paolo sighed. He'd heard that tune played too many times. Sometimes the rapists even sounded as if they actually believed the crap they were spouting.

'You said two reasons. What was the other one?'

'Witnesses from the club said she left with him of her own free will, leaning against him, which she might well have done if her drink had been laced with Rohypnol.'

'So, another rapist walked free.'

CC gave a half smile. 'Alleged rapist, sir.'

'Yes, thank you for the reminder,' Paolo said, returning her smile. 'Do we know what happened to the victim afterwards?'

CC nodded. 'I did a bit of digging. She had a nervous breakdown. Spent a few months in psychiatric care and then moved away. I've spoken to her mother, who is understandably angry about the whole affair. She says her daughter is a complete wreck. Can't sleep at nights, jumps at the slightest sound, can't work, has lost all her friends. I asked where she was living now and was told in no uncertain terms it was none of my business.'

'Poor woman,' Paolo said.

'The mother or the daughter, sir?'

'Both, but I was referring to the daughter. Any other information that might be of use to us?'

'Only that Brent Harrison picked her up in the same nightclub that Colin Jameson had gone to with Harrison and the rest of his workmates for the stag do.'

After CC left, Paolo went back to searching in his mind for the illusive clue, but couldn't get that feeling of conviction back again. Whatever it was that had been tantalising him, had vanished for the time being. He could only hope it would resurface later.

He turned to the piles of reports and graphs that were now so much part of modern police work, privately wishing the originator of the system a few months in the depths of hell. He put down the piece of paper and smiled as his imagination ran riot. Yes, maybe whoever had decided filling in forms was more important than bodies on the beat could suffer the same fate as that king he'd learned about in history all those years ago. Who was it now? Edward the something or other, died from an intimate connection with a red hot poker.

His head snapped up. There it was again. Something on the outer edges of his mind screaming at him. He sat back to allow himself to relax and let the memory surface.

His door flew open and Jack came in.

'Sir, you've got to hear this. That batty woman from the youth centre's dead. She was pushed under a bus!'

Paolo's eyes opened. 'When?'

'This morning, sir. Report's just come in. Several people who were waiting at the traffic lights say she was standing waiting for the lights to change when she suddenly went flying forwards.'

'She couldn't have tripped?'

'Witnesses say no, sir. Unfortunately, they all say something different about what actually happened. No one claims to have seen the person who pushed her, but they are all adamant that she *was* pushed. One second standing still, the next right into the path of an oncoming bus. The driver says the same thing.'

'How did you get to hear about it?'

'It came up as a standard report for us to look into, but I recognised her name, so thought I'd better tell you. She did try to speak to you yesterday, if you remember, sir. Once on the way in to the youth centre and once on the way out. I wondered if she was killed because of what she'd been trying to say.'

Paolo studied Jack's face. He looked innocent enough, but his words seemed to carry the edge of a threat in the way he'd phrased them.

'You could be right, Jack. In which case, I might have missed hearing something important. On the other hand, it could have been an accident.'

Yeah, right, Paolo thought. I stand more chance of being next in line to be the pope than that being true. It's connected, I know it is. Just because I don't like the messenger, doesn't mean the message is a lie.

'You did tell her to call the station, sir. Maybe she did.'

Paolo nodded and stood up. 'Let's hope so,' he said, 'but there's only one way to find out.'

He followed Jack back into the main office, wishing he didn't find everything about the man unlikeable. Why couldn't someone else have received the report? Then he wouldn't have had to put up with the veiled insinuation that he'd missed an opportunity. On the other hand, if the report had landed on one of the other desks, would the recipient have known its value? It was only because Jack had been with him yesterday that he'd recognised the name.

You screwed up, Paolo. Accept the fact and move on.

He called for attention and told his team about the report Jack had been given.

'Clementine Towers tried to tell me something yesterday,' he began, then caught Jack's eye. 'In fact, she tried twice to give me information, but I didn't stop to listen. It now appears that she may have been deliberately pushed into the path of a bus and died on impact.'

He sighed. 'I didn't take her seriously because of our past interactions where, quite frankly, she came across as more that a bit unhinged. That's not an excuse, by the way, I'm just stating the reasons I didn't listen to her. I was wrong not to do so. This is twice now that someone has wanted to tell us something but they have been murdered before they were able to get the information to us. In my mind that connects Derrick Walden's death with Clementine Towers.'

The intent look on Jack's face made Paolo follow his line of vision. He was staring directly at Dave, but why? Jack's next words gave him the answer.

'But you did tell her to call the station, sir. Maybe someone here took the call and can tell us whatever it was she wanted to say.'

Paolo watched Dave's face. The colour fled from it and then surged back.

'Yes, sir,' Dave said. 'I took the call.'

Paolo looked back at Jack just in time to see him pass a look of triumph across to the officer whose desk was next to Dave's. Of course, now it made sense. Jack had few friends in the office, but the man smirking back at him was one of them. Jack must have already known Dave had taken a call from Clementine Towers before he'd come in to report her suspicious death. What else did he know? Paolo guessed whatever it was, wasn't going to put Dave in a good light.

'I'm sorry, sir,' Dave said. 'I thought it was another of her weird calls. She wouldn't tell me anything at first, just kept saying she needed to speak to someone in a higher position to me.'

'Should have said you'd put her through to your uncle,' Jack said.

Paolo spun round. 'That's enough, Jack. Comments like that help no one, least of all yourself. Carry on, Dave. Did you get anything from Miss Towers?'

Dave shook his head. 'Very little, sir. She was rambling on about evil walking around and the bad people hidden in good places making the world ungodly. You know what she's like when she gets going, sir. She did say she'd been following various people and now she knew things that would give us nightmares if we knew them, too. Went off on one about licentious people hiding behind innocent disguises.'

Paolo sighed. He could imagine exactly how that conversation had gone. If he'd taken the call, he'd have switched off mentally after a few seconds and left Clementine Towers to rant without actually listening to a word she said.

'Relax, Dave. I know what she's like when she gets going. I don't think there's anyone here who would have acted differently if they'd taken the call.'

As he said this, Paolo looked pointedly in Jack's direction, but he was staring down at his desk. Paolo hoped it was because he was too embarrassed to look up, but had a horrible suspicion it was more likely because he was hiding the delight he felt in Dave's discomfort. He'd have to get Jack transferred to another branch. He was too disruptive and worked against the team morale Paolo had worked hard to build over the past few years.

'As I said, I dismissed her as someone not to be taken seriously, but I did scribble down a few notes while she was on the phone. I'll go back over them,' Dave said. 'Maybe there's something in there that's worth following up on.'

Paolo heard a noise that could easily be mistaken for a cough if he hadn't known it came from Jack whose shoulders were shaking with silent laughter. Paolo looked back at Dave. His face showed how humiliated he felt.

Paolo went back to his office determined to put a stop to Jack's constant sniping. While rummaging in his drawer for a transfer request form, he remembered that niggling feeling about a possible clue to do with George Baron's post mortem. He finally found the forms he needed and cleared a space on his desk so that he could start filling them in. He decided not to call Jack in now. Tomorrow would be better, Paolo decided, after he'd had a good night's sleep and should be calmer than he was right now.

In the meantime, he could call Barbara and see if there was anything she remembered that might provide that elusive connection he knew was there.

She answered on the first ring. 'Paolo, that's good timing. I was just about to call you.'

'Really? What about?'

She laughed. 'No, you go first. I think your reason for calling might be more important than mine.'

'OK, it's to do with George Baron's autopsy, but Derrick Walden's murder.'

'Not sure I follow you, Paolo. Which PM are you asking about?'

'I'm trying to make sense of it myself, Barbara. There's a tiny voice at the back of my mind that says something we mentioned during George Baron's autopsy will tell me something about Derrick Walden's murderer.'

Barbara went quiet for a while. Paolo didn't speak, knowing she was thinking, trying to pinpoint what he needed to know.

'Sorry, Paolo, I've run through both PMs in my head and can't find a similarity between them.'

'Not to worry, Barbara. I expect it will come to me eventually. What was it you wanted to talk to me about? I got the impression you had something on your mind the last time I was over in your office.'

'Paolo, did I say anything stupid when I came out from the anaesthetic last year?'

He recalled her whispered words of 'I love you' as he was leaving her hospital room.

'No, not as far as I can recall. Why do you ask?'

'No real reason,' she said. Paolo could hear the relief in her voice. 'I've woken a few mornings recently with thoughts in my head that seem to be more memories than proper dreams. It's a relief to know they must have been dreams after all.'

Paolo could hear the unspoken question. 'If you did say anything odd, I must have already left.'

'Phew! Glad I asked,' she said, but her voice sounded a bit shaky.

Did she believe him? Possibly not, but Paolo was quite sure that what he'd said was what she wanted to hear. He put the phone down and thought about the women he'd cared about in recent years.

He really wasn't at all sure about his feelings for Barbara. They'd met at the wrong time in his life for him to be able to respond in the way she'd needed and he regretted that as much as she did.

Then he'd met Jessica and had been thinking their relationship might prove to be a lasting one. So much for that idea. She'd be leaving soon and tonight was to be their farewell dinner. He was taking her to the Italian restaurant where their love story had first blossomed.

And then there was Lydia. His first love and, for many years, the only woman he'd ever wanted to be with. He thought back to the kiss that Katy had interrupted. He'd not been able to speak to Lydia since then. He had to face the fact that she'd been avoiding him. That was only to be expected, he supposed, but would still have liked to clear the air with her.

Paolo knocked on Jessica's door, wishing things were different. He was going to miss her after tonight, but knew she had to follow her dream. The opportunity offered to her was too brilliant to turn down.

The door opened and Jessica stood there looking amazing in a fitted silver grey dress.

'Why didn't you use your key?' she asked.

He held it out. 'Symbolism, Jess. It didn't feel right using the key when . . . well . . . anyway, I wanted to hand it over to you here, not make a big deal of it inside.'

He was surprised to feel a lump in his throat the size of a mountain and wondered how he was supposed to get through the evening without swallowing. He followed her into the flat he'd come to know as well as his own.

'Take a seat,' she said. 'I've just got to change my shoes and I'll be ready.'

As she said the words, Paolo's phone rang. Praying it wasn't work, he answered without looking to see who was calling.

'Sterling.'

Jessica had stopped midway to the door and looked back with an enquiring look, as if to ask if their last evening together was about to be ruined.

'I know who I called,' Lydia said. 'Paolo, we need to talk.'

Chapter Twenty-nine

The next morning Paolo got to the office early by virtue of hardly having slept the night before. Jessica's face, when she'd realised who was on the phone, had displayed a coldness only matched by the ice in Lydia's voice when he'd had to tell her it wasn't a good time to talk.

The net result had been a disaster all round. Lydia had ended the call with a terse word of farewell that had sounded more like drop dead than cheerio. Jessica had gone out of her way to show how little it bothered her that Paolo was receiving *that* sort of call from his ex-wife. Her determination to avoid talking about why Lydia had phoned meant the subject was sitting right there between them for the entire evening.

Four times he'd tried to clear the air and four times Jessica had insisted no explanation was necessary – after all, as she kept pointing out, he was now a free agent! The quick peck on the cheek at the end of the evening put the seal on a night Paolo hoped never to repeat.

Realising he'd been sitting at his desk for nearly an hour without so much as opening a file, Paolo pulled the nearest one across the desk and set to work. He was vaguely aware of a phone ringing in the main office, but the sound gradually forced its way into his conscious mind. It rang and rang, then just as he was about to get up and go and answer it, the ringing stopped. A few minutes later, the persistent noise started up again, ringing only a few times before silence descended again. When the sound intruded again, five minutes later, Paolo knew he'd have to answer it or he'd never be able to concentrate on what he was doing.

He strode through to the main office to find out whose phone it was. The place was deserted, but he could hear voices on the other side of the main doors, so knew his team would be bursting through at any moment.

The offending phone was on Dave's desk. He lifted the receiver. 'Sterling.'

'Paolo, thank goodness,' Rebecca said. 'I thought I'd never get an answer. I've been trying to reach Dave. Is he there?'

'I think he might be about to walk in now. Hang on a sec, Rebecca.'

Paolo looked over towards the entrance as people began filing in. Jack, Andrea, CC, several uniformed officers, but no Dave.

'He's not arrived yet. Was he late leaving home this morning?'

'He didn't come home last night,' she said. 'I thought he might have gone straight to the office this morning. We're supposed to be meeting the wedding planner with my mother in an hour's time. She'll go ballistic if we're late.'

Paolo looked again towards the door, willing Dave to walk through. He became aware of Rebecca's voice.

'He rang and said he'd be back in time for dinner last night,' she said, 'but he never showed up. Were you two on stake out?'

'No. Did he tell you where he was going?'

'Just that he'd found something in his notes that he needed to follow up on. Are you saying he wasn't with you?' she asked.

Paolo continued staring at the door, even though he knew in his gut, Dave wasn't going to show.

'Have you tried his mobile?'

Rebecca sighed. 'I've been ringing it on and off since last night. It goes straight to voicemail. Paolo, you sound worried. What's going on?'

He knew he had to appear unconcerned but wasn't sure he could pull it off.

'I'm not worried, Rebecca, but he didn't tell me where he was going. Let me ask around the team. I'm sure he'll have discussed his intentions with someone here. I'll call you back. OK?'

He put the phone down and called for attention.

'Listen up, everyone. Did Dave tell any of you what his plans were when he left here yesterday? His fiancé has been on the phone this morning. Dave didn't make it home last night.'

He saw Jack lean over and whisper something to his neighbour, causing the man to snort with suppressed laughter. Before Paolo could lay into either of them, CC distracted him.

'Yes, sir. He told me he'd found something in his notes to do with Clementine Towers call. He was going to check it out on the way home.'

'He didn't say what it was?'

She shook her head. 'Nope, just that it . . .' She stopped and looked around. 'Can we go into your office?'

Paolo nodded and led the way. CC followed him in and shut the door behind her.

'I didn't want to say this out there and give that idiot the satisfaction of knowing his words were having an effect on Dave,' she said.

Paolo didn't need to ask who the idiot in question was. He glanced at the transfer forms on his desk. It was definitely time to get rid of the rotten apple ruining his team.

'Didn't want to say what?' he asked, sitting down and pointing to a chair for CC to do the same.

She slumped onto the seat, looking more distressed than Paolo had ever seen her.

'I don't tell tales. You know that, sir, don't you?'

Paolo nodded.

'Well, I'm going to make an exception this time. Jack Cummings has been spreading rumours about Dave's competence and making sure Dave hears the worst of them. What gets said in the office out there in front of you is just a tiny bit of what Dave puts up with every day.'

Paolo held up the transfer forms. 'I'd guessed as much. I'm putting Jack forward for a transfer.'

230

She smiled. 'Good. Dave feels like everything he does is under the spotlight and that he's not measuring up. He took Clementine Tower's death hard. I told him he was being daft, but he felt almost as if he was responsible.'

Knowing how he felt about Derrick Walden's murder, Paolo understood what Dave was going through.

'He said he was going to earn his place,' CC said. 'He didn't know if what he'd found was important, but wasn't going to take a chance by not following it up.'

'But he didn't give any indication who he wanted to see or where he was going?'

'No, but I'll tell you this much, sir, he was planning to be home within an hour. He called Rebecca while we were going down in the lift and that's what he said to her.'

'CC, go and search through Dave's desk. He might have written something down to give us an indication of where to start looking. I'm going to put out an all points request on his car. I have a really bad feeling about this.'

By the afternoon, Paolo's bad feeling had grown into a cold certainty that Dave had walked into a dangerous situation and couldn't find a way out again. Who the hell had he gone to see? What could Clementine Towers have witnessed that caused her death? What had Dave remembered, or found in his notes, to send him off without telling anyone where he was going?

Paolo thumped his desk with frustration. What the bloody hell had made Dave go against everything he'd been taught from the time he entered the force? Always make sure someone knows where you're going and who you intend to interview. But he knew what, or rather who, had sent Dave off hell bent on proving his worth.

When Andrea tapped on his door half an hour later, he was glad to have something else to think about. Right at the moment, the only thought in his head was that Dave was in trouble.

'Sir, you asked me to look into Chaz's conviction and his reasons for beating that man so badly.'

He forced a smile. 'Sit down, Andrea. I take it you've got all the info?'

'Yes, sir. It's actually quite a sad story from Chaz's point of view.'

Paolo felt his eyebrows rise. 'GBH with intent is a sad story? I can see that's the case for the victim, obviously, but for Chaz? I don't get it.'

'He was only young, sir.' Paolo opened his mouth to speak, but Andrea held up a hand. 'No, please, sir, let me finish. He was only young and engaged to be married. His fiancée was on her way home one night during the winter. She'd had to work late that evening, so there were only a few commuters around as she walked home. Normally she would have been in a crowd of people.'

Andrea looked down at her notes before continuing. 'She was attacked and dragged into an alley where she was beaten and raped. The alley was pitch black because the streetlights were out. Presumably, that's why the rapist picked that spot. Anyway, during the rape, a car went past in the road running at right angles to the alley and the headlights showed the man's face quite clearly.'

She glanced up, a look of rage on her face, and then dropped her eyes again to read.

'She was able to describe the man in detail to the police. He was well known to the local force with a record as long as your arm for rape and other violent crimes. They arrested and charged him. At the trial, it was expected to be a slam dunk, but the man's wife stood up in court and perjured herself by claiming he'd been at home with her on the night in question.'

'How do you know all this?' Paolo asked. 'It couldn't have been in Chaz's court record surely?'

She smiled. 'Some of it was, but I got most of the facts from the court transcript for the rape case.'

Paolo nodded. 'OK, go on.'

'As the jury weren't allowed to know of the man's previous convictions, they accepted the defence claim of a sad case of mistaken identity. Everyone should feel sorry for the victim, but justice cannot be served by locking up an innocent man, blah, blah, blah . . .'

'And he walked?'

Andrea nodded. 'Exactly. He got away with it, but I don't think that's why Chaz beat him so badly he ended up in hospital with a fair few broken bones, damaged spleen and fractured skull. I did a bit more research and found out what happened to Chaz's fiancée. This is the part that is really sad, sir. After her rapist was acquitted, she left the court with Chaz. They had to take the tube to get home. As the train approached, she pulled away from him and jumped in front of it.'

Chapter Thirty

Paolo had been back to the Triple B club to see if Dave was being held there, but Chaz had gone out of his way to be helpful, allowing access to every room and possible hiding place. He'd even opened broom cupboards and the larders. Not that Paolo believed for a minute Chaz would be stupid enough to keep Dave at the club, or even at his home.

Paolo had men watching Chaz round the clock, but so far he'd done nothing they could pull him back in for. But Paolo wasn't even sure Chaz *was* the person Dave had gone to interview. Somehow, it just didn't sit right with him. If it had been Chaz, surely Dave would have taken someone with him?

No, in Paolo's mind, whoever Dave had gone to see was someone outside those already in the frame. If it had been an obvious target, Dave would have raised it with him. The fact that he didn't, made Paolo think Dave hadn't really believed it himself and had been unwilling to hold himself up for further ridicule by suggesting whoever it was.

His musings were interrupted by CC knocking on the door and coming in for the update meeting he'd scheduled. Until Dave was found, all resources had to go into the search for him.

CC sat down at his desk, looking every bit as worried as Paolo felt.

'Where's Andrea?' he asked.

'Mike from IT rang just as we were about to come in. She'll be here as soon as she's finished the call. I'm hoping he's uncovered something from the Nemesis blog we can use. The stuff we've got so far tells us a lot about what goes on in the torture room, but not a fecking thing that might help us find Dave. I want to kill whoever has him. Sitting in here, staring at my computer screen, doesn't feel like I'm helping to find the bastard. I'd rather be out there hunting down Dave's car.'

'I know, CC. I feel the same way, but us running up and down streets taking part in the search for his car isn't going to help. We've got good people doing that.'

'I know, sir, but they've found nothing,' she said. 'Problem is, unless it's parked on a busy street, it could easily be missed.'

Paolo nodded. 'I know, but we have to be sensible. We'll deal with the stuff we're good at and leave the hunt for Dave's car to people whose job it is. Have you had any joy with delving into past cases of sex attacks on men?'

She shook her head. 'Not a bloody thing. Either men don't report them, or there are few incidents of the kind we're looking for. I've gone back several years and there's no trace of a pattern. If it had been a man targeting women, I bet I'd have found a pattern established by now, but in this case, not a thing, even though we know exactly what type of attack we're searching for.'

Paolo sighed. 'Keep looking. I'm convinced whoever Dave went to see is our killer. The clues are out there somewhere, CC; we've just got to keep searching for them.'

He looked up as Andrea opened the door and came in to sit beside CC.

'Sorry I'm late, sir. Mike has managed to get through the encryption and has discovered the blog originator's email address. He's working on tracing the person who set up the email account. Only problem is, the blog started four years ago, so that email address might no longer be in use. Doesn't mean he can't track it back to the owner, but it will take more time.'

Paolo thumped the desk with his fist. 'Fuck it! Time is the one thing we don't have while Dave is out there.' He looked over at CC. 'OK, if the blog was set up four years ago, maybe that's when the attacks started. Concentrate your search from three and half to four and a half years back, CC.'

She nodded. 'Will do.'

He pulled a pad towards him and picked up a pen. 'Let's look at what we know and what we still need to find out,' he said. 'It looks as if Nemesis targets those guilty of rape, but who have evaded punishment. Agreed?'

Both women nodded.

Paolo wrote that down, and then glanced up again. 'So how did Nemesis find out who the rapists were if they got off without being found guilty?'

'Court records?' Andrea suggested.

'No, that doesn't follow,' CC said. 'Jason Corbett and Glen Scott were both released without charge, so there are no court records for either of them.'

Paolo nodded. 'There was also the mix up in names with Colin Jameson and Brent Harrison. Nemesis went after Colin Jameson, even though his name has never appeared in court documents. He was picked up by Nemesis in place of Brent Harrison because they looked alike in the dark club.'

Andrea sat forward. 'So Nemesis is going by sight or description, not by name?'

Paolo tapped his pen on the desk. 'Remember in the Jason Corbett parts of the blog? Nemesis wasn't surprised that Jason had given a different name earlier that evening. I think you're right, Andrea. Nemesis is going by description and knows where to find them. The question is who is providing the information? It can only be the rape victims. So, who are they telling?'

'All the rapes were reported,' CC said. 'So it could be someone on the force. I can look into that and see if the same person's name turns up in all cases.'

Paolo scribbled that down. 'Good thinking, but what about Trudy Chappell? She didn't report her rape. We only found out about it because Dave and I pushed her to find out what George Baron had done.'

'Well, we all know here in the office, sir, because it came up in the team report.' She stopped, seeming to realise what she'd said. 'I'm not saying it was one of us on this floor, but maybe someone chatted to a colleague outside of the briefing.'

Paolo nodded. 'It's possible, but I still need to ask Trudy Chappell herself if she told anyone other than us. Andrea, you stay here and take over CC's research. I want you on call in case Mike comes back with anything we can use. CC, you come with me to chat to Trudy Chappell. She might find it easier to tell you about what she did after she was raped than she would talking to me.'

Paolo pulled up outside Trudy Chappell's quaint cottage remembering his last visit when Dave had been the one driving. Where the hell was he? The thought of him being tortured in the same way as the other men made Paolo want to throw up. But, no, surely that wouldn't happen? Nemesis's whole purpose in life seemed to be punishing rapists. If there was one thing Paolo would be prepared to swear to, it was that Dave definitely didn't fall into that category. The thought gave Paolo a tiny bit of relief. Maybe Nemesis was just holding Dave.

The treacherous thought *and then what?* Paolo pushed firmly to the back of his mind. He'd cling to the belief that Dave wouldn't suffer the rapists' fate and would be released unharmed.

CC tapped on the driver's window. 'You ready, sir?'

Paolo came to with a start. He'd allowed his mind to drift and hadn't even realised CC was no longer sitting in the passenger seat. Apologising, he got out and locked the car.

As they waited for Trudy to answer the bell, Paolo watched CC's face as she had a good look up and down the street.

'Nice area,' she said. 'Wouldn't suit me, but I can see why Trudy Chappell fought so hard to keep her home.'

Paolo felt his eyebrows raise. 'Even to the extent of blackmail?'

She smiled. 'No, I didn't mean that.'

The door opened and Paolo was astounded to see the improvement in Trudy. The bruises, if there were any left, had been skilfully hidden under immaculately applied make-up. Her hair was clean and styled and, although casually dressed in jeans and a shirt, she looked more like the woman he'd first met at the Triple B club. He almost didn't want to question her, in case it brought her crashing down again, but he had to. Dave's life might be at stake.

'My solicitor says I don't have to speak to you. He says as I've admitted my guilt I don't have to answer any questions until the trial.'

Paolo nodded. 'He's quite right, Trudy, but the blackmail case isn't why we're here. This is Detective Sergeant Cathy Connors. Would you mind if we came in for a moment?'

'If it's not about my trial, what's it about?' she asked, suspicion vibrating in every word.

CC smiled. 'It really would be better if we spoke to you inside, Miss Chappell.'

Trudy looked on the point of shutting the door, but something in CC's attitude must have changed her mind. She stood back.

'Come in then, but you've only got five minutes. Not a second more.'

Back in the small sitting room Paolo noticed immediately how much bigger it seemed to be.

'Your dolls and stuffed animals have gone,' he said, but regretted the words almost immediately when he saw the stricken look on Trudy's face.

'I grew up,' she said. 'I gave them all away to the children's home.'

He realised straightaway she meant the rape had changed her outlook and wished he'd bitten his tongue out rather than add to her distress.

'You might as well sit down,' she said. 'Ask your question and then please leave. I take it you're here about . . . you know, what George did.'

Paolo must have looked surprised, because she laughed. 'I'm not stupid. If it's not about the blackmail case, that only leaves . . . leaves . . .'

'You're right,' CC said. 'We're here because of what happened to you at the hands of George Baron. Miss Chappell, we only have one question, but it is a very important one. A colleague's life is at stake, so we really do need you to answer it. Who did you tell after George Baron raped you?'

'What do you mean? Whose life?'

'You remember the young detective sergeant who came here with me?' Paolo said.

She nodded. 'Nice looking man. Kind eyes.'

'We think whoever killed George Baron might be holding him,' Paolo explained. 'Please tell us. Who did you tell about George and what he'd done to you.'

'No one,' she said. 'Well, no one in particular. I called Rape Crisis. In truth, I called several times and I've spoken to half a dozen different people since that first call. They're all volunteers, so I rarely get to speak to the same person, but they are all so kind and supportive, they've helped me get my life back on track.'

CC leaned towards Trudy. 'You told no one else? No friends or family?'

She shook her head. 'No! I don't want any of them to find out. You won't tell them will you? It won't come out at the trial, will it?'

Hearing the panic in her voice, Paolo spoke quickly to put her mind at rest.

'No, nothing will come out. You've pleaded guilty, so the trial will be more about sentencing than anything else, but even if it wasn't, the rape has no bearing on the blackmail. That happened after the event.'

Tears ran through her make-up. Paolo realised how fragile the image of recovery had been. She'd been putting on an act to appear more in control that she really was. He hoped one day it would no longer be an act.

He stood up. 'Trudy, I'm really sorry we put you through this. If you remember that you did tell someone other than Rape Crisis counsellors, please let me know,' he said, handing her one of his cards.

Trudy came with them to the door, but the composure she'd

239

shown when she'd opened it was sadly lacking as she closed it behind them. Paolo heard the sobbing start as she replaced the chain and slipped bolts into place.

They walked in silence to the car, but as Paolo clicked to release the central locking, he saw CC shake her head. He waited until they were both seated before questioning the reason for her negative action.

'What aren't you happy with?'

CC sighed. 'There are no male volunteers at Rape Crisis. Well, there might be, but they certainly wouldn't be allowed to answer the phone lines. The last thing a woman would want to hear if she'd been raped would be a male voice asking her to talk about it.'

Paolo started the ignition. 'You're right, of course, but if Trudy didn't tell anyone else, what's the alternative?'

'Either she did tell someone, who leaked it to our killer, or we have an internal leak. I can't see anything else that makes sense.'

As he drove back to the station, CC's words kept replaying in Paolo's mind and, once again, just out of reach, was a niggle about George Baron's autopsy. By the time they got back to the station, he was glad to be distracted by the need to concentrate on parking the car. His head was beginning to ache from the effort of trying to recall something when he didn't even know what it was he was hoping to remember.

They'd barely walked through the door into the main office when Andrea rushed over. He could see by the look on her face that she wasn't about to give them good news, but her words still raised hope in his heart.

'Sir, I'm so pleased you're back. I've had a call from Mike about the Nemesis blog.'

'Please tell me he's found the owner of the email address.'

She shook her head. 'I wish I could. No, sir, I think this might be bad news. Mike says a new page has just gone up on the blog. He's working to unencrypt it as a priority. He said he'll send it over as soon as he can, but I can't help thinking it might be to do with Dave.'

Chapter Thirty-one

An hour later Paolo heard a tap on his door. Andrea came in clutching a piece of paper, closely followed by CC.

'From Mike?' Paolo asked, pointing at the paper.

Andrea nodded. 'But it's not about Dave.'

Paolo's initial relief that he wasn't about to hear of torture inflicted on his detective sergeant was closely followed by fear for him. Where the hell was he being held?

'Sit down and read it out, Andrea.'

Nemesis in Action Blog

That woman dared to accost me in the street.

'I've been watching you. My car was right behind yours when you went to the home of that club owner. I know what sort of person you are. I've spoken to the police about your behaviour,' she said.

I wondered what she'd said to them. Surely if she'd told them anything of value they would have come for me by now. She looked so smug I wanted to smash her head against a wall, but there were too many people around. Fortunately, she's known as an eccentric, so nobody takes any notice of her ranting. The people scurrying past probably felt sorry for me being picked on as her latest target. Or they were glad she wasn't directing her verbal abuse at them. She's like the nutter on the bus that everyone prays won't sit next to them.

'And what did our friendly boys in blue have to say to you?'

'The one I spoke to didn't take me seriously, but I'm going to the police station now. I'll soon have you sorted out. I'll demand to be taken to someone higher up.'

She turned away from me and strode off, I presume to get her car. I almost let her go. Would anyone have taken any notice of her rambling? Probably not, but if she'd got as far as telling someone I'd gone to George Baron's house, the police would have to look into it. I couldn't allow that to happen.

I followed her with the intention of catching her unawares as she was unlocking her car, just as I'd captured George Baron in the act of locking his, but she got caught up in the press of people waiting for the lights to change. I saw a bus thundering along and seized my opportunity and shoved her in the back.

As she shot forward, I screamed. 'Oh God, someone just pushed that woman,' I said. 'I saw a man's hand reach forward.' Then I moved back a few paces and said I'd seen a woman's hand. In no time at all, the place was in chaos. Some were yelling it was a man; others saying it was a woman. Even those at the back of the crowd claimed to have seen a hand in Clementine's back when they couldn't have seen anything at all.

When enough people were arguing about what they saw, I drifted away from the scene.

'Well, that's proof of how Clementine Towers met her end,' Paolo said. 'Not that there'd been any doubt in my mind before today.'

The thought of Dave in the hands of someone so ruthless made Paolo feel physically ill.

'Andrea, what's the news on tracing the owner of the Nemesis blog? I thought Mike had unencrypted the email address used to set it up.'

She nodded. 'He has, sir, but it's a generic email address. One of those free ones where you don't need to give any information. You could set it up in your cat's name and no one would be any the wiser.'

'Are you saying he can't find out who Nemesis is?'

She shook her head. 'No, I'm not saying that. Mike explained it to me. He can trace it back but it's taking time. He knows that email address was set up using a Newcastle IP address and is running checks on that.'

'Newcastle?'

'That's what he said. It was definitely set up in Newcastle. He'll let us know as soon as he has something more concrete we can act on.'

Paolo sighed. 'I know, but it's taking so damn long and we need to find Dave before it's too late.' He turned to CC. 'I take it there's no news on his car?'

She shook her head. 'Not so far. We've got every available body out looking for it.'

As Andrea and CC stood up to leave, Andrea's phone rang. She mouthed the word Mike at Paolo, then sat back down to take the call.

Paolo watched with mounting hope as she scribbled down information and barely gave her time to close her phone before demanding to know what Mike had uncovered.

'The email address was set up by a J. Whitechapel.'

'I want the whereabouts of every J. Whitechapel who lived in Newcastle when the blog was set up,' Paolo said.

Andrea stood up. 'I'm on it, sir, but this Whitechapel person might not have lived in the City. It could have been set up at work.'

Paolo nodded. 'I realise that, but at the moment a name and a city is all we have to go on, so let's work with the info we have.'

CC stood up as well. 'I'm going to go and see if the Whitechapel name turns up nationwide in any complaints over the last few years.'

'Good idea, CC. I can't believe Nemesis has stayed under the radar for so long.'

She was almost at the door when Paolo called her name. She turned back, a questioning look on her face.

'The second you hear about Dave's car, I want to know.'

She nodded. 'Of course.'

An hour later, Paolo's phone rang and he snatched it up, hoping to see Dave's name on the display, but it was Jessica's.

She was probably at the airport by now, he thought. He was about to answer the call, when CC came rushing in.

'Sir, they've found Dave's car.'

He hit the decline call button. Finding his friend and colleague was more important than long drawn-out goodbyes.

Chapter Thirty-two

'Where is it?' Paolo asked.

'In the municipal car park not far from the youth centre,' CC answered.

'Do they know how long it's been there?'

She nodded. 'He must have gone straight to the car park when he left here. According to the attendant, it's been parked there ever since. I'm thinking he might have been going to the youth centre.'

Paolo shook his head. 'No, he'd have parked in the centre car park if that was the case. Dave never walked a yard if he could drive.' He got up and walked over to the large map of Bradchester hanging on his office wall. 'I'd say he could have been going to any of the streets within a ten to fifteen minute walk of the car park.'

'No further out than that, sir?'

'I would very much doubt it. The question now is why did he park there and not outside the place he wanted to go?'

CC shrugged. 'Maybe he didn't want to advertise he was coming,' she suggested, but without any conviction in her voice.

'It's possible, but I don't think that's the reason. I think the only reason Dave wouldn't have parked outside was if it was a restricted parking area.'

'But he was on police business, sir. He could have just put one of our signs on the dash.'

'He could have, yes, but remember he might have thought he was chasing one of Clementine's fantasies. The fact he didn't tell us where he was going makes me think he didn't believe in the information himself. Maybe he didn't want to draw attention to his car, which would happen if the permit holders called the station to complain about their space being taken up by a police car. By leaving his car in the municipal car park, if it turned out to be a wild goose chase, he wouldn't need to mention it and get held up as a laughing stock.'

'By charming Jack Cummings,' CC spat.

Paolo nodded. 'Amongst others, yes. CC, get on to traffic . . . no, scrap that. I'll get on to traffic to find out which streets have permit-only parking. Pick up a locksmith and go to the municipal car park. I want you to search Dave's car. I'm praying he's left something in there to point the way.'

When CC left, Paolo reached down into a drawer in his desk and pulled out a folded map of Bradchester. Technology was all well and good, but sometimes good old-fashioned paper worked better. He picked up the phone and called the traffic division to explain what he needed.

As he was given the information, he used a yellow highlighter to show up all the streets where permits were needed for parking.

'I hadn't realised so much of Bradchester was restricted,' he said, as he coloured in another two roads and a cul-de-sac.

'It never used to be like this, but the council changed most of the residential streets some time back,' the traffic officer said. 'I've got another couple for you, sir.'

By the time Andrea burst into his office half an hour later, Paolo's map had more yellow streets than those left blank. He thanked the officer and ended his call.

'Tell me you've got something good for me,' he said.

She nodded. 'I think so. I've been running searches on J. Whitechapel, trying all the names I could think of beginning with J: Jacob, Jarvis, Jeffrey – I went through them all and came up blank.'

Realising she was still standing, Paolo pointed to the chairs. She sat down, dropped her files onto his desk and shuffled through the pages, pulling one out and passing it across to Paolo.

'But then I found this J. Whitechapel who worked for the DHS in Newcastle during the time the blog was set up.'

Paolo sat up. 'DHS? Which department?'

'Allocation of National Insurance numbers. It's the perfect place to work if you need to set up a new identity and move to a different area.'

'For example, to Bradchester,' Paolo said.

Andrea nodded. 'Exactly, sir, but that's not all I found out.'

'Go on.'

'The J. Whitechapel who worked for the DHS wasn't a man, but a woman. Full name, June Rosalind Whitechapel. When I ran that name through the computer I got a direct hit on a rape case in Newcastle two years before the Nemesis blog was set up. June was picked up in a night club. Her drink had been spiked with Rohypnol. When she came to, she was tied up, gagged and blindfolded. The rapist held her for almost three days before untying her. He told her if she moved before counting to thousand, he'd slit her throat. She did as she was told. When she got the blindfold off, it turned out, the rapist had taken her back to her own home in her own car. He'd used the keys he'd found in her handbag to go in through the front door. He was even seen by neighbours helping her from her car into the house. No one thought anything of it until she called the police. According to the report filed, she was raped, tortured, starved and dehydrated, but her assailant was never caught.'

She put the papers down. 'It was thought at one point it might have been a revenge attack by her ex-husband. They'd been through a nasty divorce, but he had the perfect alibi. He was out of the country on business at the time and had all the documentation to prove it. But I've got a theory, sir.'

'Go on,' Paolo said, forcing himself to concentrate on Andrea's words as yet again George Baron's autopsy was screaming at him.

'The details of June's rape is such a perfect match with our crimes, I think Nemesis could be her ex-husband.'

Paolo nodded. 'It's possible. What's his name and do we have a picture of him?'

'His name is Marcus, but I don't yet have any images. I've requested them from Newcastle and they're sending some over.'

'Good, we should be able to match or eliminate him.'

As he said the words, with blinding clarity, Paolo realised what had been bugging him for days.

'Andrea, don't go. I need to make a call.'

He picked up the phone and dialled Barbara's number, praying she wouldn't be conducting an autopsy and unable to speak to him. He sighed with relief when he heard her voice.

'Barbara, sorry to disturb you, but I've got a quick question regarding George Baron's rape.'

'Sure,' she said. 'Fire away.'

'You pointed out the angle of penetration and mentioned a foreign object being used on him. Is it possible the perpetrator could have been female?'

'It's possible, of course, but she would have to be very strong to have overcome him and render him helpless.'

'Or an expert in martial arts?' he said.

'Yes, that's a distinct possibility.'

He thanked Barbara and ended the call.

'Andrea, have you got a picture of the Newcastle rape victim in the file?'

She rummaged through until she found one and passed it across the desk. Paolo studied it. She was younger then, with a short blonde crop in place of the mid-length brown hair she had now and must have been fitted with contact lenses, because she was no longer wearing glasses, but the image he held was definitely that of April Greychurch.

Chapter Thirty-three

Paolo stood up and almost fell over his chair in his haste to get round the desk.

'Andrea, grab your things. You're coming with me.'

He forced himself to stand still long enough to retrieve his phone from his pocket and call CC. Strangely enough, he could hear the ringing tone outside his office and getting louder. He ended the call as CC walked in.

'You were calling me, sir?'

'Yes, we've worked out who Nemesis is. It's April Greychurch. We need to get to the youth centre immediately. You take Jack Cummings in your car. I'll organise uniform backup.'

CC grabbed his jacket as he went to pass her.

'Wait, sir. Look at what I found,' she said, pulling a piece of paper from her pocket.

'What is it? We don't have time for this now, CC. Dave's life's at stake.'

She held on tight to his arm. 'I realise that, sir, but Dave isn't likely to be at the youth centre. Please, look at this.'

He took the scrap from her and read the words: *CT says AG was having affair with GB? Call on AG home.*

'Change of plan. You and Andrea find April's home address and call it through to me. I'll meet you there.'

CC nodded. 'Where are you going, sir?'

'To the youth centre to pick up April, but I'm going upstairs first. I want an emergency warrant to break into April's home if she won't cooperate.'

Paolo ran into the main office, yelling at Jack to follow him. He didn't bother to wait to see if Jack was with him or not, but took the stairs two at a time to get to Chief Constable Willows' office. Without bothering to knock, he burst into the office. As he did so, he felt his phone vibrate to show he'd received a text message. He pulled the phone out and glanced at it. CC had sent April's address.

'Sir, I know who's holding Dave. I'll need a warrant to search this address,' he said, holding out the phone for Willows to write down the details.

Willows nodded. 'I want to hear the moment you've found him. Got that?'

Paolo, already racing towards the door, looked back over his shoulder. 'Will do.'

He almost collided with Jack who had just reached the top of the stairs.

'What kept you?' Paolo said, pushing past him and going down even faster than he'd climbed up. 'Come on!' he yelled.

He reached his car and was already turning the ignition by the time Jack appeared at the front of the station. Paolo gunned the engine and took off, screeching to a halt long enough for Jack to climb in.

'The next time I tell you to move it, make sure you're a damn sight faster than you were today,' Paolo said, cutting in front of cars at the traffic lights.

'I didn't realise it was so urgent,' Jack said.

Paolo didn't bother to answer. All that mattered was finding Dave safe and well. Surely April wouldn't have hurt him? If her aim in life was teaching rapists a lesson, why would she hurt Dave? That bloody voice in his head that Paolo couldn't shut up, no matter how hard he tried, kept whispering to him: *for the same reason she killed Derrick Walden and Clementine Towers. She doesn't want to be found out.*

Paolo pulled into the parking area at the youth centre and

didn't bother to look for a designated place. He threw the keys into Jack's lap.

'Lock up and come upstairs to find me,' he said.

Climbing out and leaving the door open, he ran into the building and raced upstairs. April was calmly typing when he burst in.

'What the fuck have you done with Dave?' he yelled.

'What on earth are you on about, Paolo? How would I know where he is? Cute, he might be but—'

Paolo didn't give her chance to finish. He was round the back of her desk while the words were still forming. Grabbing her arms, he dragged her out of the chair and shook her.

'Where is he? Where is he?'

The red hot rage poured molten lava over his soul. If she didn't answer, he would . . . he would . . .

Letting her go, he took a step back and forced himself to speak calmly. 'April Greychurch, formerly known as June Whitechapel, I'm arresting you on suspicion of the murder of . . .'

The words came out by rote. He was vaguely aware of Jack arriving and putting handcuffs on April, but Paolo's mind had turned to quicksand. Thoughts arrived and sank without trace before he could grasp them. After a few minutes, he realised Jack was talking to him.

'Sir, I've asked you twice now. What do you want me to do with her?'

Paolo gave himself a shake and forced his mind to respond.

'Take her downstairs and put her in the back of my car. We're going to her house,' he said, pleased to see a look of alarm spread across April's previously impassive features.

He turned to the uniformed officers he hadn't even notice arrive.

'I want this office and the one next door searched from top to bottom.' He scribbled down the names of the known victims. 'Anything even remotely connected with any of these men, or anything that refers to the name Nemesis, I want bagged and tagged.'

One of the young men looked up at that. 'You mean the goddess, sir?'

'Sorry?' Paolo asked. 'What goddess?'

'Nemesis. She's most commonly described as a daughter of Night, though some say she's the daughter of Erebus. According to the poet Hesiod . . .' His voice trailed away. 'Sorry, sir, my father's a classics scholar. I sort of picked up the info.'

Paolo felt as if the clues had been staring him in the face all along, but only now were they clear to him. Nemesis was a goddess, not a god. If he'd realised that sooner, would it have made a difference? Would he have guessed he was searching for a woman and not a man? No point in speculating.

'Carry on,' he said. 'All finds to be reported directly to me.'

He raced downstairs to the car, his mind liquid fire. A huge improvement over the thick soup it had resembled earlier. As he climbed in, he glanced at April.

'We're going to your house. Are you prepared to give directions?'

She nodded.

He turned away and started the car, passing his phone to Jack.

'That's where we're going. Get directions just in case she tries to mess us about.'

In the end, Jack's help wasn't necessary. Following April's instructions, they were soon turning into a street of semi-detached houses, which was already full of marked and unmarked police cars. Paolo noticed all the permit-only parking signs with a perverse sense of satisfaction. He'd been right about that, at least. They were also about ten minutes' walk from the municipal parking area where Dave had left his car. Further confirmation, if any were needed, that Dave had called on April before he disappeared.

He pulled up as close to April's house as possible and stopped the car. CC was already there, alongside half the Bradchester force. As he climbed out, CC showed him the warrant to search the house.

'We were just about to set to with the battering ram, sir, but now that she's here, we could use her keys.'

Paolo leaned in and picked up April's handbag which had been

252

placed on the floor next to Jack's feet. He opened it and located a massive bunch of keys.

'Jack, you take care of April. Bring her inside. We might need her to explain where things are.'

He handed the keys to CC. 'Come on; let's get the place opened up. You know, all these houses have integral garages and space in front for another car to park. Why would they also need permit-only parking?' he asked as they made their way towards the property.

'I don't suppose they do, sir, but it's another way for the council to raise funds. Tell the residents they have to pay for a permit to stop anyone else parking outside their homes.'

By this time, CC had unlocked the door and they were able to get inside. Paolo gave the order for the search to begin.

April's house looked like any other semi on the inside. Lots of dark flat pack furniture, interspersed with a few more expensive pieces. Jack took April into the lounge and made her sit on the couch. Paolo followed them in.

'I want to know where Dave is. All the other questions can wait, but that one can't. What have you done with him?'

She shook her head and Paolo felt the urge to grab her and shake her once again, but he knew if he did he wouldn't be able to stop this time.

'April, don't mess with me. Where is Dave?'

Silent tears slid down her cheeks, but with her hands shackled behind her, she couldn't wipe them away. Andrea moved forward and sat next to her. Paolo watched as she wiped away the other woman's tears.

A shout from the direction of kitchen distracted him and he turned away. When he looked back, Andrea nodded in the direction the noise had come from.

'Why not leave her to me for now, sir? You go and see what they've found.'

The look she gave him said clearly, I think I can get her to talk. Paolo nodded.

He headed towards the officer standing outside a door adjacent to the one leading to the integral garage. The man looked a bit green around the gills, as if he was trying hard to keep his lunch down.

'What have you found?'

The officer shook his head and took a step back to allow Paolo to enter the room. If he'd had any doubts at all of April's guilt, the photos lining the walls of the room left little to the imagination. Men of all shapes and sizes were shown in the same position, face down on the table standing in the middle of the room. Against one wall was a table and a comfortable armchair. Did April sit and watch them while they recovered?

Paolo walked over to the table. A variety of dildos, in sizes ranging from small to extra-large, sat next to a tazer. The clicking of a camera made him turn to see the crime scene photographer at work.

'Pretty sick mind here,' Paolo said.

The photographer nodded, but didn't reply. Paolo didn't blame him. He went back out into the hall and found CC heading down the stairs. She shook her head before he could ask about Dave.

'Not a sign of anything untoward up there, sir.'

Paolo pointed back towards the room he'd just left. 'No, I think it all happened in there.'

Frustration made him smack the wall with his fist. 'But where's Dave? What's she done with him?'

He went back into the lounge, ready to do whatever it took to make April talk, but found that where he would have bullied her and probably got nowhere, Andrea had used kindness and unlocked the floodgates.

'She's ready to confess, sir.'

'OK,' Paolo said, 'but first I want to know where Dave is.'

April looked up. 'I'm sorry,' she said. 'I never wanted to hurt him, but he found my room.'

Chapter Thirty-four

'I tried to get him to leave. I tried really hard, but he wouldn't give up. Just kept on and on asking sly little questions, trying to trip me up.'

'Where is he, April?' Paolo asked again.

It was almost as if she couldn't hear him. She was staring straight ahead into a vision only she could see.

'When I opened the door and he was there on his own, I thought I could fool him, but he just refused to go away.'

Paolo stepped forward, not sure what he intended to do, but determined to get her to answer his question. CC's hand on his arm pulled him back.

'Is Dave still alive, April?' she asked.

She shook her head and Paolo's gut clenched. He'd known all along Dave must be dead, but hadn't wanted to believe it. He wasn't sure he could get the words out, but owed it to Dave to pull himself together.

'Tell me the rest,' he said, astounded to hear his voice sounding so steady. How could he be disintegrating on the inside and yet still function on the outside? He glanced over at CC and saw the same pain he was feeling reflected in her eyes.

'I opened the door and Dave apologised for calling on me at home. Asked if he could come in for a few minutes. I don't usually let men into my home, but I felt safe with him. He had lovely manners.'

She smiled as if at a pleasant memory and, once again, Paolo wanted to shake her.

'He said Clementine Towers had told him she'd followed me to George Baron's house, but it was pretty clear after a few minutes that she'd given him the impression George and I had been lovers. As if! I told him she'd been mistaken and he seemed to accept that.'

She fell silent for a moment, then looked up at Paolo. 'He was very good at his job. I thought I'd got away with it, but then out of the blue he asked why I'd pushed Clementine under the bus. Of course, I said I hadn't, but I think he'd seen my slight hesitation, because he smiled and said he believed me, but I could hear from his voice that he didn't. Not really.'

'What happened then?' Paolo asked when she fell silent once more.

'He pretended he needed to use the bathroom, but I guessed he just wanted to have a look round. The problem was I hadn't locked the door into . . . you've seen it, haven't you? My special room?'

Paolo nodded.

'So, you see, I couldn't let him wander around the place, but he insisted he really needed to use the bathroom. I told him where it was and watched through the crack in the door to see what he did.'

She bowed her head. 'I really didn't want to hurt him. If he'd just gone to the bathroom like he'd said he wanted to, I wouldn't have had to hit him.' She pointed to the poker in the grate. 'I waited until he opened the door to my room and then crept up behind him. I thought I would just knock him out, but then I realised he would bring you all here, so I had no choice. You do see that, don't you? I had no choice, so I hit him until he stopped moving.'

'Where have you put his body, April,' Paolo asked, keeping his hands at his side with great difficulty. He felt like reaching for the poker and dealing with April in the same way she'd treated Dave.

She looked up. 'He was a good man. Not like the others. I took him out into the woods and found a lovely spot to bury him. It's not far from the edge of the river, overlooking the picnic area. He'll like it there. It's very peaceful.'

Paolo nodded to CC, who left the room to organise a search party to locate the makeshift grave.

'You thought Derrick Walden knew about you, didn't you? Is that why you killed him?'

She nodded. 'I overheard him on the phone to you.'

'You killed him for nothing,' Paolo said. 'He was calling me about something completely different.'

She shrugged. 'He'd been snooping round too much. Eventually he'd have discovered my secret.'

'So, no regrets about Derrick?'

She shook her head. 'No, not really. I was doing the world a favour, you know.'

'By killing an innocent man?' Paolo asked.

For a moment April looked confused. 'Oh, you mean Derrick? No, I meant sorting out the rapists so that they never did it again.'

'How did you know who to target?'

April smiled. 'Their victims told me. I'm a Rape Crisis counsellor at weekends. I make notes about those who get away with it and then go looking for them.'

Paolo nodded as if he'd expected that answer. 'But you only target those who've used a date rape drug, don't you?'

'Usually, but I made an exception to that with George Baron. When Trudy called after her boss raped her, I recognised her voice. Because I knew who she worked for, I felt I should act. Even though she would never find out it was me, I did it as a favour.'

'But George Baron realised who you were, so you had to kill him?'

She shrugged. 'He was vermin. No loss to mankind, even less loss to womankind. Men are such evil hypocrites. Do you know what my ex-husband said when he found out I'd been raped?'

Paolo shook his head.

'He said I'd asked for it. By going to a nightclub dressed as I'd been that night, I'd asked to be attacked.' She glared at Paolo. 'The police said pretty much the same thing. Oh, not in words, but in their attitude. What was I doing going to a club on my own? How often did I go out alone? What had I had to drink? All the questions putting the blame on me instead of the pervert who'd hurt me.'

'So you decided to get retribution as Nemesis?'

She nodded. 'I went back to the club where I'd been picked up and turned the tables on my rapist. I only ever meant to punish the person who'd hurt me, but then I thought, why not apply an eye for an eye justice to others who've got away with drugging and raping women. And it felt so good to dish out to those bastards what they'd inflicted on others. None of them ever went to the police. Not one.'

'But you made a mistake with Colin Jameson.'

'No I didn't. I always made sure I picked the right men. I got good descriptions of them. Found out which clubs they used to prey on their victims and went after them.'

Paolo held up his hand to stop her from saying anything more. 'The night you picked up Colin Jameson you took the wrong man. The one you were after was a work colleague. They looked very much alike.'

She shook her head. 'No, that's not possible. You're lying.'

Paolo stood up. 'I'm not lying, April. While you're rotting in prison, patting yourself on the back for ridding the world of rapists, spare a thought for Colin Jameson whose life you ruined. Think about his wife who still loves him and is trying to help him put his life back together again. Think about his child who will never know what his dad was like before you decided to play at being the goddess of retribution.

Chapter Thirty-five

Paolo stood at the graveside with CC on one side and Andrea on the other. He was pleased to see a full turnout from the station, although not as delighted that Jack Cummings had turned up in funereal black and was walking around with his head bowed. Maybe he blamed himself for what happened to Dave. Paolo hoped so, because he certainly blamed Jack and would never be able to forgive him.

He looked over to see Chief Constable Willows standing next to Dave's parents. The chief glanced around, spotted Paolo and nodded. Paolo would have felt better if Willows had scowled at him. As much as he believed Jack's attitude had been the cause of Dave going off on his own to prove his worth, Paolo knew part of the guilt rested with him. He should have transferred Jack out of his department as soon as he realised the level of resentment he was harbouring towards Dave. Still, the papers were filled in and ready to file as soon as he returned to work. He didn't want the man in his team and was pretty sure Jack would be pleased to go.

Paolo felt the heat of the sun on his back and inwardly cursed the good weather. If there had been any justice in the world, today would have been graced with torrential rain, thunder pounding the heavens and lightning streaking across the firmament. Instead, they had a glorious sapphire sky with not a cloud to mar it.

As the priest mouthed the words of the service and Dave was buried for the second time, Paolo thought back to the moment they had unearthed his body in the woods. In the end, they'd had to make April show them exactly where she'd buried him.

He looked around at the cemetery and wondered how Dave would feel about being interred here. In one respect, April had told the truth. She'd chosen a beauty spot to hide Dave's body. With a bank of wild flowers behind and the river sparkling below, Dave's first grave had been far more beautiful than this one. Paolo wondered if he would have preferred to have been left in that idyllic setting.

CC was openly crying. Andrea was trying to stem her tears. As she'd said a few days back, she hadn't been on the team for long, but Dave had gone out of his way to help her settle in.

Barbara was standing a few yards from Willows. She looked over at Paolo and he knew she understood exactly how he was feeling. He remembered the first case he'd worked on with Dave and how he'd upset Barbara every time he'd opened his mouth. They'd grown fond of each other with time, once Barbara had realised Dave's outward misogyny hid a sensitive nature scared of rejection.

It had been Rebecca who'd brought out the real Dave and made him seek help to get rid of the macho persona he'd tried to hide behind. She, too, was in tears, supported by her parents. Paolo wondered how she would cope and made a mental note to call on her in a few days. He'd give her time to . . . to what? Get over it? Paolo knew there were some things you never got over. He was still grieving over losing his daughter Sarah. Nothing would ever staunch the hurt that flowed from that wound.

The service finally came to an end and Paolo moved towards Dave's parents.

'I am so very sorry for your loss,' he said. 'Dave wasn't just a colleague; he was a good friend. I'm going to miss him.'

Mr Johnson held out his hand. 'He was very fond of you, too, Paolo. Never had a bad word to say about you.'

'My brother says you took good care of my son,' Mrs Johnson said, glancing over towards Chief Constable Willows.

Paolo followed the direction of her gaze and saw that Jack Cummings had made his way over to that side of grave and was deep in conversation with the chief. Good, Paolo thought. I hope he's asking for a transfer.

He turned back to Dave's mother. 'I wish I'd taken better care of him,' he said. 'If I had, he wouldn't have gone to that woman's house without me.'

A smile trembled on her lips. 'No, he probably wouldn't have, but you weren't his nursemaid. He knew what he was doing. I'm proud of him.'

Paolo nodded. 'You have every reason to be. He was the best of my team. The one I turned to more than any other.'

Mr and Mrs Johnson excused themselves as another member of the mourning party arrived to give words of condolences.

'We'll see you later,' Mrs Johnson said.

Paolo returned a noncommittal answer. He didn't think he could bear to join the others at the hotel function room hired for the wake. He walked away, intending to go back to the station, but had only gone a few yards when he heard his name being called.

He turned to find Chief Constable Willows bearing down on him.

'Leaving already? Aren't you going to say a few words at the hotel? Dave would have wanted you to, I'm sure.'

Paolo could almost hear what Dave's comments would have been on hearing that and nearly laughed, but managed to restrain himself.

'I don't think—'

'For his parents' sake, I'm asking you,' Willows said. 'You are the one who knew him best of all of us.'

'Sir, I really don't . . . I'm not the best . . . I'm not good at . . . all right, but I'm not making a long speech. Dave would have hated that.'

Willows smiled. 'No need for a speech at all. Just be yourself and say a few words about what it was like working with him.

Young Cummings has been telling me how you watched over my nephew and nurtured his career.'

'Cummings? Look, sir, I've been meaning to talk to you about him, but now isn't the right time.'

Willows smiled. 'No, not the right time at all. Today is for Dave, but I agree with you we need to discuss Jack Cummings career path. He admires you tremendously.'

'Does he?' Paolo asked, hoping Jack wouldn't have much time left to do so, but Willows next words took that dream away.

'Yes, he does. So much so, he's asked to be taken under your wing. I've told him he couldn't ask for a better mentor. I know you'll do the best you can for him.'

END